C000154585

Sir Tristram and the Great Commotion in the West

Philippa Moseley

This novel is dedicated to the memory of the West Country rebels who in July and August 1549 fought valiantly against overwhelming government forces for their legitimate rights, with tragic results.

For Aldyth, with love

Sir Tristram and the Great Commotion in the West
Copyright © Philippa Moseley 2007

ISBN 978-184426-415-5

First published 2007 by
UPFRONT PUBLISHING LTD
Peterborough, England.

Printed by Printondemand-Worldwide Ltd.

Historical Note

In 1534, Henry VIII broke away from the authority of the Pope, and made himself Head of the Church. Otherwise, England continued to be a Catholic country, with each region having its own particular heritage of worship. Few people had any desire for radical change. When at Henry's death in 1547, his under-age son, Edward, and a fanatically Protestant-minded government took over, it was decided England should become a rigidly uniform Protestant country. The immediate destruction of every aspect of traditional Catholic Christianity, without prior consultation, was taken very hard and resulted in rebellion.

All the significant incidents and main characters in the novel are authentic, with the exception of Thomasine and Robin Dyer.

Nothing is subsequently known of William Wynslade or John Kestell after the rebellion, except that the former was said to have become a wandering minstrel, known as *Sir Tristram,* and the latter married Jacquet Coffin. The end of the story is the author's surmise of one imaginable outcome.

Acknowledgments

David Fletcher, Susan Pine-Coffin, Susan Scrutton, Mary McColl, Dorothy Hill and Carrie & Stephen Sylvester

Sir Tristram and the Great Commotion in the West

Philippa Moseley

Sir Tristram and the Great Commotion in the West

I am an old man now, sixty-one come the autumn, but active enough and still living in Great Torrington, beside the River Torridge.

I never did marry after the Great Commotion, for all that Patience kept a look-out for a suitable bride. Two of my friends lost their wives in childbirth, and a third from the sweating sickness, yet all were happily married again within a year. But my Thomasine could not be replaced so easily.

It isn't that I haven't an eye for a well-made young woman with bright eyes, soft skin and a pleasant kindly manner. But a new wife would have had a very hard time of it, for although Thomasine and I never lived here together, I dream of her so often she has almost become a reality, a part of my life I could not do without. It is always the same dream.

The moon is full on a clear night. I am hurrying along the river path from Taddyport to Rothern Bridge, and there she is, seated on the spur of grass and shingle, jutting out into the Torridge. Her kirtle is hitched above her bare legs, and her waist-length chestnut hair hangs down her back in a thick plait.

She's waiting to see the otters swimming by moonlight.

Soon they come – a line of bubbles followed by four sleek, shining dark heads gliding across a rippling ribbon of white light stretched between banks of alder and sallow which climb up to the dense, high wooded hills south of Torrington.

Each time I approach her quietly, and call softly, 'Thomasine!' She looks round and smiles, then fades away. When I look back at the river, the otters too have gone.

A small cloud covers the moon for a moment, and a stillness – black and deep as death – envelops my mind. The moon reappears, the river ripples on, a twig snaps in the undergrowth, and some tiny creature plops into the water.

No, a new wife could never have tolerated a man as haunted as I am.

I attend St Michael's church in Great Torrington, not because I'm devout, but because, like most people in this town, I can ill afford to pay the government two hundred and sixty pounds a year for non-attendance. To tell the truth, I long ago cast aside religion, both Catholic and Protestant, as organised and practised by our ecclesiastical establishment. At this present time, the year being 1591, we are a Protestant country. In my lifetime we have been Catholic, then Protestant, Catholic again, and finally Protestant. I reckon we shall remain Protestant at least until our Good Queen Bess dies.

From time immemorial, religious leaders of all persuasions have ordered us to think and act as they command, or suffer dire punishment. To this day none of them has learnt that a human being will not be dragged, – nay, should not be dragged – by the collar into God's presence. He must find the way freely for himself, and worship as he thinks fit.

Sadly, I believe freedom of belief has not proved to be the most urgent necessity of mankind. People think they value it, even die to gain it, but secretly they fear it. Most of them prefer being told what to think, and in times of scarcity and insecurity they band together into hostile religious groups. Their leaders insist on uniformity of belief and descend into communal violence against any dissenting voice. They become strangely blind to all compassion and beauty. Such people have happily ripped up priceless illuminated manuscripts, taking years of labour in the making, to serve as brewer's barrel stoppers.

During the fatal summer of 1549, thousands of Devon and Cornish men rebelled and were sacrificed on the battlefield or the gallows for the sake of enforced uniformity. And what did they gain? Nothing but a reputation for savagery and a determination on the part of the government to deny their human rights. And forty years on, nothing has changed. A man can keep his mouth shut, as I do, or he can find the courage to speak out

3

and be imprisoned, tortured, hanged or burned for his pains. Kings and bishops detest rebels. Thus it is written – thus will it always be. Amen.

Since that Great Commotion of 1549 the South West has been bludgeoned into becoming solidly Puritan by Francis Russell, John Jewell and Richard Tremayne – and by families such as the Carews, Dennises, Grenvilles, Pollards and Raleghs, all of whom were granted extensive church lands and goods during the Reformation. Sir Richard Grenville lost no time in hanging Cuthbert Mayne in Launceston for daring to preach Catholicism. And in Cornwall, only the Arundells of Lanherne possess the power and riches to keep a Catholic priest in their private chapel. Even our Queen Elizabeth fails to keep Catholic and Protestant from each other's throats or from threatening her person. I pity her, for I daresay she has too much spirit to be a sound Puritan, and too much reason to be a staunch Catholic.

I was deeply involved in the Rebellion, and like many others, can tell a sombre tale concerning a siege and many battles. I can also relate many a tragic incident of individual human endeavour. Yet all wars have a third dimension. They tempt, encourage and enable the vilest of bullies to use the licence of war to loot, betray, rape, torture and murder to their own advantage. And the cleverest of these devils delight in adding a subtle form of mental torture to the general misery, rejoicing in corrupting goodness and destroying happiness. They are like flies attracted to a dung-heap. Such a one was it my fate to come up against during the Great Commotion.

All my life I have harboured a shameful secret. I have avoided violence and feared pain, not only for myself, but for all sentient creation. I have dreaded to look on or even to imagine the suffering of the weak and the vulnerable. Above all I have abhorred cruelty, that offshoot of the lust to power. To fear such things is to be less than a man in the eyes of the world. Yet to appear to be a man is what I have striven for. Only my mother, Jane Trelawney, and my friend, Dick Popham, knew what I still conceal behind a false bravado. When I was a child my mother used often to stroke my hair, saying, 'Oh, Will, don't allow suffering to disturb you so much, or you will never know contentment yourself. My greatest desire is for you to be happy.' She died when I was ten years old.

Two years before her death, she taught me to play the Cornish harp. She had a beautiful soft voice, ideal for singing romantic lays derived from the ancient Cornish legends of King Arthur and of Tristram and Iseult. I inherited her talent for music, and soon mastered the art of adjusting the pegs and strings of my harp. My father applauded my musicianship, but warned me not to spend time on playing and singing to the detriment of more manly skills. He feared his only son might not become a good soldier. He himself, though far from being an aggressive man, had won fame fighting in the French wars, even becoming an Esquire of The White Spurs, a rare honour.

I was but nineteen when I became lord of the manor at Constantine, some six miles from Helston in Cornwall. I had to make repairs to the barns and stables, stack yards, thatched shippens and dairy. By the spring it was done, and I could sit in my cosy parlour feeling proud of my achievement. My father had allowed me to take charge of my inheritance before reaching my majority, owing to my stepmother, Agnes, finding me too troublesome to remain at Tregarrick, my father's home at Pelynt in Cornwall. Since she had no child of her own, and I closely resembled Jane Trelawney, my father's beloved first wife, Agnes could no longer bear to have me about her.

The Wynslades came from Buckland Brewer in North Devon. My grandfather died at Wynslade Farm in the hamlet of East Putford, but my father, John Wynslade, moved as a young man to Pelynt. After my mother died he married a widow, Agnes Prest, to give Tregarrick a mistress and his son a mother. He was glad to leave her in charge of all domestic matters, for he was a busy man, looking after his estates and involving himself in public affairs. Agnes ran the manor and her stepson with a rod of iron. She was most devout, a small, neat, fiercely energetic lady with a sharp tongue and a suspicious, critical nature, which led me to discover that excess of religion didn't necessarily go hand in hand with sweetness of character. In contrast my father, though sometimes lax in religious duty, was a just, kindly, well-liked landowner.

By the age of twelve years I had grown into a tall, strong but ungainly lad. When I was not at my books with Father Moreman, the learned priest at Menheniot, who'd been Dean at Exeter College, Oxford, my time was spent out of doors with my friend, Dick Popham, from Woodbury, east of Exeter. My father had long been acquainted with Jack Popham, four of whose sons were content to work on the farm. The fifth son, Dick, had a special way with horses, and at the age of fourteen became our stable boy. We soon discovered he was also a marvel at making and mending all manner of things. In addition he was adept at archery, and it was owing to his excellent tuition that I became a good bowman. This did much to have me accepted as a true Cornishman.

To begin with, I was a most cack-handed pupil. Dick said my height was an advantage, indeed a necessity, for a longbow is as tall as a man, and an arrow half that length. My bow, made from the trunk of a yew, was strung with three strands of hemp dressed with glue, and I wore a glove to shield my fingers when I drew back the string. I also wore a bracer on the inside of my bow arm to protect against the released bowstring.

I learned that an arrow could be fletched with feathers to stabilise it in flight. Alternatively, an arrow could be fitted with a heavy fore shaft which need not be feathered. My arrows were made of red deal with three feathers. It fascinated me to watch Dick fitting a metal head into a shaft by socketing. He could shoot six aimed shots a minute at a range of some two hundred yards, though he said an arrow can go twice as far in the hands of an expert bowman. Longbow arrows speed about fifty yards a second, and a steel-headed arrow can penetrate armour.

Dick informed me that all fit young lads are by law obliged to take up archery, and I should aim to be admitted to the most famous band in Europe, the Cornish Archers, who had several times brought down the flower of the French cavalry. Dick made me practise with little good result, until in my fourteenth year I suddenly got the hang of it. There was a knack in keeping my bowstring steady with the right hand, and pressing my body's weight against the bow held in my left hand.

Dick also taught me how to run, pacing myself carefully over many miles. 'Why do I have to run so far?' I would ask.

'Because even an archer must know how to flee', Dick said. How right he was.

My father judged Dick to be the most intelligent and most reliable of servants. Agnes too found him useful. She grudged the time he spent with me, and was for ever calling him to run errands and undertake repairs. If not summoning him she would be calling me to ride with her to visit a neighbour or to attend Mass at Pelynt. Dick and I dreaded the sound of her high-pitched voice, and would often pretend not to hear.

Most hated of my tasks was being forced to accompany Agnes to St Nonna's Well, above the West Looe River. My first visit to this beautiful place had been on a sunny day in early June, prior to my stepmother's arrival, with Dick and a few of the farm boys. I was only eight years old, and they told me we were going to Ninny's Grotto, where lived the frogs Ninny liked to eat. You could put your hand into his house to try and catch the magic water, but if you weren't quick enough, Ninny might see you and turn you into a frog.

We took the track northwards past Pendriffey and Muchlarnick to the steep-sided river ravine filled with impenetrable trees in every shade of green. Walking some way along the ridge in the drowsy sunshine, we reached a small gate almost strangled within a myriad wild flowers – forget-me-nots, stitchwort, campion, bluebells, speedwell and herb-Robert. Giant stone steps plunged down a precipitous grassy slope to a fenced-off damp plot overhung by a young oak with golden leaves. Against the hillside a small stone house with a neat arched entrance had been built to house a well-spring which trickled – drop by drop, year after year, century after century – into a wide granite bowl engraved with Maltese crosses enclosed in rings.

I was so fascinated by this water that I held my hand inside too long, and my companions, to tease me, rushed up the steps, shouting 'Ninny's coming! Ninny will catch you!' but I didn't follow. I was entranced by this magical, secret place, and lay on my back amidst tall willow-herb and buttercups, staring up at the hot blue sky and tasting my wet fingers. Eventually Dick returned to find me, saying how surprising Ninny had let me be. It became apparent that Ninny would always let me be, for I often visited his grotto by myself, and put my hand into his house without disaster.

Thus two years later, when Agnes asked me to ride with her to the holy well, I had no notion she meant Ninny's Grotto. On reaching the gate I rode on, hoping she wouldn't see it. But she shouted, 'Stop! St Nonna's well is down here!' I refused to go with her, and remained on the track, disappointed that she'd found my secret place, and that Ninny, who ate frogs, was really St Nonna, who performed miracles for Agnes. Once when I had a rash on my arm, Agnes insisted on taking me down to the well and sprinkling me with water, while saying a prayer. The rash disappeared the next day, but I had my doubts about the holy water. When I asked my father who was St Nonna, he admitted he'd no idea. But Agnes piped up, 'Shame on you, John. She was one of our foremost saints, being the mother of St David of Wales.'

He grinned, saying, 'She must have been a well-travelled lady, with excellent building skills. I can't be expected to know all your Cornish saints, Agnes. There are saints enough in Devon to be going on with.'

'Devon!' scoffed Agnes. 'Can you name a single church in Devon named after a Celtic saint?'

'Well now, let me think…' My father paused, and then, winking at me, he rattled off a string of names, ending with Nectan, Brannoc and Fili. For once Agnes had nothing to say, and he added, 'You see, my dear, Devon is not such a heathen place as you will have it.'

My stepmother had made me recite the names of the saints and their feast days which she'd had me learn by rote – Cadoc, Piran, Geroe, Neot, Meriadec, Indract, Budoc… so much gibberish they had seemed to me.

Before Agnes came, my father's many friends were made very welcome on feast days at Tregarrick. After dinner on dark wet afternoons, as they sat round a roaring fire eating raisins or hot chestnuts, I was always asked to play my Cornish harp and to sing well-known Cornish songs. As a young lad my preference was for cheerful songs, but it was usually the sad ones our guests wanted to hear. There was nothing I enjoyed more than singing after a day's work. But Agnes declared singing was no fit pastime for a young man, and as she wasn't a hospitable woman we ceased having many visitors.

By the time I reached the age of sixteen my relationship with my stepmother had become a sore trial. My only relief from her had been a month each summer with my grandparents at Wynslade Farm, near Torrington. They were acquainted with the Coffyn family, who owned much land in North Devon, and I had made friends with Richard Coffyn and his pretty, gentle sister, Jacquet.

We would often go riding in the wooded valleys or on the moorland above Hartland. Especially fascinating to us was the rugged, dangerous coast on either side of Hartland Point. The worse the weather the more we liked it. We would stand staring down at what looked like black fields of jagged rock paving the cove and washed over by white foam. Solid squared boulders stood upright or tilted at strange angles on this paving. My grandfather said the strata had been pushed up in this fashion by ancient earthquakes. The vicious howling wind, he told us, could throw a ship into the air, smashing it to smithereens. We shivered with delicious horror at the thought, wishing we could see one.

I recalled a particular excursion to Hartland Point one summer. As we rode down the treacherous incline to the sea, Jacquet's horse took fright, and she lost control of it. Had I not managed to seize her reins in time, she would have been propelled over the edge of the high cliff. Richard told me later that Jacquet was eternally grateful, and worshipped me for months after this incident.

My Constantine manor was pleasant enough, but lacked a mistress to make it a home. There had been talk at Tregarrick of my marrying Honor Becket of Cartuther, near Liskeard, whose father was a staunch Catholic and rich enough to satisfy Agnes. I cherished a more romantic vision of marriage.

But no sooner had I arrived at Constantine, in March 1548, than my thoughts and those of everyone round about were concentrated on the forthcoming visitation to Helston of the Archdeacon of Cornwall, William Body, a man with an unsavoury reputation. In July 1547, Archbishop Cranmer had published his proposals to abolish all superstition and practices against God's glory and commandments, among them being feast days, masses for the dead, bells, holy water, palms, rosaries, processions and candles. People were particularly incensed at the thought of losing their many saints' days, the only days when everyone could take a holiday and enjoy themselves with games and feasting. I couldn't understand why such things were harmful, and indeed no one in our parish actually believed these changes would become law in the immediate future.

My excellent tutor, Father Moreman, shared many a meal with us at Tregarrick, and occasionally brought a friend or two with him. They would talk long into the night on religion and philosophy. By the time I was fifteen years of age I had become aware that religious beliefs are not fixed in stone, as Father Lambe, our priest at Pelynt, would have us think. Great religious upheavals had been taking place throughout my childhood among educated men at the universities. The new ideas were way above the heads of the commons. For that matter, I didn't comprehend some of them myself. I had always listened to the discussions round the dinner table, and Father Moreman talked to me about religion during my lessons.

As a young child I had asked him, could we not all simply try to follow the commandments of Jesus, and then there would be no quarrels? Father Moreman had laughed, saying it was exactly what people were meant to be doing, but unfortunately each man was inclined to make his own interpretation of the gospels. Priests had been given the authority by God to guide our moral life, but kings did not wish to have the Church telling them how to behave, and how to order their kingdoms. At the same time, the commons had begun to question the authority of the priests, and therein lay the seeds of rebellion. Strict punishments were devised to maintain obedience to the laws of the Church.

'Read the gospels, and think for yourself, Will', said Father Moreman when I was older. 'But at the same time keep a wary eye on authority. Avoid above all the arrogance of so many Christians, who think God has given them the key to all knowledge and wisdom. Never forget that the greatest wisdom does not consist in thinking you know everything, but rather in having the humility to admit to knowing very little. The best saints are not necessarily the most learned.'

I gathered my father had long been of the opinion that the superstition of the commons had overreached itself, and was prone to being ridiculous at times, particularly in regard to relics.

'Why do the people', I asked Father Moreman, 'Attach magic properties to the bones or possessions of saints?'

He explained that uneducated folk dearly needed to feel that such relics would afford them protection, for instance, against the harsh forces of nature.

'Think of the fishermen, Will, who have to set forth in our rough seas in winter, or let their families starve, and you can understand why.'

One acquaintance I remember Father Moreman bringing was a long-faced gentleman named Nicholas Udall, once headmaster of Eton College, and now Regius Professor of Divinity at Oxford, who wanted to meet my father. This learned man lectured us in a compelling fashion, which no doubt would have brooked no contradiction at his school. But Father Moreman and my father both enjoyed a good argument. Having recently heard of the proposals to sweep away all traditional religion almost overnight, they were much concerned. Nicholas Udall, himself a Cornishman, scoffed at their worries, and spoke of his fellow countrymen in a patronising manner, maintaining they were mostly ignorant, credulous, unlettered folk, who'd allowed themselves to be influenced by certain malicious papist priests to cling to wicked superstition. 'Besides', boomed Udall, 'These childish habits lead to loud minstrelsy, profanation of the Sabbath, and, worst of all', here his voice dropped in horror, 'Increase of bastardy!'

Father Moreman laughed heartily, but conceded that some gradual reform was needed. Since the King had cast off the Pope and become head of the Church, the Archbishop had been encouraging priests to lead their congregations gently away from what he called papist practices.

'I myself have been teaching the children at my school in Menheniot the Lord's Prayer, the Creed and the Commandments in English, so they will be able to understand the new service in due course.'

'An excellent procedure for one or two pupils', pronounced Udall in his rich, fruity tones. 'But one must remember that for the most part Cornish children would take years to learn English. And the adults, especially the elderly, will never master it. How much better if the people were simply to petition for a Cornish prayer book.'

'On the contrary', said Father Moreman, 'My children do learn English rapidly.'

'Indeed they do', agreed my father. 'All Cornish children could learn English if they had access to education. Yet, instead of encouraging learning, the government is seeking to abolish our chantries, together with their priests, thereby denying children the chance of basic schooling.'

'No, no', said Udall impatiently. 'New grammar schools will be founded to provide sound Protestant teaching in place of the present popish nonsense.'

'I doubt the government will be setting up a little Eton in each Cornish village', said my father with the dry sarcasm he often used with his amiable smile.

'Of course not', replied Udall, taking him seriously. 'We do not require a grammar school in every village. Grammar schools are only for those who will benefit from education. The general run of Cornish villagers need no education other than being taught the Protestant doctrines. Rather than a priest mumbling away in Latin at the altar, there shall be lengthy sermons to instruct people in all they need to know.' – and here he pointed a bony finger at my father – 'Instead of images and paintings of heaven and hell, there shall be the Commandments and suitable texts from the scriptures hung upon the walls.,

Father Moreman and my father were not Cornish, but they had resided long enough in the county to fully understand the Cornish attachment to their traditional religious customs.

'It is a constant surprise to me', said John Moreman, 'That every common man in Cornwall has not succumbed to despair, such is the hardship he endures from generation to generation. The Church promises eternal life if he believes and obeys all the articles of religion, but his unwavering devotion is maintained by just such religious devices as images and paintings, music and bells, miraculous tales of saints, relics and the mystery of candlelight. These things provide the sense of awe which speaks so profoundly to the Celtic soul. Amongst the commons the power of the church lies in its magic rather than its doctrine.'

'Idolatry, nothing but idolatry, prejudicial to God's glory and commandments!' snorted Udall.

Father Moreman told my father later that Udall had visited him uninvited in order to sound out his views on the Protestant reform. In his immaculate black robe, with his glossy black hair combed back so carefully behind his large white ears, Nicholas Udall looked impressive. He may have been right in some respects, but I felt an extreme revulsion for the man, particularly his commandeering voice and vulpine smile.

When in February 1548 further proclamations were issued, this time by the government – abolishing pilgrimages, ashes, candles and bells for sick communion, the Easter sepulchre and creeping to the Cross – there were more serious stirrings among the commons. Then came rumours that government commissioners had orders to start smashing statues and stained glass in cathedrals. It was said that Dr Heynes, Dean of Exeter, had already removed all the statues in the cathedral. Thus by the time the visitation on April the fifth was announced, the commons in Helston, together with many from Constantine, were determined to resist all religious change.

Father Martin Geoffrey, the priest at St Keverne on the Lizard, had visited me to warn that his parishioners were in threatening mood and intended marching to Helston to make their wishes known. Father Geoffrey himself was incensed, because the archdeacon said that Archbishop Cranmer considered the people of Devon and Cornwall to be ignorant, understanding nothing of their religion. Their anger had been made worse because Archdeacon Body, well-known as a grasping scoundrel, had been chosen as the government representative.

I took immediately to the genial, straightforward character of Father Geoffrey. He seemed to me to be a good man, caring deeply for the welfare of his flock. Gradual change with the consent of the majority might be acceptable, but the wholesale destruction of every aspect of the faith was a cruel insult to the deep devotion of the Cornish people. 'One has to realise, Sir William', he said, 'That those of my parishioners, living in wretched hovels of earth and thatch, lying on beds of straw, wearing rough-spun clothes and often going hungry, should not be denied their saints' days, their traditions and the glory of the Catholic ritual, the only brightness in their lives. That wretch, Body, rants on about holy days being an excuse for wasting good summer weather in sloth and drunkenness. The church is slyly seeking to abolish most of the saints' days between July and October. Confining our brave seamen and tinners to winter holy days! Is that not utterly mean-minded?'

I recalled the day I'd spent at St Keverne in a howling Cornish gale, with rain so icily sharp it could rip the skin off your hands.

'It's not right', continued Father Geoffrey, 'That covetous gentry are now adding the riches of the churches to the lands they've already stolen. And to add insult to injury, I have even seen a gentleman riding with saddlebags fashioned from a richly embroidered cope!'

At that time I had no means of knowing how true were the tales flying about, but I was well aware that Body was not a man to conciliate the commons. Father Geoffrey had asked me to deter my tenants at Constantine from violence. He himself intended bringing his parishioners from St Keverne, and suggested that I take on the leadership of the demonstration to give it the stamp of respectability. This, I refused, for I considered that Father Geoffrey, as a well-known and respected priest, was the best man to confront Body. He'd assured me that the voicing of complaints in a peaceful manner was lawful. But I doubted that a large crowd of disgruntled Cornishmen would keep the peace. Having only just arrived at Constantine, and being so young, and a stranger to the people, I was not the man to restrain a bunch of hotheads.

I did however warn one particular yeoman I knew, William Kylter, a most likable fellow famous for standing up fearlessly to injustice. Indeed, he spoke up so impulsively it was a wonder he wasn't behind bars. Kylter already had good reason to dislike all government commissioners, for he'd been among a number of young bowmen conscripted by King Harry's government in 1536 to help put down a rising in the North, known as the Pilgrimage of Grace. He'd returned to Constantine full of disgust for the treachery of the government. The conscripts had been instructed to wipe out without pity every man, woman and child who harboured sympathy for the cause.

Kylter imagined he'd been brought to fight destructive ruffians marching to London to put innocent civilians to the sword. To his surprise he'd found a peaceful band of Christian men under the disciplined command of an honest gentleman named Robert Aske. The protesters had been promised pardon and redress by King Harry himself.

Instead, they were hanged as insolent rebel dogs, foremost among them Robert Aske himself.

King Harry had died in 1547, succeeded by his nine-year-old son, Edward, with his maternal uncle, Edward Seymour, Duke of Somerset, as Regent. In Cornwall we knew not what kind of man Protector Somerset would turn out to be. As yet we'd heard no great ill of him. It was the Archbishop who was foisting this new religion on us, but I was sure the Protector would deal hardly with the commons if violent opposition should take place.

I remember Kylter, a very tall, strong man with thick blond hair and dark blue eyes, standing in the spring sunshine outside the manor with his thirteen-year-old twin brothers, two small versions of himself, who followed him around with hero-worship. When I mentioned the Archdeacon, he answered with a broad grin on his handsome face, 'We must needs rid Cornwall of such vermin as Body'. I begged him to resist uttering angry words, let alone violent deeds, for all that Body would deserve them, being such a tactless, merciless fellow.

But Kylter was always careless of danger, and there was no more I could say. He had already told me that the previous day Body had gathered parish priests and churchwardens at Penryn, where he'd sternly made known to them the government's demands, and instructed that all statues in their churches be removed without delay.

As the hours passed on the fifth day of April, and still no news came from Helston, I prayed earnestly that Father Geoffrey had managed to keep the peace.

At last, just before midnight he arrived, his reddish-brown weather-beaten complexion drained of all colour. It was hard to imagine him ever smiling again, and probably he never did. He sank into a chair, unable to speak until I'd dosed him with brandy.

'You were right, Sir William. Kylter and his friend Pascoe Trevian have killed Body.'

After a long silence, I asked, 'How did it happen?'

'I arrived with my band of men, having marched half the night from St Keverne. We were told that Body's servants were already smashing up the statues in St Michael's. We could hear hammering going on, and saw a crowd of some thousand armed men – tinners, fishermen, graziers and tillers – gathered outside the church. When someone shouted that Body was hiding in a house at the bottom of the hill, there was no stopping those angry men from pouring down the street and dragging Body from his refuge. I didn't see him being killed, but was told Kylter and Trevian had done the deed. The people then moved to the market place and stood quiet to hear the words of a Helston man, John Resseigh, who stated they would have no laws touching religion other than those made by King Harry, until his son reached his majority.'

'Will you return to St Keverne tomorrow?'

'I will.'

'Though you had no hand in the murder, might they arrest you?'

'Certainly they will. One of Body's men sought me out as the crowd was dispersing, and informed me the government would know who to blame. "It is you devilish priests", he shouted, "Who are inciting the people to stubbornness and violence against the King's godly proceedings. You shall answer for Body's death."'

'Jesu!' I said, 'Make straight for Porthleven tonight, and find a boat to make your escape.'

'No, Sir William, that's not my way. If they arrest me, I'll have a chance to defend my views, to explain why my people cherish the ancient rights of their religion, and should not be bullied into reform. Kylter and Trevian will hang, of course, poor souls, but there will be others I may be able to help to a pardon.'

Father Geoffrey left the manor at dawn. I rode to Helston to find that the Justices dared not arrest anyone until they were assured that a government force was on its way. Eventually when it came, Kylter and Trevian, together with twenty-six others, were imprisoned at Launceston castle, and a government commission sentenced nine of these to be hanged, drawn and quartered alongside Kylter and Trevian.

I travelled on a sunny day to Launceston with a horse and cart to visit Kylter before his trial, taking with me his widowed mother and twin brothers, Peter and Paul. I gained admission and found Kylter outside on the castle green with several other prisoners. When told his family were waiting to see him he begged me to ask them not to come in. He didn't wish to break down when confronted with their tears in front of the other prisoners and the gaolers. 'Go out and wait with my family a short distance from the tower. There will be a message for my mother before she goes home.'

I joined the family in the park in view of the castle tower, wondering what would happen. Within half an hour a flattish white stone of some three or four pounds in weight came hurtling over the top of the tower. On it was written in some black substance, *Weep not. Be proud I died a true Cornishman. God bless you all.*

Later I heard that Kylter and another strong prisoner had been competing with each other within the castle walls as to who could lie on his back in the grass and hurl the heaviest stone over the tower. The gaolers were astonished at Kylter's strength, and deemed his hanging to be the waste of an excellent man.

On the day, a great crowd turned out to see him off. I was there in front when they brought him to the gallows. Catching my eye he grinned like a mischievous schoolboy and raised his arm. He admitted his guilt with pride, and was defiant to the end, saying it was worth dying to have rid Cornwall of such a villain. I turned quickly and pushed my way through the teeming crowd to find my horse and cart. On the way home I retched and retched again over a hedge, but my stomach was empty of everything but fear and loathing.

Father Geoffrey was given no chance to speak up at the trial in Launceston. He'd already been arrested and sent to London to be tried himself and sentenced to be hanged, drawn and quartered at

Smithfield. For days I kept seeing his smiling face in my mind, and then tried to shut out the image of his terrible fate. I began to be afraid of what such fanatical tyranny would bring for all decent folk, and wondering where I would stand in such a world.

The riot at Helston heralded the beginning of what was long spoken of in the South West as *The Great Commotion.*

After the hanging a festering mood prevailed among the commons in West Cornwall. Each village waited with dread for the government commissioners to arrive. For the first time in my life I scarcely noticed the wondrous Cornish spring, when every hedge, field, moor and even granite rock sprouted wild flowers – nor the early summer, when the tumultuous grey seas of winter became calm expanses of sapphire and emerald shot through with silver in the sunlight.

The excitement of new life and fertility had always focussed on the church. It was the time for feasting, singing and dancing – for church ales and Easter processions. Yet that year there was no true joy in the festivities, only a grim determination to practise all the old traditions for the last time. And it was to be the last time we heard the Whitsun Mass in Latin, for in May a new order of service in English was proclaimed for the following year.

Because of the religious changes it was hard for me to settle to the normal life of a landowner in Constantine, or to be a good neighbour to the nearby gentry. There was an air of suspicion as each family, fearing an armed rising by the commons, had to decide which camp they would support. Many hoped to reap some reward of land or riches from the upheaval, and bided their time.

In mid-June, Dick came to Constantine with a message from my father, requesting me to visit Tregarrick to sign a petition. There was mounting unrest over the hanging of Father Geoffrey and the imprisonment of Father Moreman in the Tower of London for preaching against the government proposals. It was inconceivable that Father Moreman, of all priests, had been arrested, for he'd long been teaching the children in his school at Menheniot to recite the Lord's Prayer, the Commandments and the Catechism in English, and he'd been open to other changes. Everyone we knew judged he should have been made Bishop of Cornwall. So who had instigated his arrest? My father suspected it was Nicholas Udall's doing.

Father Moreman had told my father in confidence that in 1541 Udall had been dismissed from the headship of Eton for theft. Silver images and college plate were found among his possessions. In addition, there had been complaints about his over-zealous flogging of pupils, and he had spent time in the Marshalsea prison. Father Moreman hadn't thought of exposing his crimes, but probably Udall feared he might. It was safer to have him behind bars. I was to discover during the Commotion that some of the leading participants were not above shady and jealous actions to benefit themselves.

His parishioners were enraged at being deprived of their much-loved and learned priest, and were now determined to resist all change. Another priest, Father Richard Crispyn, a Canon of Exeter Cathedral, had also been imprisoned in the Tower. Tyranny had come in earnest to the South West, and no one dared to speak out too loud against the new laws.

Dick also informed me that the Becket family had approached my father regarding a marriage between Honor and myself. They desired to settle the matter quickly in view of the uncertainty about the future. Honor was a good enough girl, but not for me. I would have to go and face my father. It would be difficult to refuse her, for I knew he longed for a grandson.

The third piece of news Dick brought was that a distant relation of ours, a girl of sixteen named Thomasine Wynslade, was now living at Tregarrick. He didn't know the reason for her coming: all he could tell me was that she seemed a very strange, shy person, and Agnes was none too pleased with her. Then Dick laughed, saying Agnes had nearly choked on her soup when Thomasine asked if the Tregarrick household would be going down to Looe to take part in the May Day festivities.

'"And what, may I ask, would we be doing at Looe?" – "Dancing all night", says Thomasine. –

"The Wynslades do not dance in the streets like vulgar peasants." – "I see no harm in it", she replies. "My father used to take me to dance at Hartland, and he promised that one day we would go to Padstow to join the hobby-horse dance."

I travelled to Pelynt with Dick, not looking forward to seeing Agnes, but very curious indeed to meet Thomasine. My father being out when we arrived, it was Agnes who greeted me with her long-suffering air. 'I've had nothing but trouble from that so-called relation of yours. Come and meet her if you wish. She's upstairs, sewing.'

She took me up to the parlour, but the room was empty. On the settle lay a large, partly hemmed length of fine linen and a sewing basket. In exasperation Agnes exclaimed, 'Deus! Where's that girl? She was told to wait here. On no account was she to leave the parlour. But, as always, she's disobeyed and slipped away.'

'Don't fret, Agnes', I said, 'She'll appear sooner or later. Dick says she's a distant cousin from North Devon. I didn't know we had relations at Frithelstock.'

'I doubt she's any relation. Your father insists she is. Goodness knows why he took her in. Imagine, she arrived in a peasant's dimity gown, wearing a head kerchief and red hosen, with no baggage. I had to lend her clothes. We had cutlets in wine for dinner, but she would not touch meat. I had to order her a dish of eggs. In her father's house, it seems, they ate little more than pottage and black bread. And she was running with fleas!'

'An unusual girl!'

'Worst of all, she's no Christian. She can't say her catechism, has never been to confession, and doesn't even know there are seven sacraments. I've heard tell Thomasine's mother was a witch, and the villagers at Hartland threw her into a pond. She died later from a fever.' Here Agnes lowered her voice, almost hissing, 'I suspect her daughter's a witch too. I found her crushing wormwood and mint in a bowl. And she insists on bringing wild creatures into the manor.'

'Wild creatures?'

'Small animals she finds, snared or abandoned.'

'No harm in that. There's room enough in the outhouses.'

'Your father lets her have her way. She'll get bitten one day, and serve her right. Oh, she's as wild and uneducated as any peasant. I'm having to teach her everything. She goes barefoot half the time, though your father has bought her good boots. Look! There they are, by the settle.'

'Is she able to learn?' I asked.

'Able enough, if she were only willing. Last month she went out at dawn with the servants, if you please, to go a-maying. She was glad enough to carry in the hawthorn and rowan, but not so keen to help grub up the brambles. I sent her to Looe one day to do some errands, and on the way back she lost a jar of beeswax, some goose quills and half a pound of pins, dropped somewhere down by the river…'

As Agnes ranted on, I was barely listening. I'd noticed ten small brown toes protruding from under

29

the window curtain, and couldn't wait to see their owner.

'There's no trusting that girl to do anything. I'll go and find her', concluded Agnes.

When she'd gone, very quietly I picked up Thomasine's shoes and drew aside the curtain to reveal a strangely beautiful, slender girl with sunburnt arms and neck and a great mass of tangled chestnut hair. We stared at one another for a few seconds, as I held out the shoes. She looked confused, but then her brown eyes answered my smile.

'Good day, Cousin Thomasine. Agnes sends you these with her compliments.'

Taking her little black boots, Thomasine sat on the settle and put them on.

'I'm William Wynslade, newly arrived from Constantine, near Helston, in West Cornwall. And you are…?'

'Thomasine Wynslade, arrived two months ago from East Putford, near Torrington, in North Devon', she announced with a little curtsey.

'Why were you hiding?' I asked.

'I always want to hide when I meet new people.'

'And are you still frightened?'

'No.'

'You've been living at Wynslade Farm with my grandfather. I know it well. I used to spend a month each summer at East Putford. We are distantly related, I believe?'

'So distant, Agnes says, it's of no account. We lived at Frithelstock.'

'And your family fell on hard times.'

'My father made the mistake of moving north of Hartland, near Titchberry. The land wasn't fertile, and the first winter the wind raged so strong it blew down part of our house. My mother took sick...' She stopped, and I wanted to hear more. Then she continued, in a slow, dreamy voice, 'I remember miles of greyish purple moorland where hares ran unmolested, and buzzards soared above the quiet combes. A few swallows would shelter all the year round in the deep cliff holes. D'you know the coast from Windbury Point to Hartland Point?'

'Well enough.'

'I never saw a soul at Hartland Point. There was only the cry of the curlew above the deep glens and the harsh screech of gulls. In winter I loved to watch the wicked waves leaping and crashing against those weird upright pillars of black granite.'

'Yes, those strange shapes in ironstone used to fascinate me.'

'I remember the quiet days too', continued Thomasine, 'With sunlight glinting on the grey slate, and pink thrift growing out of the rocks, and the sea pretending to be dead, but you could still feel the deep roar under the surface.

We moved back to Frithelstock when I was eleven years old. Mother died, and father grieved and took to drink. Once he beat me in a drunken rage, and I ran away to Torrington,'

'Why Torrington?'

'To seek help from Mary Lee, the mayor's wife, who'd been a very good friend of my mother's in their youth. She spoke to your grandfather, and he offered me a home at East Putford. Now the old man is ailing, your father has kindly taken me in.'

'He'll take good care of you.'

'I've not been taught the manners of a lady, or how to be a good Christian. My mother only taught me how to read and write and sew. Since her death I've been much alone, left to wander as I please. Creatures of the wild have been my only friends.'

'D'you like it here at Tregarrick?'

'I may become used to it. But I miss my river. There's no river here to compare with the Torridge – the way it runs south towards Okehampton, and then at Hele Bridge cunningly changes its mind and makes that great loop up to Torrington and Bideford as though it can't, after all, bear to leave North Devon. And who can blame it? It's like a great shining, coiling snake, twisting and winding its way. D'you know Rothern Bridge?'

'Of course, the bridge with four arches.'

'There's a wide piece of shingle and grass at the foot of that steep slope below Rothern Bridge. That's where I used to sit quite still at dusk, waiting for the otter cubs to come and play. First I would see a chain of bubbles, then four or five brown heads in the water. The mother would raise her shining sleek body out of the river, followed by her dripping cubs. They played, sliding down the smooth bank of mud, rolling over on their backs squeaking, with their tiny pink pads in the air. Sometimes the dog otter would join them. He would stand upright quite close to me, listening intently, whickering and mewing. In warm and clear weather I would stay out all night to watch them. There can be nothing more beautiful than watching otters swimming by moonlight.'

'Were they aware of your presence?'

'Perhaps. I would lie quiet for hours. Did you know that otter cubs don't like water at first? Otters were once land animals like their relations, the brocks. Once I rescued a half-dead cub from a holt between the roots of a sycamore tree. A pale grey velvety creature with a square muzzle and tiny ear holes. He must have been ten or eleven weeks old, for he'd already eaten fish. But he still needed milk. When he saw me bringing his food he would crawl towards me, chirruping like a small bird. He liked eel best. When he was old enough I put him back in the river at Waddy Cleave. D'you know it?'

'I remember a ruined chapel there, dedicated to the goddess Diana. My grandmother said I must keep away from Waddy Cleave, for it was a wicked heathen place.'

'After I'd put my otter back in the river, he would come to my whistle. I didn't see him during the winter, but in the spring he appeared and knew me still. Sometimes the otter hunters came with their savage terriers, and I feared for his life. Did you ever see an otter killed?'

'Yes.'

'Shame on you.'

'Only tagging along as a very young lad.'

'It's wicked!'

I too had thought it a cruel death, but had never said so until now.

'I've seen no otter spraints or fishbones by the river here. I walked through Tregarrick Wood to the mill, and up Trefany Hill to Gill Hill Wood, and down to the West Looe River.'

'Not barefoot, I hope! Where else have you been?'

'Nowhere else. Agnes forbids me to go far alone. Sometimes I have to accompany her to St Nonna's Well to pray.'

'You mean Ninnies Grotto! She used to take me there very often.'

'Yesterday we found the well house blocked up with heavy stones. She was so vexed. "I'll strangle that Protestant devil with my own hands", she said. And I believe she would.'

'Agnes is over-zealous in the cause of religion. – Have you brothers or sisters?'

'None surviving.'

'I too am my father's only child. The Wynslades will die out if we're not careful.'

'Agnes is young enough to bear children.'

'She seems unable to have children.'

'D'you love your stepmother?'

'Agnes has done her duty by me. She's a pious lady, much given to good works.'

'She's teaching me to be a good Christian, but there are many things I don't understand. For instance, why it is that only the priest is permitted to drink the blood of Christ at the Mass. And why so many masses for the dead? What good can it do? Besides, I can never remember the names of the Celtic saints.'

'I forget them too. The Cornish have a surfeit of saints.'

'Last week Agnes made me say sixty Paternosters as a penance.'

'What had you done?'

'Let loose an aerymouse into the parlour when she had visitors.'

I laughed. 'She's terrified of bats.'

'When were you last at East Putford?'

'Two summers ago, when I was seventeen.'

'Why have they pulled down that beautiful rood screen in the church? It looks so bare. And removed the stoup and left a crumbling hole in its place.'

'They think such things smack of popery. It's mindless destruction.'

'Who is the Pope?'

'Paul is his name. Pope Paul the Third. We are well rid of popes.'

'I watched two men carrying statues of Celtic saints from the church down the hill to the river and throwing them in. I shouted that I would fetch them back, and was told I'd be hanged for my trouble.' Thomasine paused, and then said sadly, 'Your father will find me a burden. I have no inheritance.'

'My father has always been glad to help someone in trouble. And', I said, smiling, 'My stepmother has gained a daughter.'

'Agnes says I'll never be a lady. I've no respect for my elders.'

'She's not easy to please. I too have my differences with her. It was partly why Father suggested I move to Constantine. It's best not to cross Agnes.'

'I can't help crossing her. She summons me each morning to tell me my tasks. Always more sewing of altar cloths and corporals, and the stitches have to be so neat, or she makes me unpick them. Not that I mind hard work. At Frithelstock I carried water from the well in two buckets on a yoke.'

'Surely you had a servant to do such work?'

'We couldn't afford a servant. I looked after my father when he became too drunk to work. From a woman in the village I learned to make simples. She took me to find coltsfoot, comfrey and pennyroyal, and many other plants. I cured my father's boils with oil of bay.'

'What else can you cure?'

'I can cure melancholy with oil of violet', stated Thomasine proudly. 'And pain with essence of poppies.'

'Agnes would be glad of your remedies. Have you one for constant ill-temper?'

Thomasine laughed. 'No, she chides me for collecting plants. I mustn't wander in the woods unescorted.'

'While I'm here I'll escort you. We'll ride further up the Looe river and look for otters, and soon you shall visit me at Constantine, and teach me how to make simples. Just now I have to help my father deal with this commotion at Menheniot.'

'Your father has suffered much over the hanging of Father Geoffrey.'

'He was a good man who had nothing to do with the murder of William Body, though God knows all of us were glad enough to see that evil rogue dispatched.'

'I once saw a man hanged at Bideford. I got caught in the crowd and couldn't move. To think they can make a person suffer so, and yet people were laughing and making lewd jokes. Even a man's neighbours will enjoy seeing him die.'

'I've no stomach for it. Twenty-six men were hanged for the Helston riot, besides Kylter and Trevian.'

'What had those other men done?'

'Some had assaulted Body, but the rest had only gathered to complain.'

'Why do the people laugh and shout obscenities at a hanging?'

'Because it makes them happy to think it is not they who are suffering. Each person knows that on the morrow it might be him condemned to the gallows. But today he can return home to his dinner and rejoice in his safety. It is only hollow laughter you hear.'

'I'm more like to weep.'

'You can feel the agony. The poor devils who laugh are so inured to suffering that one of the few pleasures they have is to see that others are suffering more.'

'Your father talks of a new prayer book in English, which we must use from next Whitsun.'

'Yes, the archbishop has devised it with the help of Protestant scholars from the continent. But most of the Cornish people don't speak English. They understand the Latin service and don't want it changed.'

'I remember as a small child watching them pulling down Frithelstock Priory. Only the farmhouse was left standing. Men arrived at dawn to empty the chambers and closets and storehouses. First they brought out three huge coffers bound with iron, and then many fine hangings, embroidered linens and leather-bound books. Once the Priory was cleared and the glass removed, workmen came to knock down the walls, and for two days we heard the noise of hammering and falling rubble. It was wicked to smash up the finest building in the village. My mother used to take me into the Priory chapel on Good Friday with a basket of wild flowers to place on the Easter sepulchre, and we would watch the great rood being scrubbed in wine and water. I loved to hear the priory bell for mass, and to hear the canons chanting in the chapel.'

'Yes, my grandfather was much distressed when the priory was demolished, and the canons turned out with nowhere to go.'

'A canon once took me into the priory barn to see the wool fells laid out neatly in piles for weighing. Such soft, soft wool, and the poor sheep looking so cold and bare after the shearing. That priory stood for over three hundred years, and now there's nothing left but a few walls and a pile of stones. We children were told to keep away from the ruins. They said it was a dangerous place, where Satan would catch us. But I explored the deserted rooms.

The wind whistled through the gaping windows, and bits of parchment blew around the scriptorium. Sheep had dropped dung all over the sanctuary.'

'A sad sight indeed.'

'Under some stones I found a gospel book with a red satin cover, worked in silver thread. I have it still, but I can't read the Latin. – Agnes says the commissioners are going to pull down the chantries. What is a chantry?'

'Usually a small private chapel attached to the house of a wealthy family. It saves them having to battle through rain and thick mud to reach the church. Masses are said daily in the chantries for the souls of the departed. But now we are forbidden to pray for the dead.'

'What harm is there in it?'

'No harm at all if kept within bounds.'

'What else does a chantry priest do?'

'He's usually responsible for teaching the children to read and write and instructing them in religion. When the chantries go there will be no more education for poor children in the remote villages.'

'Will we enter heaven more easily if we abandon ancient religious customs?'

'I doubt it.'

'Your father is determined to stand by the people. Will you support him?'

'Yes. I'm here for a family conference. My father's sister, Joanna, and her husband, Humphrey Bonville, are coming from Ivybridge, in South Devon, today.'

We were interrupted by the arrival of my father, who was usually more inclined to laughter than to gloom. But that day his face was drawn with care. 'Ah, Will', he said, 'You've come at last. I see you've made yourself known to your cousin. – Well, Thomasine, what d'you think of my lad?'

'I've not had time to decide', she said, giving me a sidelong glance.

'You'll be good friends, I'm sure.'

Thomasine took up her sewing, and my father and I sat down to talk. 'What's the mood among Helston folk?', he asked.

'Ugly. The hanging of Kylter and Trevian and the others has seen to that.'

'There will be more riots, I'm sure. The trouble is, too few of the gentry care about the commons. They've embraced the new religion to benefit themselves.'

'Which families have done so?'

'The Carews, Denyses, Pollards, Rowleys – and of course, the Godolphins and Grenvilles,'

'Who is for the old religion?'

'The Arundells, Trevians, Beckets and Trelawneys in Cornwall, and the Smythes and Burys of Devon. We're thinking of asking Humphrey Arundell to sign a petition to the Protector.'

'What kind of man is this Protector Somerset?'

'Very earnest in the new religion. But willing to listen. He wishes to persuade rather than force, but is hampered by his councillors.'

'And if the Protector will not accept your petition?'

'He must, or face armed rebellion.'

'Wasn't Humphrey Arundell on the jury that condemned the Helston rioters?'

'Unfortunately, yes. But he was against the hangings. And he has a longstanding quarrel with the Sheriff of Devon, that grasping Lord John Russell. I had my fill of Russell four years ago, when I was part of the Devon musters for the French war. He led the attack on the fortress of Boulogne, and a more brutal man you couldn't hope to meet. I don't much care for Arundell, but he'll have to do. He'll be acceptable to the Devon protesters as our chief leader, since his mother is one of the Calwodleigh family of Devon. The mayors of Bodmin and Great Torrington have agreed to sign. That should add weight to the cause.'

As we talked, Agnes marched into the parlour in a fury. 'How dared you disobey me Thomasine? I've been searching everywhere for you, when I've better things to do.'

'Don't scold, Agnes', I said. 'I found Thomasine myself, and we've had a pleasant talk.'

'This is no time for pleasant talks. We have serious matters to discuss. We're being robbed of our religion. Those evil Protestants will stop at nothing. And do you realise, Will', she said, fixing me with her round black eyes, 'The church at Liskeard has been desecrated. And in our own church at Pelynt we're no longer permitted weekday masses. Father Lambe is forbidden to preach, lest he incite us to Romish practices. Mass is no longer a sacrificial offering. It is but a memorial service. And we're advised to change the dedication to our Blessed St Nonna, for they dare to say she never lived!'

I interrupted the stream of her indignation to say that Thomasine had told me the well at St Nonna's had been blocked with stones.

'That holy well has cured the ailments of our parish for generations. I hope, Will, you intend to help your father fight for our rights. We must act now, before every vestige of our faith is stamped out.'

'Of course I'll sign the Petition. Father says Somerset is a moderate man.'

'He's no moderate! He's a fanatical Protestant like the rest of the King's Council. He made a fortune out of monastic lands, even built his house with the stones of Clerkenwell Priory and St Paul's Cloister. That man is in league with the devil himself!' Agnes was almost shrieking by now. 'We need to rouse the whole of the South-West to take up arms for our Blessed Saviour. Petitions will not suffice!'

'Steady on, Agnes' broke in my father..' There's no question of fighting or killing.'

But Agnes continued regardless. 'At Menheniot the parish has voted against Cranmer's Prayer Book. They'll strike down their new vicar if he uses it!'

'Hush! We must prevent such threats. They haven't read it yet. I'm told it doesn't deviate so greatly in doctrine from our missal. We're no longer to believe that the bread and wine is changed into the Body and Blood of Christ. The anointing with oil at Baptism and Confirmation is done away with, as are the Sacraments of Extreme Unction, Penance and Marriage.'

'Shouldn't we persuade the commons to try out the new service before taking action?' I said.

Agnes's eyes flashed with anger. 'Contaminate our church with that scandalous book! Father Moreman commended us to resist it on pain of death.'

'Perhaps it should have been written in Latin', I ventured.

'Latin or English, it's the work of the devil', insisted Agnes, 'And all to satisfy the greed of that wicked man John Russell. He owns most of Devon and Cornwall and has even built himself a grand house in Exeter. He's broken up the shrine to St Rumon at Tavistock and sent the gold and silver and jewelled ornaments to the Tower. He's assuming to himself the power the Courtenay family had in the West, but cares nothing for our interests.'

'It's Peter Carew I'm more concerned about', said my father. 'The Carews should be siding with our people.'

'His Uncle Gawen is the Commissioner sent to suppress the chantries. The money's needed, so he says, to defend ourselves against the French. But what need have we to fight the French? King Harry went to war and was left with nothing but debts.'

We gained some relief from Agnes's ranting when at the sound of horses she moved to the window.

'That'll be Joanna and Humphrey', said my father. 'Come, Agnes, we'll go and greet them.'

I remained behind and asked Thomasine her opinion. She laid down her sewing, saying, 'I know so little about religion.'

'Agnes has no doubt been instructing you!'

'Oh yes, daily, but I don't like her idea of religion.'

'Religion is the great issue these days. You'll be required to support one side or the other.'

'I'll support your father, who's so good to me. He has difficult decisions to make, but Agnes is so decided already. Such anger frightens me.'

'Unfortunately my father is too generous to Agnes.'

'And your Aunt Joanna? Is she as good as he?'

'Joanna is kindness itself. She loves everyone, especially children. She's had six, and there's another on the way. But she's easily swayed in her opinions. She's liable to wake a Catholic and go to bed a Protestant! She'll believe anything if you tell it with conviction!'

'Are her children with her today?'

'Not this time.'

'I shrink from meeting new people.'

'Joanna will put you at ease. You mustn't let Agnes bully you.'

'Agnes wishes to marry me off just as soon as I've learnt some manners. But who would take a penniless girl?'

Agnes ushered in Joanna, my buxom, cheerful aunt, overdressed as usual - vision of ribbons, pleats, feathers, curls, pearl buttons and huge false sleeves – a colourful contrast to my stepmother, in a severe white linen coif and dark unadorned kirtle. Placing a large basket on the table, she embraced me with her usual affection.

'Dear, dear William, how good to see you again' she said. 'I could swear you've grown taller since Christmas.' Then she kissed Thomasine, and stood back to look at her. 'So you are Cousin Thomasine, of whom John speaks so well. What a pretty child you are, though you could do with more flesh about you. We shall love one another, I'm sure, and soon you shall come to visit us.'

'Sit yourself down on the settle, Aunt Joanna', I said, removing the folded banner.

'Is that your banner, Agnes?' asked Joanna 'Do let me see it.'

Agnes opened out the banner. 'I still have to attach the lining, when Thomasine puts her mind to finishing the hem.'

Joanna fingered it carefully. 'What work must have gone into this!'

'A whole year's work.'

'How gruesome, though. So much blood!'

'Our men need to be reminded of Christ's sacrifice. There is only one way to God, and that is through suffering. This world is nothing, Joanna. Our salvation in the next world is all that counts. Death is the gateway to heaven.'

'That may be so, but I've no desire to pass through it yet.'

'Amen to that', I said, smiling. 'The Wynslades have never been reconciled to suffering.' Agnes scowled at us both.

Breathing heavily, Joanna seated herself on the settle, and opened her fan.

'You look blooming as ever, Aunt Joanna!' I said.

'I'm well enough' she said, fanning her face vigorously, 'But this June heat doesn't suit my condition. If you look in my basket you'll find a box of comfits for you to share. And some little gifts to keep you warm in winter.'

I thanked her, but Agnes only said, 'We have no need of more woollens, Joanna.' She was always ungrateful towards my aunt, much to my annoyance.

To cover my embarrassment, I said, 'What have you done with Uncle Humphrey, Aunt Joanna?'

'Your father is showing him a horse he bought recently. He thinks it will do very well for Thomasine.'

'Thomasine can't expect a horse of her own' stated Agnes sourly.

'Why ever not?' exclaimed Joanna.

'John should be considering more important matters just now.'

'Yes, Agnes, we're so worried about the religious situation. Many of our friends say we must accept the changes, for we can't expect to fight the government. We have our children and property to consider.'

'Does your religion mean so little to you that you'll allow it to be wiped out by government decree?' demanded Agnes.

'Of course my faith is dear to me. But I'm told the new Prayer Book in English is not so revolutionary as people make out. It will enable the congregation to take a greater part in the service. The Archbishop himself has devised it and...'

Agnes interrupted, as though speaking to an idiot, 'Don't deceive yourself, Joanna. Next Whitsun you'll no longer be attending Mass. In its place will be an empty memorial service as though Christ never promised us His Grace as we partake of His Sacrifice...'

'John and I were of course taught as children that the bread and wine were transformed into the Body and Blood of Christ. But if the Archbishop says it's not so, who are we to contradict?'

'Did not Christ say at his Last Supper, "This is My Body" and "This is My Blood" as he broke the bread and poured the wine into the cup he shared with his disciples? Did he not, Joanna? See, you have no answer!'

'Yes, he did say it, but Humphrey tells me Christ meant the bread to be a symbol of his Body...'

'A symbol!' screeched Agnes. 'D'you think God is unable to perform this miracle? God raised Christ from the dead. That's evidence enough.'

'Yes, yes, you're right', agreed my poor aunt, almost in tears. 'I am so confused.'

Disliking the way Agnes was bullying Joanna, I said, 'To be honest I have never believed it. Yet I see no harm in others believing it.'

'Heresy, Will! Do you want to suffer the horrors of hell? You had better...' Agnes broke off, as my father entered with Humphrey, a cautious man whose smooth round face and shiny bald head gave little away.

'Come, Thomasine and meet my brother-in-law', and my father propelled Thomasine towards Humphrey, saying, 'You see, I've gained a daughter at last.'

'And a beautiful one at that!' said Humphrey gallantly. 'You've been living at Wynslade Farm. I gather my father-in-law is sadly ailing.'

'I wanted to stay and take care of him', said Thomasine, 'But he said it was no place for a young girl.'

'North Devon is pleasant enough in summer, but dark and murky in winter. So many trees dripping into so many streams.'

'I loved it', said Thomasine.

Humphrey seated himself, saying, 'Now, to the main purpose of my visit. 'Where do you stand, John, should there be further commotion over the new religion?'

'How can you ask, Humphrey?' said Agnes. 'We'll lead the commons in armed rebellion rather than give in'.

'Calm yourself, Agnes!' chided John, before answering. 'I can't condone murder, Humphrey, but neither can I condone unlawful imprisonment. And how ill-advised was the government in sending that rogue, Body, to Cornwall.'

'You're right. Nevertheless, be cautious about lending your name to a petition. You know the foolhardy risks our West Country folk will take when their fears are aroused. It could turn into a bloody contest. You would be hanged as a traitor, and a good man lost for nothing.'

'We merely wish to present a Petition.'

'If you must, keep it strictly to religion. No asking for the rights of the people concerning other matters. Those who have tried it in the past have been severely crushed. To tell the truth, I can't understand why you're involving yourself with a petition. You've often said you'd be glad to see certain superstitious practices removed.'

'John has never said anything of the sort!' snapped Agnes.

'Yes, I have, Agnes, but only one by one', admitted my father.

'Archbishop Cranmer will never accede to your proposal. He regards the commons as obstinate simple-minded peasants. My friends, Hugh Pollard and Thomas Denys, both reasonable men, strongly advise against putting your name to a petition.'

'I must, to show how deep is my concern for our people. They're protesting in sheer desperation.'

'Sheer desperation about what?'

'Obviously you don't understand the country folk.'

But Humphrey would have none of it. 'Your petition will be rejected', he said impatiently.

'Remember what happened to that Pilgrimage of Grace.'

'In the first instance we're only sending a petition, Humphrey, not planning a march.'

'Well, John, I have to make it clear, don't count on active support from me. I have my family to consider, and can't afford to lose the few lands I possess.'

'John has a family and lands too', said Agnes.

'The more reason to desist from rebellion. The church needs some reform. We should all acknowledge it.'

'You should be ashamed. This is heresy!'

'Of course we care for our faith', insisted Joanna, who hated the upset Agnes always caused. 'Weren't we the first to complain when that wicked Dr Heynes destroyed all the statues in the cathedral?'

'I've even had altercations in the street with government officials', added Humphrey.

'But your protests haven't halted the reforms', said my father. 'Dr Heynes is busy bullying the cathedral canons, and the one man who could have kept them faithful – Father Crispyn – is in the Tower. Individual disapproval will get us nowhere. Only a peaceful protest of the whole South West will have any effect. It's the legitimate right of the people.'

'Provided it's led by a member of the nobility. Who will fill that role?' demanded Humphrey.

'Humphrey Arundell has agreed to lead us.'

'Arundell! I wouldn't put my trust in him. He even denied his young brothers money left in their mother's will, and he never pays his servants' expenses to London.'

'He's been a good military commander.'

'Aha, so you are thinking of armed rebellion!'

'No, Humphrey, you twist my meaning. Thomas Pomeroy has agreed to sign our petition, and John Payne, port reeve of St Ives, also John Bury, Robert Smythe and Richard Coffyn.'

'John Bury's a Devon man, isn't he?'

'He holds lands in North Devon, in addition to Tavistock and Ugborough.'

'Richard Coffyn's a North Devon man too, isn't he?'

'The Coffyns hold extensive lands west of Torrington.'

'These men have no influence outside the South West. I beg you, John, to refrain from signing any petition. Think of Will's future.'

'I have also to think of the future of our people. Each year we landowners become more hard pressed, and so we go to squeeze every last penny out of the commons. They lead a life of grovelling poverty. Superstitious though it is, their piety keeps them going. The old style of worship lifts their miserable souls.'

'Rebellion will deprive them of life itself.'

'They may wish to take that risk.'

'Are you to become our enemy, Humphrey Bonville?' demanded Agnes.

'Please, dear Johnny, do think again', begged Joanna. 'We may suffer through being related to you.'

'Don't you ever think of anything but your children and your property, Joanna? Think rather of your soul's salvation. Fight against these devilish Protestants and you'll be sure of an inheritance in heaven.'

'If every man, woman and child in the South West rose in rebellion, the government would simply send an army to quell it', declared Humphrey.

'John says the government needs all its forces to fight the French and the Scots.'

'Mercenaries, my dear Agnes. Mercenaries will be hired to put us down.'

'Mercenaries! Foreign troops against our own people!'

'It's done on the Continent all the time. It will be done in the South West.'

'Would you stand by and allow foreigners to murder us, Humphrey?'

'Oh, how I hate quarrels!' wailed Joanna. 'We mustn't allow this commotion to divide our family. Why can't the clergy and the Commissioners meet together and come to some compromise?'

'Compromise!' said Agnes. 'Catholics will never compromise! And there are too many cowards like you and Humphrey who want to hide while others fight for your religion.'

'We shall see how events turn out in the next few months. I'm not looking to seize my sword yet', said my father.

'So you'll let your timid little rabbit of a sister influence you? Like a rabbit, she knows nothing of life outside her constant breeding.'

Joanna heaved herself up from the settle, and staggered tearfully from the chamber, exclaiming, 'I'll not stay in this house a minute longer to be insulted.'

Humphrey rose to follow his wife. 'Unless you apologise, Agnes, we shall never enter your house again.'

'No! I'll not apologise.'

Humphrey left, and my father said angrily, 'Agnes, why must you taunt Joanna every time she visits?'

'I can't abide her snivelling ways.'

'Go to her, Agnes. She's my sister. I'll not have her upset.' My stepmother didn't move, and I hated her for being so mean and obstinate. My father walked to the door. 'Come, Agnes, I beg you.' And now I could hardly contain my own anger, that he had to plead rather than order his wife.

Perhaps she felt the weight of our hostility, for she followed my father out of the room, saying, 'As you will, but it doesn't change my opinion of her.'

Feeling ashamed of our family squabble, I said to Thomasine, 'Agnes and Joanna have never seen eye to eye.'

'Your aunt has a good heart', she replied. 'I don't blame her wanting to save your father.'

'He's taken up the cause of ill-used people all his life. I hate the idea of bloodshed in the name of religion, but I'll sign the petition to support my father.'

A week after my aunt and uncle had returned to Ivybridge, my father broached the subject of my marriage. Before returning to Tregarrick I'd been lukewarm about wedding Honor Becket. Since meeting Thomasine I'd become wholeheartedly against it. That this distant cousin of mine was penniless, too young and unsuitable as yet to be the mistress at Constantine, did not deter my intention of marrying her one day, if she'd have me.

For the first time in my life my father was, if not angry, first amazed and then certainly disappointed in me. 'You need a more capable wife than Thomasine, a woman who can fulfil the task of running a manor. Much of the time Thomasine lives in a world of her own. She hates the routine so necessary to the running of a household. She has no proper sense of time and place. The Wynslades aren't so wealthy that they can keep the army of servants a rich estate can afford. You'll be a laughing stock at Constantine. Dislike Agnes as you may, we all know how efficiently she manages Tregarrick. If she didn't, I would have to charge our tenants even more. Money has never been so scant as it is now. I've always liked to keep open house, to enjoy my life and to see our family, tenants and servants enjoying theirs as far as possible. Agnes has shown us a stricter regime is necessary.'

'Thomasine is learning. In a year or so she'll manage as well as Agnes.'

'I grant Thomasine is an intelligent girl, and when she gives her mind to it can fulfil a task as well as Agnes. But she will never devote herself entirely to being mistress at Constantine.'

'She will in due course.'

'You're my only son, Will, and if, in these troubled times, anything should happen to you, I'd have no heirs, and the Wynslade line would come to an end.'

At this point Agnes came into the parlour, and sat herself down quietly.

'It's your duty to take a wife now, to help you run your estate, and to give you children.'

'Why should my life be in danger?' I replied. 'I'm healthy enough. Surely I can wait awhile before marrying.'

'I wasn't thinking of your health. This commotion in Cornwall, and general unrest in the South West, is likely to continue. God only knows what will happen next year when the prayer book becomes compulsory.'

Agnes, who could never remain quiet for long, burst out, 'You've ever been a contrary lad, Will. We've all but arranged the day that you should wed Honor this summer. How can you refuse her?'

'No, I will not marry Honor. We would never be happy together', I said firmly.

'Happy!' scoffed Agnes. 'What does that mean? Marriage isn't walking hand in hand for ever among the buttercups. It's for sharing hard work from morning till night, and for bringing up children in the true Catholic faith.'

Not wishing to squabble, I kept quiet. Silence had always infuriated Agnes, for she revelled in a fight. She was accustomed to win every contest of wills, but there was no victory against obstinate silence. So Agnes took it out on my poor father, telling him more or less what a worthless son he had, until he turned on her saying, 'Will is very dear to me, Agnes. If you want a son in your own image you'd best produce one.'

At that she began to weep, and left us. Her childless state was the only subject which could move her to tears, and her tears could be turned on and off at will.

It was time I returned to Constantine, but I was loth to leave Thomasine. We had been out riding every day, and only then, freed from the malign atmosphere generated by Agnes, did I hear her laugh and observe what a high-spirited and delightful girl she was. I wanted to give her a gift before departing, but couldn't think of anything that would really please her. She cared little for clothes or trinkets. Then one day while visiting a farmer's family I'd known since childhood, we were shown a litter of recently weaned spaniel puppies scampering round their yard. Thomasine fell in love with the smallest pup, a golden bitch. Recklessly, without considering the consequences, I bought the spaniel for her. Thomasine was overjoyed, and said mischievously, 'Her name shall be Nonna.'

An apt choice, but not one to please Agnes. We took the dog home, hoping her icy heart would melt at the sight of it. There were three working dogs at

Tregarrick, housed in a shed, but naturally Thomasine wanted to keep the pup indoors as a pet. Agnes would have none of it. It must be lodged in a separate shed while it was young, and eventually put with the other dogs, which were all bitches. Thomasine was miserable, but I said there was the whole summer for her to spend time outside with Nonna, who by the winter would have become accustomed to the other dogs and could happily share their shed.

I remained at Tregarrick for two more days, helping Thomasine to settle Nonna. My father took to the dog and was sorry Agnes wouldn't allow it in the house. He'd promised I should have a pet when I was nine years old, but my mother's illness, followed by his marriage to Agnes, had prevented it. Like Thomasine I took a childish delight in watching Nonna playing in the yard with the other dogs, who treated it with indulgence. Sometimes we took her to the Warren, where we sat hidden behind the stone wall while the dog raced around, sniffing at all the rabbit holes in ecstasy. We were all happy except Agnes, and it puzzled as well as irritated me that she should be so unmoved by the antics of a sweet new life. I had never seen her smile at our chicks, new-born lambs, piglets or calves – or even a foal. Dick, who helped care for all the damaged creatures Thomasine brought home, in a disused shed some distance from the house, was prepared to help her keep Nonna out of Agnes's way. Thus I was able to return to Constantine knowing all would be well.

Just before leaving I told my father I was still determined to marry Thomasine.

'Agnes is so much against it', he said unhappily.

'Agnes will be as glad to be rid of Thomasine as she was to be rid of me', I pointed out impatiently. 'We all have to consider Agnes above all else in this house. I wish to marry Thomasine, and Agnes will have to put up with it.'

'Perhaps Thomasine will do as well, in spite of her strange ways. But there will be trouble with Agnes.'

'It's high time to stand up to your wife, Father. You indulge her too much.'

'You must understand she's a disappointed woman. I have to allow for that.'

'You allow for everything. Agnes has ruined our family life. Your sister only comes to Tregarrick because whatever insults she receives, she still loves you too much to stay away.'

However, I knew my father would do nothing to remedy the situation. He preferred to give in rather than incur her hatred.

I departed for Constantine, promising Thomasine I would return in August.

At the end of 1548 my father wrote that they wouldn't be keeping Christmas with the usual festivities, owing to the uncertain religious situation.

After the hanging of Martin Geoffrey, Father Lambe at Pelynt became reluctant to flaunt any Catholic practice which might be construed to be popish, and he advised his parishioners to do the same. Agnes judged him a fainthearted milksop, but it was not her life at stake.

I longed to be with Thomasine, but it would have been hard to find anywhere in the house at Tregarrick to be alone together without Agnes spying on us. Out of doors it was muddy and cold, and usually wet. With spring came days of sunshine and showers. Then on the first day of May, my favourite month, came two weeks of unusual warmth, so I hurried over to Pelynt to rescue Thomasine from Agnes.

Stealing out of the manor each afternoon like thieves, for Agnes particularly disapproved of our enjoyment at this time of religious dissension, we would cross over Sowden's Bridge, and ride down towards Looe, through Trenant woods alongside the river, which widens out before joining the East Looe River. We would sit on a patch of damp, sweet-smelling grass amongst wood anemones and primroses till the evening, kissing and keeping a lookout for an otter. If anything caught her eye in the river, Thomasine would hitch up her kirtle about her waist, kick off her shoes and wade out into the shallows.

'Holy Virgin!' I said. 'If only Agnes could see you now!' I said, laughing.

As the sun began to drop behind the thickly wooded hill on the west side of the river, we would eat the eel pies and hard-boiled eggs, or the bread and cheese with spring onions, Thomasine had begged secretly from the kitchen.

On our last evening we decided to devise our own ritual of betrothal. I suggested visiting Ninny's Grotto. Recalling my childhood fascination with the magic spring, I was seized with the romantic notion of our sprinkling the healing water over each other to symbolise our eternal unity. Thomasine had never tried inserting her hand into the well house, nor had she really seen the place, for Agnes had always made her wait at the top of the steps. She had no love of Ninny's Grotto. However, she agreed to go.

It was, I remember, unusually warm and still for an evening in late May. Thomasine rode pillion with her slender arms about my waist. In the sleepy hush that descends on the land after a long day of sunshine we plodded lazily from Sowden Bridge up the river under the fresh green canopy of tender new leaves, feeling the urgent stirrings of life above and beneath us.

The gate to Ninny's Grotto was so compassed about with wild flowers we almost passed it by. Tethering the horse to a tree within reach of a patch of juicy grass, we descended the uneven steps. The fenced-off plot of feathery grasses and tall willow herb was dry. Even the shallow puddle which normally accumulated in front of the well house had all but disappeared.

Thomasine took off her simple gown and, kneeling in her white chemise at the entrance of the well house, stretched her arms inside. Her chestnut hair fell on either side , mingling with long leggy stalks of blue forget-me-not.

'Cup your hands under the spring until you have collected enough water to sprinkle me', I said.

I lay back on the grass and shut my eyes. Presently Thomasine tipped the few drops she'd collected in her small palms over my face. She licked her fingers as I'd done all those years ago, saying, 'What a strange taste!'

Then I put my hands in the well house and waited for them to fill. Now Thomasine lay down, and I poured my offering over her face, and very gently licked off the drops of magic from her eyelids, nose, cheeks and chin. 'The water tastes like nectar', I said.

'So now, are we betrothed?' asked Thomasine.

'Not quite.' And drawing a gold ring from a small pocket in my breeches I slipped it on her finger. 'My mother's wedding ring', I told her. 'See the names engraved, *John and Jane MDXXVII,* on the inside. We'll have our initials engraved on the other side, since our names are too long.'

We sat very close together, gazing down beyond the grassy slope at the ravine below, where the river ran secretly amongst the trees. The sun had disappeared, leaving the wooded hill opposite dark and mysterious. The sky remained a tender unearthly pink, and the air was soft and warm, enveloping us like a gossamer blanket. By and by a crowd of rabbits appeared, determined not to miss their playtime, in spite of predators waiting to pounce or swoop down.

Night closed in gently, and presently we found ourselves beneath brilliant stars, matched on the ground by the white stars of stitchwort standing out from the dark undergrowth. Two tawny owls began to call to one another. Then a moon arose, flooding the ravine with light. Thomasine slipped down her chemise, and with my fingers I traced the outline of her silky moonlit breasts, her narrow rounded hips and long firm thighs. 'Are you cold?' I whispered.

'Just a little', she replied. I gathered her into my arms and in that hallowed place we consummated our betrothal.

Later, as Thomasine slept, I listened to the rustlings in the undergrowth and the movements of my horse up above on the track. Then abruptly I became aware of being watched. Raising my head slightly I looked towards the lower steps, bathed in moonlight. The upper steps were shrouded by overhanging trees, yet it was just possible to make out the shape of a dark skirt on the second step down. I stared terror-struck as the icy moments passed, for whoever or whatever it was must have been able to see my face, but I could see nothing but blackness above the skirt, and in my imagination two piercing eyes. Was she a supernatural apparition, or was she...? Instinctively I guessed it was Agnes. I sat up, and as I did so the skirt glided quickly up the steps. I could have leapt up and followed, and had an unpleasant altercation with my spying stepmother.

Instead I kissed Thomasine, and she woke with a yawn. I determined to say nothing of Agnes.

'We must return home, or they'll be sending out a search party', I said.

If the government or any authority in the South West hoped that the commotion over religious reform would die down in the year following the hanging of Father Geoffrey, they were sorely mistaken. All through the autumn, winter and spring, as the churches were despoiled and arrests were made, discontent smouldered among the commons. In March 1549 the new prayer book was passed in parliament to become law on Whitsunday. Messages began to flow between our leaders in Cornwall and in Devon too, in an effort to co-ordinate a peaceful protest march to London.

The day after I returned to Constantine my father summoned me back to Tregarrick. On my arrival, Agnes informed me in excited fury that all the furnishings of the great Priory Church at Bodmin had been removed – censers, chalices and crosses, vestments of silver damask, and missals. 'Can you imagine such wickedness. They've stolen a pyx, a grail and a processional, in addition to all those fine satin and velvet hangings from Bruges. It's heartbreaking. But fortunately the bones of our blessed St Petroc have been secretly hidden away.'

'Some consolation to the parishioners', said my father drily. 'But relics have little value.'

Naturally Agnes was incensed. But knowing his opinion of old, she didn't pursue the matter.

The week before Whitsun came an excessively handsome, well-dressed, neatly made young man from Helland announcing himself as John Kestell, secretary to Lord Arundell. With a broad smile some might call disarming, and others might call insolent, he informed my father there was to be a great gathering of protesters at Kynock Castle, an ancient fortification near Bodmin. Its purpose was to plan a march to London under the leadership of Arundell. Kestell was very polite as he spoke to my father and myself, yet with no hint of subservience in his manner. There was always rough work to be done at Tregarrick, and on this occasion we were dressed little better than peasants. I caught Kestell once or twice looking me up and down with derision.

As he left the manor he noticed Thomasine sitting on a bench in the courtyard, braiding her hair. I was but a short distance away, standing at the door. He approached her, declaring he'd never seen a prettier serving maid, and if she'd not been employed by Sir John Wynslade he'd like to carry her off to Helland. I reprimanded him sharply for taking liberties with a lady.

'Oh, I never take liberties with a *lady*', he replied, and rode away laughing.

'If he'd not been Arundell's secretary I should have demanded an apology and had him locked up for a few hours', I said to Thomasine.

She only smiled, saying, 'You'd have had to catch him first. It's nothing to make a fuss about. I don't dress like a lady; he couldn't help his mistake. And he did have such a charming smile.'

I felt humiliated. Would Thomasine think less of me for letting Kestell get away with insulting her? One or two of my acquaintance would have taken a horse-whip to Kestell. To my shame I wasn't up to such violence, and it would have destroyed my father's already difficult relationship with Arundell. I was relieved that Kestell didn't live locally.

Our actual serving maid at Tregarrick was a loyal and honest young woman called Amy, daughter of one of our tenant farmers. Her sister, Susanna, was married to Luke, a tenant of Arundell's on the Helland estate. Amy told me they'd adopted Kestell, having found him abandoned as a babe on the steps of the parish church.

He soon came again with another message for my father. He didn't see Thomasine, but I came face to face with him in the porch. No greeting passed between us. I stared into his dark eyes, and this time saw unconcealed contempt, envy as well, and hatred too – an expression to be repeated every time I encountered him over the next few years. On my side I felt intense dislike, and fear too, a rare experience for me, for so far in my life I'd liked or at least tolerated all the people I'd met in spite of their faults, except for Agnes. Kestell departed with a smile, yet he'd thrown down an unspoken hostile challenge. He might as well have spattered me with mud, for he left me feeling soiled, and though during all my acquaintance with him we never exchanged more than a few words, this feeling stayed with me. I sensed instantly that he was one of those few people so confident in their own charm and intelligence that they had no sense of inferiority. And indeed this type of man usually attains a high place on the strength of his own egotism.

My opinion of Kestell was confirmed by Amy. 'You didn't know it', she said. 'But when Johnny arrived, he came a-searchin' for Thomasine at the back entry before goin' in to the main door to speak to your father.' She hinted that as a lad of fourteen he'd even made advances to her, his aunt, and Thomasine should look out. 'They all doted on Johnny at 'ome', she said, "Is mother'd die for him, but not I! Oh, 'e be a sly creature. Susanna and Luke think I be jealous of them for having such a wonderful son. Only I do know 'is real nature, and perhaps, Master William, you will too.'

At my father's return from Bodmin on the seventh day of June, he told us that some six thousand men had gathered at Castle Kynock. Arundell was made General, and the rest of the protesters were formed into detachments under colonels, majors and captains. The clergy were well represented, the priests of Poundstock, St Clair, St Uny and Crede being among them. Judging by the fate of other priests who'd preached against the new religion, I thought how brave were these four. Should the march fail, they too would be hanged without mercy.

The march was due to commence on the tenth day of June, when we would move towards Exeter, linking up en route with the band from Devon. But our departure was postponed when, on the ninth day of June, Whit Monday, to our utmost dismay, came news of a violent incident at Sampford Courtenay, near Crediton, which was to destroy any intention of a peaceful march to London.

On Whitsunday, the day appointed for the compulsory use of the new service, the congregation at St Andrew's, like all congregations in the land, beheld their priest no longer wearing vestments. The procession singing plainchant within the church did not take place, the altar was bare of candles, the Mass was said in English, and the host was not elevated. Whit Monday was the customary day for settling disputes and raising funds to relieve the poor and maintain roads and bridges, combined with ale-drinking, games and competitions between neighbouring villages. It had also been the custom to attend Mass again. Feelings were running high against the new service, and the priest, Father Harper, was forced to don his vestments and celebrate the Mass in Latin.

After the service a franklin named William Hellyons from a nearby village, stood up to urge against the Latin Mass in such a hectoring fashion that the people became angry and, as will happen among large, angry crowds, the unfortunate Hellyons was assaulted and then killed.

This second act of bloodshed naturally gave the government every excuse to use military force. My father was in despair. His only hope was that this incident might put an end to the planned march. But the commons of Devon and Cornwall were up in arms, and declared their solidarity with those at Sampford Courtenay. Arundell had already gathered recruits from every region, some three thousand men, he maintained, and sent us a summons to come to his headquarters at Yewton Arundell, where he owned a house. We also learned that Peter Carew, of Mohuns Ottery in Devon, a skilled and ruthless soldier, had been given charge of the overall suppression of our rising, together with his Uncle Gawen, of Tiverton Castle.

There was no going back now. My father was never so reluctant to go anywhere before, but he endeavoured to be optimistic. I was even more reluctant, as I'd begun to regard our rebellion as a lost cause. Agnes, however, had no doubts. 'It serves that fool, Hellyons, right', she rejoiced. 'Now you must go and fight for our faith, John, with no more talk of time-wasting peaceful petitions bringing empty promises from the government.'

'After Sampford Courtenay the government will be sending an armed force. Unless we gain the support of Exeter we'll never achieve our aim. Murder will beget murder.'

'What better way to die than for the glory of God!' exclaimed Agnes, and I shuddered at her bloodthirsty manner. It was as though she relished the idea of my father and myself dying. Certainly she would have been glad to see me buried.

By this time Agnes was barely speaking to Thomasine and me, so disgusted was she at our betrothal. The atmosphere was poisonous – in earnest it seemed, for Dick suspected Agnes had tried to poison the spaniel. It had been unwise of Thomasine to insist on the name Nonna, for it aggravated Agnes daily. Yet I could understand that it was Thomasine's way of asserting herself for once, since she was treated like a slave when my father was not around.

The day before we were due to leave, my father called me into his private room where he kept his documents and conducted the business affairs of his estates. 'Since I know not what will be the outcome of our venture', he said, 'I have felt obliged to make provision for Agnes, should I die, which you will agree is fair. Rebellion brings with it forfeiture of property, and I could not leave Agnes homeless. Thus I have enfeoffed Tregarrick with a jointure to Agnes for her lifetime. Two friends came to witness my carrying into the house a turf and a bough, according to our ancient custom. It's all signed and sealed. Tregarrick Estate will revert to you on Agnes's death. In the meantime, of course, Constantine is yours. Should it be confiscated by the Crown, Agnes will have to share the running of Tregarrick with you.'

I doubted my stepmother would share anything with me, but I agreed that this arrangement was fair enough.

Now the time had come for the march, Thomasine began to act somewhat strangely, as though unwilling to admit we were to depart so soon. My kind-hearted girl probably had little notion of what horrors might lie in store for the protesters, and even less comprehension of the fury and hatred aroused by the present differences in religion. My father had already said to me how sorry he was that Agnes's fanatical desire to destroy anyone who deviated, be it ever so little, from the true Catholic faith, had turned Thomasine away from religion. For a girl sadly deprived of a Christian upbringing, he could have wished her to experience a far more loving and forgiving faith, than had pertained in Cornwall during the last few years. While everyone around her had been thinking for months about fighting against Protestant destruction, Thomasine seemed to think only of our love and her wild creatures.

I rose before dawn on the sixteenth day of June to make ready for departure. Thomasine had also risen, and I seized some quiet minutes alone with her in the parlour as the sun's first rays fell across the flagstones. I sat on the settle, while she sat on the floor, leaning against my knees.

Suddenly she said, 'You remember that messenger of Lord Arundell's, John Kestell? Well, he came again yesterday while I was in the kitchen garden picking strawberries. He looked over the wall, and I offered to fetch your father. He said he'd only come to apologise for calling me a serving maid. He also said that Lord Arundell had promised after the march to appoint him bailiff at Helland, and to give him a good cottage to dwell in. He would become a gentleman, and wished to marry a lady to help him on his way. I took his meaning and declared I was already betrothed. He smiled, saying a betrothal could be undone, and he would be back to try his luck.'

'What did you say?' I enquired.

'That by then I would be the lady of the manor at Constantine.'

I laughed bitterly, saying, 'Insolent good-looking fellows like Kestell imagine they can charm any woman they fancy.' But I felt uneasy. Thomasine might feel flattered, even if she hadn't been taken in.

'I don't fancy him at all, and anyway, I'll never be a proper lady.'

I stroked her hair, saying, 'I don't ask for a lady. I want the same strange young girl whose brown toes protruded from under that curtain.'

'Agnes says I've cast a wicked spell on you.'

'I like the wicked spells you cast. You're the most beautiful witch in Cornwall.'

'I'd like to cast a spell on Agnes, so she would get taken by the piskies and never be heard of again. We're only happy at Tregarrick when she's out. I dread your going on that march. Agnes will never like me, however much I try to please her.'

'You'll never please her if you keep bringing sick animals home.'

Thomasine leapt up and brought a basket to me from the corner. 'Look at my vuz-peg. Isn't he sweet. His wound is healing well.'

'Another hedgehog, Thomasine! And last week a one-eyed black kitten. No wonder Agnes is vexed.'

'It was starving, Will. How can anyone not feel pity?'

I peered at the small spiny creature, asking, 'What does it eat?'

'Beetles. But he takes any scraps I give him. — Did you know vuz-pegs could swim?'

'No. How long can they live?'

'Five to seven years if they're lucky. Agnes says she'll ask Dick to drown all my pets.'

'Father won't let her.'

It was then that Thomasine surprised me by saying, 'This evening let's go down to the river again, and wait for that otter we saw.'

'This evening I'll be on the march to Okehampton.'

Her only reply was, 'Promise you'll never, never hunt an otter again.'

'You feel too much for them, Thomasine. When animals fight to the death they feel little pain. Most animals die by being attacked by other animals. I've watched a fox gobbling down a duck.'

'They must feel pain when they're sick and starving – I suppose you think me stupid?'

'Just soft-hearted, my sweet Thomasine, far too soft-hearted for this world.'

We were silent for a while, until Thomasine asked suddenly, 'When shall we be wed?'

'On my return from London.'

'Agnes is trying to persuade your father against it.'

'He won't listen to her.'

'She'll stop us, I know she will. She always gets her own way with your father. She'll see to it that you marry Honor Becket.'

'You and I are already betrothed. It's as good as being married. You worry too much about what Agnes thinks.'

'You don't know how much she hates me! When you're with me she curbs her tongue. But when we're alone she calls me a whore as well as a witch.'

'A whore! There could never be a girl less like a whore than you.'

'If you and your father don't return from London, Agnes will turn me out of Tregarrick.'

'Don't fret. We shall return. It's not a crime to march peacefully under a religious banner.'

'That horrible banner! Wait till you see it, embroidered with the bloody wounds of Christ, and in the centre a great heart dripping blood into a chalice.'

'My stepmother has always wallowed in the blood of Christ. There used to be a banner of the five wounds in Pelynt Church when I was a child. I often wondered how many red wool stitches had gone into embroidering all that blood.'

'I see no joy in her religion at all. It's all guilt and blood and death. I'd want to march behind a banner emblazoned with sunshine and blue sky and lambs and doves, to celebrate life.'

Thomasine rose to put the hedgehog's basket back in the corner. As she did so, my father entered in agitation, followed by Agnes carrying her banner.

'What's the matter?' I asked. 'Is there further bad news from Arundell?'

'Worse than I could have imagined. He's had a reply to the petition. Our demands are not even mentioned. If we lay down our arms and return home we'll all be pardoned. Remember that pardon at Helston last year?'

'How can the government fail to take note of articles signed by our priests and mayors?' I wondered.

'The petition was too peremptory. I told Arundell that the Protector would never abide by King Harry's will. If he did, he'd have to hang half the citizens in London as heretics.'

'And quite right too!' said Agnes. 'If only those first Protestant reformers had been burnt in King Harry's time, we'd have had no changes in religion.'

'The time has come, Agnes, to stop burning people for their religious views.'

'One can't afford to be soft-hearted when it comes to defending the faith. It's all or nothing for Christ. Your family' – and here she glared at me – 'have ever been waverers.'

In addition to the disappointing news regarding our petition, we heard that the appointment of Peter Carew as a government commander had angered the rebels gathered near Crediton. They'd entrenched and rampired the highways, and barricaded them with tree trunks, also fortifying two barns, one on each side of the River Clyst. When Carew arrived and charged the rampart, one of his men set fire to the barns, and as a result the rebels refused to parley.

My father could see no possibility of avoiding further violence.

'Once you get to Exeter all will be well', Agnes assured him.

'No, Agnes, all will not be well. Blackaller, the mayor, has refused to declare for our cause. He fears the rebels will loot the town, and though the majority of citizens are against the reforms, he will not condone what he calls treason. Yet he knows Arundell and I and the other leaders only agreed to lead this march to keep the hotheads in peaceful order. Even Bishop Veysey has refused to support us.'

'Coward!' said Agnes. 'He should be ringing the bells and calling the citizens to muster. Once the Protestants take control he'll soon lose his copes and stoles and chasubles, and all those servants he keeps in expensive livery!'

I could scarcely believe that Exeter had gone against us. Not only Devon and Cornwall but the whole of the south of England was stirring, and yet our capital refused to move. 'Is there no one in Exeter who'll support us?' I asked.

'Some of the citizens may come out to join us.'

'What does Arundell intend to do now?' demanded Agnes.

'Lay siege to Exeter. There's no sense in it. Precious time will be lost when we should be on our way to London. Oh, I am sick at heart, Agnes. While we lay siege to Exeter, that blackguard Russell is camped at Honiton, calling us traitors and rebel dogs. With him is a chaplain, Myles Coverdale, who preaches daily against us in the surrounding villages.'

'Russell will never raise an army in the West', said Agnes.

'If he can't, the government will send mercenaries, as Humphrey predicted. – We must prepare to depart now. Are the provisions all loaded?'

'Of course – smoked and salted meat and fish, cheese and plenty of hard biscuit.'

'Once the food has run out we'll have to rely on the goodwill of farmers. It will be difficult to stop hungry men stealing. In France, dire punishment, including hanging, awaited anyone who looted. But I wouldn't want to go down that road with our rebels. We must hope farmers will sell us food, and some join the march too.'

'Which route will you take?' asked Agnes.

'Launceston and Okehampton. We're to meet up with a band from North Devon.'

My stepmother left us then, to see that all was ready. We had sturdy Cornish ponies to carry our baggage. My father, Dick and I, together with three other men, were to ride, while the rest travelled on foot. We expected to reach Exeter in three days.

My father kissed Thomasine goodbye, telling her to bear with Agnes, who would, he was sure, come round to the idea of my marrying her. When he'd gone, Thomasine said, 'If only we'd been wed before this rising started.'

'We're as good as married. We've plighted our troth with a ring and sprinkled ourselves with holy water.'

'I'm frightened of Agnes. She's so jealous of our happiness she'd do anything to destroy it. She tells lies about me to everyone.'

'My poor sweeting. I'll come back soon and carry you off to Constantine. Let me tell you one thing: now that Dick will no longer be here to stand up for you, the only servant you can truly put your trust in is Amy.' I kissed her, and then we went down to the courtyard, where, to our amazement, we discovered Aunt Joanna talking to my father.

'Here is your brave aunt come all this way, bringing us more gifts just when the roads are so unsafe', said my father with slight impatience.

'Don't mock me, John', she said. 'It was Humphrey who sent me to beg you for the last time not to join Arundell's army. Russell has sworn to exterminate every rebel. Italian musketeers are on their way to join him, and Lord Grey is bringing German mercenaries. Altogether there will be more than a thousand trained soldiers, and Hugh Pollard says Lord Herbert might bring a large force from his Welsh estates. Once you join Arundell you're as good as dead. Keep out of it, John, I beseech you, before it's too late.'

Tears were running down Joanna's face, as my father said, gently, 'Joanna, it's good of you to make this journey. But we're now so far into this commotion we can't draw back.'

'You can! The justices, Hugh Pollard and Thomas Denys, are planning to meet with Peter Carew and other leaders to try and resolve the troubles. If you persuaded your Cornish followers not to march, you would be pardoned – and rewarded.'

'Joanna, this isn't a local riot. There are stirrings of rebellion in all the southern counties. Supporters will swell our numbers as we proceed to London, and then the Protector will have to listen.'

But Joanna was desperate. 'Oh, dear, dear brother, do reconsider. It's not as though you and I were ever fanatical for Catholic practices.'

'We have to leave now, Joanna. You stay a day or two with Agnes before going home.'

'Never! We return to Saltash, where we stayed last night. Agnes would not want me here.'

I felt deeply for my poor aunt. The more love and care she bestowed on us, the more Agnes despised her.

I was glad that Dick was to come with us, but a part of me wished he could be left behind to defend Thomasine discreetly against Agnes.

As we moved off down the lane, my father and myself leading men from a wide area around Pelynt, we encountered a woman on a pony. As she drew nearer I recognised her with great surprise as William Kylter's widowed mother. Dismounting from my horse, I greeted her and noted that her haggard face showed signs of great distress.

'Oh, Sir William', she said, her words tumbling out, 'Thank God I've found 'ee in time. My boys,

Peter and Paul, 'as rinned off to serve Lord Humphrey Arundell. They'm not much more'n chillern, sir, but bein' tall, as William be, could pass for seventeen, and will get theirselves killed in no time. They went to avenge they brother's death. I beg you, sir, do 'ee look out for 'em, and order 'em home. I cant' bear to think of losin' they boys now William be gone.'

The company moved on, and I remained behind for a while to console Mistress Kylter. Taking her into our house for refreshment, I promised her I would speak to Arundell.

I crossed the West Looe River and eventually caught up with our party, now swollen to over four hundred, on the further side of the East Looe River. It was an impressive sight, the men wearing helmets and leather or canvas jackets. The majority were archers, easily identifiable in steel caps and jerkins, carrying their bows in tall rectangular shields. The rest carried various weapons – swords, clubs, halberds, spears, pikes and bills. We marched behind two men holding Agnes's banner and another bearing a pyx containing the host. Many of the men bore smaller banners that their wives had sewn, and candles. Thus we set out for the long fateful march to Exeter, crossing the Tamar River at Polson Bridge.

The weather was fine and the men were in good spirits, still singing hymns as we reached Launceston. Listening to individual conversations as we went, I became aware that for many of the rebels the march was to be an exciting if hazardous adventure. Some few might have cared deeply about the doctrinal changes in religion. But many, especially the younger men, were more incensed that Archbishop Cranmer had wiped out the festivals, games, guilds and processions which had focussed for generations on their churches, now lying stripped of all their beauty. No gadding about on pilgrimages, they were told. The cheek of it! This was their chance to demonstrate that Cornish people would not be kicked around by any government. My sympathies were all for those whose lives had never been anything but hard and poverty-stricken. But, I wondered, did they have any inkling as to what lay in store – death in battle, or death by the rope, leaving their families bereft? Healthy young men deem themselves immortal, unable to imagine that death could strike them, and even if they are aware, some gladly take the risk. But as a young man of twenty that fatal summer of '49, I'd no wish to throw my life away in a useless cause.

At Okehampton we joined up with the Devon men, and I noticed that most of them were shorter than the Cornish, who stood out for their height. Some yeomen complained at having to walk so far rather than ride, but agreed that a great host of riders in the narrow Devon lanes would not make travel easier. We would have needed more waggons to carry the bows as well as the baggage.

As we set up camp for the night I was delighted to come across Richard Coffyn, but puzzled as well, for my father had told me the Coffyns at Portledge were strongly inclined towards Protestant views. Richard explained that he felt conscience bound to support the rebellion in spite of his family's wishes. Even his sister, Jacquet, considered him ill-advised to follow Arundell, and he'd left after a great row in which his father had told him not to come running home when the foolhardy venture failed. I was sorry when, on arrival outside Exeter, we found ourselves stationed in different camps, which prevented us from meeting often. Though Richard was two years my senior, I'd always felt strangely protective towards him, owing to his frail constitution. I judged it courageous of him to have joined us.

Dick rode ahead to keep a constant lookout for Peter Carew's force, but saw nothing untoward, and we came to Exeter unmolested. Arundell had already set up four camps on the first day of July, and encircled the city with two thousand men. He'd also organised the delivery of barrels of salt beef and the buying of supplies of food – seven bushels of flour, three hogsheads of beer and four hundred dried hake – from various sources. Each camp was based at a farmhouse commandeered by Arundell from their willing owners. The largest camp spread across the banks and flat water meadows by the River Exe, where yellow flag irises grew. My father's forces were distributed between two of the camps, and we were gradually joined by volunteers from around Exeter, all keen to march to London. This was encouraging, but Arundell insisted that Exeter must be taken first. We learned from citizens who slipped out of the city to join us that the more the local men swelled our forces, the more the mayor of Exeter, John Blackaller, was determined to resist the siege for fear of looting and burning. He also feared reprisals from Russell's men should he give up the city.

Dick, who from his youth at Woodbury knew every inch of the land between Exeter and Honiton, had ascertained that so far Russell had very few men, possibly no more than a hundred. Wasting so many days continuing the siege, with all its difficulties, was madness. We should be marching on to London while the way was clear. All the leaders were of the opinion that keeping troops unoccupied outside Exeter was asking for trouble, and we determined to tackle Arundell.

'The town has springs of water', I said to Arundell, 'And will be able to sustain itself for a while. Why don't we press on while support for our cause is high in all the southern counties? We can collect supporters on the way.'

Arundell, full of himself as the great military man, refused advice from an untried youth who'd never engaged in battle. Before leaving him I ventured to mention the Kylter twins, pointing out they were only fourteen years of age. But I'd chosen the wrong moment. Arundell was much irritated by the refusal of Blackaller to surrender the city, and would not indulge me. 'Let the lads stay. They can act as messengers, and carry out other useful tasks. We'll see to it they keep away from the fighting.'

It would be hard, I thought, keeping any Kylter away from a fight. I had to be content with Arundell's decision. All I could do was to keep a watch out for the twins. Dick said they were used mainly to take messages from one camp to another. Encountering them once, I beseeched them to avoid trouble for the sake of their poor mother. My warning fell on deaf ears. The boys were enjoying the rebellion as though it were a schoolboy prank.

We soon discovered there was another person Arundell preferred to keep away from the fighting. This was Rowland Jeynens, a sweet-natured, innocent lad of eighteen years, but in most respects with the mind of a ten-year-old. However, once he'd learnt to do a task he did it well, and he was passionately loyal to Arundell. He'd been adopted into the Helland household by Arundell's mother, Joan. But for a cast in one eye, Rowland had been a good-looking, endearing child, and Joan Arundell had been very fond of him. At her death, Arundell had promised faithfully to care for poor Rowland, who would never be able to look out for himself. I had seen Kestell chatting to Rowland a few times, and I wondered what kind of influence he was exerting over the weak-witted young man.

In the meantime Blackaller had fortified Exeter as best he could. On the second day of July Arundell led many thousands of rebels in an orderly march behind our banner past St Thomas's Church and across the bridge, once more singing hymns. We halted at the West Gate, asking the citizens to surrender. But Blackaller refused. From the high ground outside the city walls we'd already watched the mayor's preparations in raising spiked barricades and placing ordnance at every gate. Arundell was disappointed, but decided we must starve the city out and harass the citizens by shouting and aiming arrows over the walls.

While marching to the West Gate I'd made the acquaintance of a most singular man, Father Robert Welsh, Vicar of St Thomas's on Exe Island, whose place of birth was Penryn, in Cornwall. He was a short, stocky man, a good wrestler, able to handle a gun and piece with skill. Yet it was hard to imagine him fighting, for he was so courteous and gentle and sensible in all his pronouncements, in fact an ideal priest. After the march I sought him out, and discovered that, like Father Moreman, he was no religious fanatic. He'd remained outside the city to support the rebels, since he was of the opinion that in all their dealings with the commons, the government was always high-handed and unwilling to listen. Then at the slightest opposition it would send in military commanders who'd no sensibility or understanding of a situation. Thus the commons were driven into desperate retaliation.

'You've heard, Sir William', he said to me, 'That counties across the south of England have been stirring in rebellion. None can stomach the laws of the King's Council. Yet, instead of wisely mending its ways, Protector Somerset has resorted to bringing in foreign mercenaries. It sickens me beyond measure to think that the government would use foreigners against its own people. On the continent, mercenaries have been used for centuries, but never till now in civil war. I am the last man to recommend armed rebellion, but perhaps that time has come.' Then he added, 'It's most unfortunate Exeter will not support our cause. But you can understand that the merchants fear losing their trade.'

Father Welsh had tried to persuade our leaders to avoid shooting at civilians in the city. He was particularly worried that since the beginning of the siege the number of rebels had been increased partly by the type of man always attracted to a fight in the hope of gain. And these troublemakers were even boasting of what they would do when the city was taken. It was mostly due to Father Welsh that the men were kept in order outside Exeter, and that later many were persuaded not to slip away to bring in the harvest. Father Welsh was anxious to leave Exeter and resume the march to London. Like me, he had little hope of wresting concessions from the government. But he felt there was a moral principle at stake, that of the right of the common man to protest against ill use. 'We shall most of us end up as martyrs to this cause', he told me, and a chill crept through my bones.

I didn't feel brave enough to offer myself for martyrdom, neither did I want it forced upon me. Secretly my only desire was to return to my estate at Constantine with Thomasine. However, I continued to seek out Father Welsh, because I admired a man so much more courageous than myself, and yet at the same time so compassionate towards those who were not strong enough to stand up for the good.

'Father Welsh', I asked, 'If you were a bishop, would you insist on uniformity of belief?'

'It would be impossible to impose complete uniformity. We can only teach what Christ taught, and hope that people will have faith in Him.'

'You are supporting the Catholic rebels, but do you have any use for the new Protestant ideas?'

'Of course there is much good in the reformed religion. For example, allowing the commons to read the scriptures and the prayer book, and ridding ourselves of so much superstition. We should be taught to use our reason, not so as to lay claim to the ultimate truth, as do both Catholics and Protestants, but because reason is the path to the wisdom of admitting with humility that there are limits to our understanding of God. We can devise as many doctrines as we like, but in the end we are left with the mystery of the unknown God. These Protestants seek to remove all mystery in our worship. They're stripping away the music and the exquisite craftsmanship in stone, woodwork, iron and glass, developed over many centuries. We could all do with more listening to God in church, and less listening to preachers threatening us with hell.'

My father and I were housed in a farmhouse, whose owner, though in sympathy with our cause, was also nervous. In order to protect him from the vengeance which Russell had promised to wreak on all those giving assistance to us, he was to say we'd billeted ourselves upon him by force.

For the first few days after our forces had set up camp around the city there was enthusiasm for the cause in the nearby villages. People went out of their way to cooperate with us. But presently this feeling turned sour. A concentration of military forces into a small area with all the problems of sanitation, disruption of labour, noise and a few unruly rascals bent on making money out of the situation, is bound to become unsustainable. It was to the credit of our men that they refrained from looting and raping. Bands of very young lads had constantly been gathering near the camps during the long summer evenings. They had generated an air of excitement, but during July they became frustrated, and made a nuisance of themselves. The villagers resented having to send away their children and elderly folk for safety. A long siege was going to destroy all the initial goodwill.

Being experienced in mining and sapping, the Cornish tinners in our camp made an attempt to attack the city by digging a gallery under the West Gate and filling it with gunpowder. Unfortunately the digging was heard by a miner within the city walls, and the plan failed. It was almost laughable that we should be undertaking a siege. The most we could do was to snipe at intervals into the city from the high ground north of Exeter.

Messages attached to arrowheads were shot out over the wall from citizens in sympathy with us. From these Arundell was made aware that Blackaller had organised the city's defence very well, and it would only fall when food ran out. But during the first three weeks of July individual rebels were constantly thinking of ways to breach the city. One of the Breton rebels camped with us on St David's Hill, beyond the North Gate, assured Arundell that he could lay down a barrage of incendiary shot which would set fire to the city and destroy it within a few hours. To my disgust Arundell agreed to try this plan. When I told Father Welsh what might happen, he was astounded and angered that anyone should dream of actually destroying Exeter.

Immediately he set about getting and persuading a party of rebels that our beautiful cathedral city should not be burnt. He marched his supporters to meet Arundell, who agreed to stop the plan, realising perhaps that dissension among his own ranks would not do. The fact that citizens had already been shot at over the wall had strengthened Exeter's resistance. Burning the city would have defeated the whole purpose of the rebellion. There was great disappointment among those who'd planned the conflagration. To some of the rebels, taking Exeter by whatever means was their sole object. There loomed the possibility that our lawful march could turn into cruel and pointless civil war without our ever setting a foot out of the South West.

In spite of this particular scheme having been stopped, Father Welsh was still full of anxiety. Besides being a good priest he was also a practical man who understood human nature, especially the mind of a man turned soldier, encamped idle and undernourished beneath a city wall. Victuals were a problem for rebels and citizens alike, for while Russell was waiting impatiently at Honiton for government forces to arrive, he was also ordering looting attacks to prevent farms selling or donating food to us.

Dick continued to make himself a most useful spy. He told my father he had a feeling he couldn't yet substantiate, that John Kestell, Arundell's spy as well as secretary in this venture, had turned informer against us. This didn't surprise my father or Father Welsh, who said many men could succumb to this temptation if paid well enough. Arundell must already have realised his gross mistake in staying so long besieging Exeter, but he refused to admit it, or to believe any servant of his could turn traitor. He'd known Kestell since he was a lad, and prided himself on the loyalty he inspired in his men. Father Welsh despaired to think we'd landed ourselves a leader without principles, who was unlikely to acknowledge a mistake, or to agree to a change of tactics.

One day Dick returned from a scouting trip to report that the young daughter of a widow he knew had been assaulted. Two rebels had broken into her farmhouse, and the younger of the two, who had a cast in one eye, she said, had raped the fourteen-year-old girl. Dick suspected Rowland Jeynens had done the deed. I was doubtful at first, knowing how gentle and timid Rowland was, but the more I thought about it, the more I realised it must have been so. The boy would certainly have been strictly warned to refrain from looting or raping the local population. But with Kestell half bullying and half egging him on, and probably bribing him, Rowland might well have been excited into rape. Kestell had the poor fellow in his power, and could now blackmail him into further evil acts. It was a sickening thought.

Kestell's nasty mind seemed to be constantly engaged in acts of betrayal and corruption. The Kylter twins, who'd been instructed by Arundell to keep their ears open, enjoyed eavesdropping around the camps. One day they told me they'd been trailing Kestell, and one night, as darkness fell, had observed him waiting at one of the posterns in the city wall, nearest Russell's Exeter mansion. Eventually the door opened and a man came out to talk quietly to Kestell and to put what they thought was money into his hands. They wanted me to come with them to inform Arundell of this meeting. But as they hadn't heard what was said, nor could be sure it was money Kestell had received, I told them they hadn't sufficient evidence. Besides, if Arundell were to question his secretary it would not bode well for the twins. Then I asked whether Kestell might have seen them hanging about the city wall. Shamefaced, they admitted he had caught sight of them. This was indeed a misfortune, and I wondered what petty revenge Kestell would take.

My father remarked to me that we should have had a man like Father Welsh as our leader: a man who could plan a battle and fight when necessary, but who was also a reader of the human heart. We could also do with a scrupulously fair man such as my father was, with the courage to speak the truth, but one who was the more able to consider a course of action carefully before embarking on it. Father Welsh had not had the chance of studying at Oxford, but I've no doubt he'd read as many books as Father Moreman, and with as good an understanding. The citizens of Exeter had often come to St Thomas's to hear him preach. He could with ease have moved a congregation to violence, had he been so minded. But, on the contrary, he begged each man to search his conscience before fighting in the name of religion.

'Would you advise us all to return to our homes if you had your way?', I asked after hearing him preach.

'No, Will, we are too far gone in this commotion. Russell will hang every rebel he can lay hands on, whether we fight on or flee.'

Dick said that Russell had been sending his chaplain, Myles Coverdale, and other Protestant preachers to the villages to spread the lie that we'd killed half of the citizens of Exeter, and looted and burnt the countryside. The fault, they said, lay with fake priests, such as Father Welsh. Russell promised he'd be the first to hang. I begged him to try and escape. Though the ports were being watched, there would be some fishing boat in Cornwall willing to risk helping him across the Channel. But Father Welsh only smiled sadly, saying he would stand by the rebels.

By the ninth day of July most of us outside the gates expected the city to surrender, for food had all but run out. Surely Blackaller would give in without a fight, for his citizens had become very half-hearted in their resistance. Dick assured us that Russell had not yet received reinforcements. Only let Exeter fall, and there might still be a chance of moving towards London. We were also encouraged by the news that Yorkshire, Norfolk and Suffolk were threatening rebellion. The government therefore needed the mercenaries to put down each rebellion, and it might be they wouldn't reach the West in such a hurry after all.

Arundell had instructed Father Welsh to write a pamphlet, copies of which were to be delivered to Dorset and Hampshire, Somerset and Wiltshire, informing people of what was happening in the South West, and encouraging them to hold fast to their rights and religious traditions; also to protest against the thieving of church plate, bells and vestments. I offered to help have copies of this pamphlet made. They were to be entrusted to the Kylter twins to deliver to a supporter of the rebels in the East Devon town of Axminster. This man had undertaken to have them distributed to the villages where they would be read out in churches. Peter and Paul were to travel across country by night, a mission they would relish. Instructed by Dick, they'd already taken one message across East Devon, and had proved how well they could conceal themselves.

I believe Arundell had grand ideas of arousing the whole of the South of England under his military leadership. His cause was much reinforced by the news of a rising of the commons and priests in Oxfordshire, which had been brutally put down by Lord Grey's mercenaries. We'd also heard of arbitrary executions in the villages and in the city of Oxford itself. Four priests had been hanged from their own church towers for refusing to cast aside the doctrine of the Real Presence and Sacrifice of Christ in the Mass.

As I wrote out my share of the copies of Father Welsh's pamphlet, I thought constantly of what might lie in store for him when Lord Grey's mercenaries arrived at Honiton. Once more I begged him to escape while there was still an opportunity; but he was not to be moved. He would not even desist from putting his name to the pamphlet. He was, I felt, signing his own death warrant.

Nearly two weeks passed, and still we waited, the tension mounting with each day of inaction. It was becoming impossible to buy victuals from nearby villages, and we had to send foragers further afield. Russell continued to put it about that we were raiding, raping and bullying people into joining us. In truth we found most villages already abandoned, and the livestock driven away or slaughtered. Our ranks had been increasing daily, and some of the volunteers from East Devon, Somerset and even Dorset, brought vegetables and dried meat with them. This they did at the risk of their lives, for by now Russell had sent commissioners to note down the name of each farm and its owner, promising rewards for killing rebels and hangings for those assisting rebels. Villages round the fringes of Exeter, such as Broadclyst, Clyst Honiton, Clyst St Mary and Clyst St George, had been entirely evacuated, and these provided welcome shelter for our men, since heavy rain had begun to fall towards the end of July.

As I was riding round the city perimeter early one morning, Dick appeared out of a damp, grey mist, his apparel sodden and wet straw clinging to his hair. His face was ashen, and he seemed on the verge of collapse. With tears in his eyes he described how he'd just been to his home farm near Woodbury, and discovered his father had been butchered by Peter Carew's men. His brothers had joined the rebels, and his mother and sister had long since fled to seek refuge with relations at Otterton, and Dick had had to make the long round trip to tell them the sorry news.

While I was commiserating with poor Dick, John Kestell came sauntering down the lane, dragging a fat squealing pig on a piece of rope. As he came up with us, he grinned, saying the animal would furnish a fine dinner for his lord. Then, his expression changing to one of extreme gravity, he reported he'd been up on Woodbury Common. Near the windmill where Russell had stationed a small outpost, he'd discovered a corpse dangling from a makeshift gallows. He'd fled the spot swiftly, for fear of his own life. It was probably some poor fellow of a farmer, he said, suspected of having sold provisions to us.

Too much concerned with Dick's misery, I didn't think further of what Kestell had told us. It was only that night in camp when it was reported the Kylter twins hadn't returned, that a monstrous suspicion suddenly overwhelmed me. In a frenzy I shook Dick awake from his well-earned rest, and begged him to go up to Woodbury Common to find the gallows near the windmill. He rode off immediately, planning to leave his horse at a certain house below the common. I felt much ashamed later for not going myself and leaving him to his sleep. But I didn't know the terrain, and would have lost myself in the dark.

When at dawn he rode back utterly exhausted, I saw from his face that all my fear was justified. The corpse dangling from the gallows was that of young Peter Kylter. His brother never returned, and Arundell assumed that Russell's men had caught him too. I was certain Kestell was responsible, and the pig was probably his reward. He had seemed genuinely upset, but I knew now he was a man who could feign convincing delight or pain in equal measure. However, it would be no use my speaking to Arundell upon unproven suspicion. It was essential that he and my father should keep on good terms.

Eventually at the end of the third week in July, Dick brought the bad news we'd been expecting. A hundred and fifty trained Italian gunners had arrived to reinforce Russell's army. Dick had been warned by an acquaintance of his in Honiton that in addition Lord Grey's eight hundred German mercenaries would reach the town within a few days. And Sir William Herbert, another fighting hothead, was not far behind with a large force from the Welsh Borders.

Looking back I can understand that both Russell and Arundell were desperate to see action – Russell because he was frustrated by the long wait, and Arundell because he was anxious to do battle before more mercenaries arrived. We had set up blockades on all the roads into Exeter, and it was Kestell who described scathingly that Russell hadn't been able to approach the city on horseback, try as he might. He'd even lost some of his men in an unexpected fierce encounter with a patrol of our archers. In typical ruthless fashion, Russell had relieved his foul temper by returning to his headquarters via Ottery St Mary, setting fire to the town and to all the dwellings on the road back to Honiton as he went.

To most of the rebels this incident was just an accident of war, and the loss of a few archers to be expected. But to those men who came from Ottery and other parts of East Devon, it was a personal disaster. Revenge was in the air, and Arundell decided to tackle the enemy. Thus it was a force of very eager men which he led to Fenny Bridges, even causing a trumpet and drum to sound as we marched. The two rebels in front had to carry Agnes's banner, poor devils. I went with them, to show my mettle in the first battle of my life.

We had fortified the bridges over the four branches of the river, but Russell's Italian gunners managed to clear our defences. Sir Robert Smythe, commander of the Cornish archers, held half of them, including myself, in reserve. Earlier in camp I'd heard him declare to Arundell he had little use for guns. He preferred the bow, with its rapid arrow discharge. He maintained that in France the Cornish archers shot ten to twelve arrows a minute over a hundred and sixty-five yards. Discharged arrows missing their mark could be collected later and used again. Gunners had to be trained to recharge, and it was a waste of valuable time. But Arundell insisted that the gun was the weapon of the future. He deplored the fact that our few guns would be inadequate against Russell's gunners.

Thus I did not take part in the initial fierce clash, in a field below the bridges. To begin with it seemed as though we might prevail, but after the first onslaught the gunners rallied, and the field was soon covered with our dead. From behind a hedge we reserves watched Russell's men starting to loot, even heaving up headless corpses to search their packs. Immediately we let loose our arrows, catching them by surprise. But their guns once again had the victory.

In the confusion I heard Robert Smythe's voice urging the few of us still alive to make our getaway. Stumbling across a field to the road, I became aware of blood running down my face. I had suffered a gash, fortunately just above my right eyebrow. Later, in healing, the wound did not knit together smoothly, giving my face an unsightly scar for life. I noticed a muddied piece of Agnes's banner trodden into the grass, and thought of Thomasine. We must have run for close on three miles to Strete before the enemy gave up the chase and turned back. We none of us had horses, not even Robert Smythe, since we'd come up as a contingent of archers carrying our bows. We left the road and took shelter till nightfall to complete our trudge back to camp.

My father told me the next day that Arundell had returned safely with his few surviving men. Three hundred rebels had been killed. Arundell had given him a copy of the reply to the petition we'd sent to London, urging us simple, credulous West Country people to repent and cast aside wicked superstitions perpetuated by seditious papist priests! We were exhorted to return to the King's obedience or we would suffer the King's punishment.

I read the document several times, becoming more and more angry until I burst out, 'The government will never give way. What's the use of sending more West Country men to their deaths? For all that we fought valiantly at Fenny Bridges, Russell's gunners gained the day. Soon he'll have eight hundred trained mercenaries, and then the forces from Wales. You and Arundell and all the leaders know we don't stand a chance. The men surviving the battle will be hanged, so will the priests supporting us, and then the people of Devon and Cornwall will have to submit to the new religion. Hasn't enough damage been done? The land for miles around Exeter will be further devastated. The harvest will suffer, and for what? Tell the government we give in, lift the siege and go home.'

My father looked at me despairingly. 'Surely, Will', he said, 'You're not suggesting we turn tail and run?'

'Exactly that', I shouted. 'Just what Robert Smythe and I and a few more had to do at Fenny Bridges yesterday. We acknowledged defeat and ran. All this talk about honour and courage, but what of common sense? What use is there in going out to be killed? In years to come, people will judge us crazy to have thrown our lives away for the sake of religious customs, to have died by the rope so that many of our covetous gentry can seize our lands and leave our families destitute. Will they praise us? – No. They'll laugh at us for the fools we are.'

'Have you no principles at all, Will?'

'Yes, if we had a chance of winning, if we had a chance of forcing the government to help the commons to a better life.'

My father must have counted my outburst as a temporary fit of madness, for the following day he talked to me as though it had never happened. I was glad to discover Father Welsh agreed with me there was no point in further battle. On principle he himself must remain faithful to Catholic doctrine, and would suffer whatever punishment came to him.

'I know, Will', he said, 'That if the rebels laid down their arms now and went home, I'd lose my living, but perhaps not my life. And if we stick to our fight I'll certainly lose my life. But can you imagine any one of us instructing these valiant men of the South West to grovel in repentance at Russell's feet? For all that your father and you and I intended to lead a lawful march to London, these men came to fight for their rights, and fight they will. Arundell certainly came to fight. He's a military man, and understands nothing else. Should you go home tomorrow, your family would be for ever dishonoured.'

He spoke the truth. I felt a coward, but as always, I wished to prove otherwise. And if to cast my life away would turn me into a brave fellow, then I must try to do it with a brave face.

During July Arundell had spent much time teaching our foot-soldiers the rudiments of battle, particularly in the matter of discipline. He'd been inclined to put the men into some kind of uniform, but my father maintained it to be an unnecessary expense. Our men could be distinguished by their not wearing uniforms. Though not a popular leader, owing to his arrogance and self-opinion, he was a most efficient military commander, and was never so content as when training his troops. It was obvious he'd consented to be our leader with the sole purpose of fighting. A peaceful march to London could never have been his aim, and I don't believe he had any real interest in religion or in the welfare of the Cornish people. He was using our protest to sacrifice his men in a personal vendetta against Russell, whom he rightly considered an upstart who was swiftly becoming the foremost landowner in the South West. 'He can't see beyond the next battle', said my father, who'd long since realised our cause was well-nigh hopeless.

On the last night of July, all our captains and the governors of the four camps held a conference at Father Welsh's house near St Thomas's outside the West Gate, together with other members of the gentry and a number of priests. They were to discuss and plan our future military action.

On the strength of being John Wynslade's son I was asked to attend, and looking round I was able to put a name to most of the men assembled there. I noted Roger Barrett and John Thompson from Cornwall, William Fortescue from North Devon, and the tailor, Thomas Underhill, who was stationed in our camp. It was he who'd forced Father Harper at Sampford Courtenay to conduct the Whit Monday Mass according to the Latin rite and wearing vestments. Though not of the gentry, Underhill was a highly intelligent man of great influence in Mid Devon, whom men were glad to follow and obey. I knew Robert Smythe of course, and Henry Bray, the mayor of Bodmin, Sir John Bury of Tavistock and Sir Thomas Pomeroy from South Devon., I was also acquainted with Simon Morton, Vicar of Poundstock, and Robert Boyce, Vicar of St Cleer. The mayor of Torrington, Henry Lee, had once spoken to me. It was his wife, Mary, who'd befriended Thomasine's mother, Alice, and found her daughter a home with my grandfather at Wynslade Farm. Best of all, I had a chance to talk to Richard Coffyn.

Arundell rose to explain our position. 'We have information', he declared, 'That the city may be forced to surrender at any moment or suffer starvation.. The majority of citizens support our cause, but it's to be expected that once the gates are opened, all of them will burst forth desperate for food. Blackaller has been told that if he surrenders we shall put a store of grain at his disposal, which must be distributed in an orderly fashion.'

Thomas Pomeroy interrupted to state that he doubted Blackaller would surrender. If Russell didn't arrive he'd fight his way out, and we'd have an unlooked-for battle on our hands. 'Blackaller', he said, 'Knows Russell's uncompromising character only too well – any sign of Exeter throwing in its lot with rebels and Russell will let loose his mercenaries on the city. Blackaller must be depending on Russell breaking through our lines to relieve Exeter.'

'Indeed', replied Arundell, 'And it's therefore our task to prevent this occurring.'

Two men unrolled and held up for all to see, a length of linen on which was drawn a map of Exeter and the surrounding area. Arundell pointed out that four of the Clyst villages and their bridges had been well fortified with ramparts, huge felled tree trunks, thorny furze and stakes. The roads from Tiverton, Cullompton and Newton Poppleford had also been blocked with tree trunks and rocks. It was essential to prevent Russell reaching the naval base at Topsham, from where ships could convey him up the estuary to Exeter. So our immediate task was to ensure that neither Russell's cavalry nor infantry should cross the River Clyst.

'We don't know yet which route Russell will choose from Honiton. He'll probably have to come cross-country over Woodbury Common, where he can more easily move his cavalry. And I suspect he'll attack Clyst St Mary and try to clear the bridge.'

Thomas Pomeroy and my father were put in command at Clyst St Mary, and I was to go with them. Henry Bray and Henry Lee were to defend Clyst St George, a mile to the south. Women, children and the elderly had been evacuated from all the villages immediately north and east of Exeter, leaving behind any young men who chose to join our forces.

When it was ascertained which village Russell was aiming for, the church bells were to be rung as a call for help, already promised from many a nearby hamlet and farm in East Devon. The more distant villages, having taken up the signal for the call to arms, would then ring their bells. Naturally a besieging force would be retained around Exeter. Several small hand-picked patrols were to be sent out each day to spy out the land and make an attack on any reconnaissance group Russell sent forth.

Kestell, too, would be out daily seeking information. I asked Arundell whether Kestell's life was not being risked too often, since he didn't assume a disguise. I pointed out that Dick Popham went spying dressed as a simpleton labourer with an incomprehensible East Devon accent, and he knew the area far better than Kestell. But Arundell dismissed my suggestion, insisting there was no better spy than Kestell, who needed no disguise. He was like quicksilver and could charm his way out of any tight corner. I'd warned my father about Kestell, but he replied that without hard and fast evidence against the man there was nothing we could do.

After the conference, Dick brought a verbal message from my uncle Humphrey Bonville, who was staying at Bicton with his long-time friend, Sir Thomas Denys, who'd no wish to take sides. If he could be of any personal assistance, we should let him know. Thomas Denys and other local gentry sympathised with our cause, especially since Russell had brought foreign cutthroats to devastate their land. Yet on no account did they intend to join Arundell, who they considered a fool for leading an irresponsible rebellion doomed to failure from the start.

Dick also brought a message from Sir Thomas Yarde, another gentleman of East Devon and a wine merchant, who was living temporarily at Bicton. He begged that we shouldn't billet our men at his house in Clyst St Mary. He did send a key with Dick, saying that Pomeroy, my father and I could use the house in an emergency. Dick informed us Yarde's young son, John, desperate to be a cavalry officer, had, against his father's wishes, offered himself to Russell as an expert rider with good knowledge of the area. Yarde was vexed, but he turned his son's rash doing to his own advantage. He'd pointed out to Russell that since his only son was risking his life against the rebels, he'd be grateful if in return his house at Clyst St Mary would be spared if an attack took place on the village. My father wasn't happy about this double game Yarde was playing to protect his property. However, he did tell our men to keep clear of the large two-storey house with its cellar full of wine.

We dug ourselves in at Clyst during a third day of heavy rain. It was a strange experience camping in a deserted village, a few men in each dwelling and some in the barns, slithering around in the mud, trying to keep dry and to take in the layout of the place. We had three gunners, who took turns manning the bridge, concealed behind a heap of furze piled on top of many stout jagged branches. The river was churning with swift muddy water, an uninviting prospect, although Pomeroy showed the men the safest place to wade across, should they have to escape. I felt sorry for those who couldn't swim.

Poor Dick was out in the wet the whole day, walking up to Woodbury Common to give us warning of any military movement. At last, on Saturday, the third day of August, Russell led a force from Honiton of some thousand men across the common, and set up camp at the windmill in late afternoon. Dick returned at dusk to tell us that a patrol of rebels had surprised the camp. They'd given the enemy a hard and bloody contest, but an unequal one. And indeed, there were only three survivors, who arrived soon after Dick, collapsing with exhaustion and minor wounds. My father declared the attack had been rash, but understandable. Any action against the detested enemy was better than endless waiting.

Half an hour later, who should appear, wearing the most dejected demeanour, but Kestell, on his way back to Arundell's camp. Almost choking with angry emotion, he described having watched Russell's chaplain, Myles Coverdale, conducting a service of thanksgiving on the battlefield, while our rebel corpses lay unburied, together with several fatally wounded moaning in agony. Before he left, Kestell informed Pomeroy that Russell had announced an attack on Clyst at dawn.

Why, I wondered in annoyance, didn't my father or Pomeroy question Kestell as to how he'd come close enough to the enemy camp to be able to see so much and to report so precisely on Russell's doing. Where could he have concealed himself on the open common? Detail such as this was never obtained from Dick. Kestell was, of course, being paid, perhaps handsomely, by Arundell, and by Russell. How he must have relished being a double spy! I was asked to give him a hand over the barricaded bridge under the darkening sky. Before he leapt down at the other end I glimpsed a look of triumphant elation on his face as he gave me a sly smile. Did he guess I knew about the Kylter twins, but had no proof? If he did, what satisfaction he must have derived from it. I had never felt like killing a man before, but that evening I would willingly have done it.

A grim mood seized the whole army as a result of Kestell's report. It was in a spirit of determined revenge that, under cover of darkness, every man took up the post he'd been allotted in the four Clyst villages. Dick had come with us to Clyst, not to fight but as usual to be our messenger and spy, a task becoming more dangerous every day. Whenever Dick went off on a mission, the image of that poor lad, Peter Kylter, dangling on a gibbet, came into my mind. What if Kestell had told Russell to look out for Dick? I confided this fear to my father, but he thought I was letting my imagination run wild,. He'd come to the conclusion that though cocky and unpleasant, probably Kestell was as tried and trusted a servant of Arundell's as Dick was to us. At the daily risk of his own life he'd brought Arundell much valuable information. I couldn't calm my fears for Dick's life, but at least many of the local people would risk hiding him if necessary, since the Pophams were well liked and respected in East Devon.

A few archers were stationed in each cottage along the main street, and many more behind walls and hedges leading down the long slope into the centre of the village. My father was to wait with a band of men on the green behind the rampart laid across the road. Pomeroy planned to take up a position behind a high wall in front of Yarde's house. At midnight the church bell was tolled. This was taken up by Clyst St George, and then by other bells. Gradually during the early hours, men we'd not seen before began to arrive, together with a few very young lads who should have been abed. Some of these came armed only with a pitchfork or a billhook. To my surprise there were so many there was barely room to accommodate them all. These were men who'd not come to fight on grounds of religious discontent alone; they came, filled with fury at the wanton destruction Russell's men had wrought on their land – trampling the crops ready for harvest, looting the farms, slaughtering the livestock, and even murdering, as had happened to Dick's father.

My father had told me that in France mercenaries were the hardest to discipline. If they weren't permitted to loot and rape they would desert in marauding bands, and it was a terrifying experience to have these ruffians descend on your village. The commons of East Devon hadn't experienced destruction on such a scale before, even in the fierce local Courtenay-Bonville feuds during the civil war of the last century. And the commons were also incensed that Russell and Grey helped themselves to their produce under the guise of coming to protect them from Arundell's cutthroats.

It was a crystal clear night, as so often occurs in Devon after a few days of deluge. The star-pricked sky, scrubbed clear of clouds, stretched over the miles of flat estuary land to the sea at Exmouth. It was a night to be out fishing instead of waiting with stiff aching limbs for the attack in the cramped space of a cottage. As the first ghostly grey light of dawn filtered through the small window, my eye fell on a rag doll perched on a three-legged stool in the fireplace, a cheerful grin sewn onto its grubby face. Chewing on a piece of hard biscuit to calm my churning stomach, I wondered idly if the doll would ever be reunited with its young owner.

On a sudden impulse I took up the toy and stuffed it into my back pack. It was to become my mascot, a symbol of childish innocence.

Suddenly in the distance we heard the pounding of hooves, and moments later horses thundered into the village, charging the ramparts straight into the body of men standing on the green. They were followed closely by mercenaries on foot. I suffered the ordeal of letting fly our arrows to wound the horses first. Sir William Francis – for later I discovered it was he who led the charge – quickly realised the mistake of trying to join battle under a hail of arrows from both sides of the street. Immediately the cavalry wheeled and turned back up the slope, causing much confusion to the foot soldiers pouring down. As the Italian gunners had not yet arrived, we almost held our own in the fierce hand-to-hand fighting. Then from a side street Pomeroy's East Devon volunteers burst eagerly into the battle, uttering ferocious shouts, which took the mercenaries by surprise. I heard desperate commands in German, and saw the enemy struggling to retreat. As the men ran, so we pursued them out of the village, and to our great satisfaction were able to capture some waggons of armour and munitions which Russell had brought down to Clyst from Windmill Hill. He had, no doubt, been expecting to defeat us easily so as to remove the obstructions from the bridge and give his army a clear passage to Exeter.

Our wounded were carried into a cottage, and our dead into a field. Then for the first time I was forced to witness what seemed to me to be the worst part of battle – the despatching of the mortally wounded. It was Dick's task to deal with the unfortunate horses brought down by arrows. At home he'd been the only one who could approach a writhing horse screaming in pain closely enough to make sure of killing it with a single shot. Nothing angered Dick more than the wounding of horses in battle, and I do believe that if my father had been able to use our horses in this rebellion he would have quit our service. Yet he must have known that my grandfather and my father had won their honours in France as part of the cavalry.

If our men judged the victory to be ours, they were sorely mistaken. We'd outnumbered Russell's force in the first assault, but ironically the thousand or so men who'd joined us during the night became an embarrassment packed into such a small village, especially as they'd had no military training. Thus they were ordered to an open space at the northern edge of Clyst St Mary as reserves. The rest of us took up our original positions. I disobeyed this order however, having been most unhappy cooped up in the small low-ceilinged cottage. I found a better place to draw my bow – a walled sheepfold on the bank of the river with a water-trough along one side, behind which I could duck out of sight.

Russell, on discovering our numbers were greater than he'd expected, was planning different tactics. If only we'd had the sense to guess what was in his mind. If we'd thought of fire we might have avoided the extreme carnage, especially of the bowmen, resulting from the second attack.

Part of Russell's cavalry charged once more down the slope, but this time the riders carried flares, which they tossed onto the thatch of each cottage. Then came foot soldiers, also throwing flares. A vicious and chaotic struggle reigned in the main street and on the green. Order of any kind broke down as coughing archers struggled to quit the smoke-filled cottages. There was a noise, the like of which I'd never heard before. As I drew my bow another sound, that of gunfire, came from the direction of the reserves. The Italian gunners must have penetrated our northern defences. In spite of their great numbers, the volunteers of East Devon would stand no chance against guns.

It quickly became a question of each man shifting for himself to escape before the whole village became an inferno. Russell had extricated his cavalry from the mellay before the fires took a hold in the damp thatch. Just below me the river was still running fast, but many of our men managed to wade or swim across and ran off dripping towards the estuary. The mercenaries didn't take to the water in pursuit. Having won the day, they waited till given the command to cross the river. An enemy gunner took the risk of challenging our one gunner defending it, and was shot into the river. In the meantime another Italian gunner waded unnoticed under the bridge and came upon our gunner from behind as he was reloading. His body too fell with a crash into the water.

Now that the enemy could attempt to cross the bridge, I had to dig myself further into the treacherous nettles growing round the trough, fearful of being seen. I could have joined the rebels escaping across the river earlier, but didn't wish to leave Clyst until I knew what had happened to my father and Dick.

For what seemed like hours I lay, not daring to move, listening to the constant movement, shouting of orders and several gunshots. In contrast, the sky above me was a serene, innocent blue with small clouds drifting across it. At length quiet reigned in the village, and raising my head I was aware of action on the opposite side of the river a yard or so from the bank. Some men were lying, some sitting, and others standing. Where could Pomeroy, my father and Dick be? My best chance would be to try and reach Yarde's house and lie low till dark. I might be seen when I stood up, but it had to be risked. Climbing out of the sheepfold, I made a dash for what cover there was, avoiding the smoke still billowing up from the cottages.

I reached Yarde's house, trusting I might break my way in with what implements I carried in my pack. As I climbed over the gate, what a relief it was to see Dick, carrying a bucket of water from the well. He stared at me in astonishment, saying, 'We thought you was burnt to death in the cottage.'

My father had been wounded in the thigh, and Dick had managed to drag him into the kitchen from amongst several bodies lying beside the wall. He'd staunched the wound with linen he'd found, and laid him on a flock mattress he'd carried down from a bedroom. My father was weak from loss of blood. ''E do believe you perished in the flames', said Dick, 'And wishes 'isself dead.'

We hastened into the house. The sight of me brought a little colour into my father's ashen face, but we couldn't rejoice for long. Even if not discovered by the enemy, there was the problem of how to move my father away from Clyst. Dick had spent some time looking out from an upper window of the tall, two-storey building, to see what was happening across the river and in the village. He'd watched the hundreds of East Devon volunteers in Clyst being surrounded by the Italian gunners, and ordered to lay down their arms. Some had attempted a breakaway, only to be shot down, whereupon the rest had obeyed and were herded one by one across the bridge. As each man leapt down on the other side, he had his hands tied behind his back and was made to lie on the grass.

'So those men lying on the grass are prisoners!' I exclaimed. 'Why would Grey encumber himself with so many prisoners, or indeed with any prisoners at all?'

Dick suggested I go up and look for myself. From the upper window I could see that some of the prisoners had been ordered to clear the bridge of its defences, and were struggling with a great tree-trunk. Was this the reason for taking prisoners? What luck I had left the sheepfold just in time! Dick joined me in a while, and we worked out that possibly the prisoners would be kept as hostages to ensure the cooperation of their families. If they made themselves useful, they might be promised a pardon. It was a cunning move on the part of whoever had decided to take prisoners.

'But what's become of the cavalry?' I asked. My question was answered as we watched horsemen emerging from woodland to the north on the further side of the river.

'They must've crossed by the ford at Bishop's Clyst', said Dick. 'John Yarde must've guided 'em to it.'

We continued looking out across the river, and saw everyone except the prisoners eating their rations, seated on the ground. The few prisoners who had cleared a passage over the bridge were now lying down again with their hands tied together. Russell will go on to relieve Exeter, I thought, leaving sufficient gunners to guard the prisoners here. Suddenly we saw Lord Grey striding to the river's edge and gazing at the land below Woodbury Common, and then up at the Common itself. After some minutes he walked back to speak to Russell. We never did discover what he'd seen. Possibly he feared an attack from behind.

What followed as a result of his fears was to give me nightmares for the rest of my life. An order was shouted. The mercenaries leapt to their feet. At the second order they whipped out their knives and began to stab and slice like savages at the helpless bodies of the prisoners. As I heard the high-pitched, agonised screaming, I clutched Dick as I'd done long ago when as a child I clutched my nurse on seeing a squealing pig having its throat cut.

We were witness to a most shameful massacre, the first and I hope the last of my life, an act to be abhorred by every decent man in the South West. There could be no forgiveness for butchering in cowardly cold blood. Grey must have judged that shooting the prisoners, though less cruel, would have been a waste of shot. It was all over in ten minutes – nine hundred men, as I later found out – in ten minutes! – mostly those East Devon men who'd so willingly answered our call for help. Too sick to speak, we went on staring fixedly from the window, long after Russell and Grey had mounted their horses and led their army away from the carnage. For Dick it was a double tragedy; some of these murdered men had been his family's neighbours and friends.

My problem then was how to bring my father to safety where he could receive treatment for his wound. If we'd only had a horse to convey Dick swiftly to Bicton to seek Humphrey's aid. But the only horses left locally belonged to families who were siding with Russell. However, in spite of the danger, Dick insisted on walking the seven miles to fetch a cart.

During his absence I tended my father, who was suffering much pain. I found honey and oats, and mixed them together with water for us to eat, and we drank the remains of the ale left in my leather bottle. It was dark when at last Dick returned in a cart, with Humphrey riding his own horse. Fortunately the sky was clear, with a moon, so they'd no need of a lantern. Humphrey had brought a straw pallet, blankets, food, wine and a remedy Lady Denys had sent to quell my father's pain. Dick and I made my father as comfortable as possible in the cart, and before setting out we climbed hastily to the top of the house. We could hear distant sounds across the river, and guessed Russell's men were now encamped on Clyst Heath.

'They'll move to relieve Exeter tomorrow', I said. 'It's the end of the rebellion.'

'No', said Dick grimly. 'Our men in the camps maintainin' the siege, and them as just escaped from Clyst – they won't run away. They'll give Russell another fight, just 'ee wait and see.'

We started on the long ride to Lympstone, my poor uncle looking so fearful I felt sorry for him. How he must have longed to be tucked up in bed at Bicton. Probably he'd only come to East Devon to satisfy my aunt, nagging him to *do something for poor Johnny and Will*.

We stopped just south of Exton for a while to refresh ourselves with meat, bread and wine. Humphrey relaxed somewhat, and I related all the events of the previous few days.

We boarded the early morning ferry from Lympstone across to Powderham, passing within sight of the castle, once the seat of the richest and most powerful family in the South West. We could have wished that Lord William Courtenay had given our cause his active support, being a staunch Catholic. But he was away from Powderham during the whole of the rebellion. If he, rather than Humphrey Arundell, had led the rebels, our tragedy might well have been averted. The only Courtenay residing in Devon was one of his younger sons, Sir John, who lived in Exeter, and though sympathetic to our cause, was fearful we might destroy the town.

Once across the estuary we felt safer, Humphrey in particular, for he had no wish to be seen by the enemy assisting rebels. Little did he realise that Kestell, a man who seemed to have the luck of the devil, had seen us leaving Clyst St Mary.

The long journey to Ivybridge was accomplished safely. Joanna provided tender nursing for my father as he sat in a great leather chair with his leg on a footstool, and plenty of hot water, dressings and fresh garments for Dick and me. How we must have stunk! Our bodies soon recovered, but our minds were still full of foreboding.

Dick was right. By early afternoon the following day, news of the last stand outside Exeter had reached Ivybridge. The battle of Clyst Heath, as it became known, was remembered for many years in Devon for the superhuman valour of the rebels. Russell had been fully prepared for the rebels to make a final attack and had stationed small bands of his men in every enclosed field round the bracken-covered hill of Clyst Heath. Thus the rebels were ambushed and had no choice but to fight almost to the last man. One of the last men was Arundell, and he lost no time in riding to Sampford Courtenay to raise fresh troops. I never liked him, but I had to respect his dogged courage.

It was not until I was imprisoned in a London gaol with Thomas Holmes that I heard details of this heroic battle. The exhausted survivors of Clyst St Mary joined up with the rebels who'd been maintaining the siege. Leaving only a few men round the city, they hastened to Clyst Heath to do battle with Russell, surely knowing, I thought, that they were going to their deaths, yet hell-bent on revenge for the massacre. Often after the rebellion was over, I remembered and grieved for poor Thomas. To have survived Clyst Heath, only to suffer the obscenities of Tyburn, was a fate beyond comprehension. To me the mercy of God was swiftly becoming an empty phrase.

We heard that Exeter had been officially relieved early on the morning of the sixth day of August. Russell was now in complete command of the city. The day before Sir Walter Herbert had arrived with a thousand Welshmen, no doubt eager for battle, and disappointed that the fighting was over. Russell gave

Herbert's men permission to loot Devon for food and anything else they chose to seize, both for themselves and to sell. There being no further spoil to be found in East Devon, and little in the area immediately north and west of Exeter, the Welshmen descended on South Devon with gleeful ferocity. A number of villages had distressing tales to tell, and though some defences were erected to protect livestock, no violent resistance was attempted, lest Russell confiscate property. The Welshmen told the people their goods should willingly be given to assist the starving citizens in Exeter! So far the Welsh ruffians hadn't reached Ivybridge. But Joanna was full of fear, since harbouring rebels had become a capital offence.

For three days we lived in rising tension, hearing wild rumours we knew not whether to believe. Everywhere papists were being hunted down, mass books and even rosaries were being seized. The neighbouring gentry could no longer be trusted. Joanna begged my father and me to go into hiding, now that my father's leg was improving.

The news, when it came, was even worse than we had supposed. Russell had lost no time in meting out punishments and rewards. 'He's confiscated all the leaders' property', Humphrey announced grimly as we sat at dinner. 'Even before any have been brought to trial. All your lands, John, have been seized by Peter Carew, even Wynslade Farm. – I'm afraid, Joanna, my dear, your father is dead.'

My aunt let out a great cry of anguish as Humphrey continued, 'He died of shock after being turned out of bed at night by a pack of Carew villains.'

'We should have brought him to Ivybridge, Humphrey. We're to blame for his death.'

'He would never have come of his own freewill.'

We were all, even Joanna, silenced for a while by this news. Russell was acting without any recourse to the law, and the worst could be expected for anyone having a connection to the rebels.

Joanna descended into a torrent of weeping, combined with hysterical utterances. 'We must all escape immediately – we must!. We can't wait to be butchered in our beds. Think of our children, Humphrey! Oh, my poor father, my poor, poor father, who never did anyone any harm. Why did you go to fight, Johnny, why? We could be living quite content as Protestants.'

At that moment I was almost inclined to agree.

When Joanna had exhausted herself, Humphrey told us that Gawen Carew had been granted all Arundell's property, and William Gibbs all John Bury's. My father's properties had already been seized, leaving us with nothing but the contents of our packs.

'Thank God you made over Tregarrick to Agnes', said Humphrey.

Yes, I thought bitterly, Agnes is now mistress of Tregarrick, and if we return will tyrannise us for ever.

My father spoke then in bitter despair. 'You were right, Humphrey. Arundell and I should never have led a rebellion. Apart from the religious tyranny, which will carry on apace, in Russell we have foisted a bloody tyrant on the South West, far worse than the government in London. He will reign as he pleases, and his son Francis after him.'

Humphrey agreed, but then said, to our surprise, 'After what's happened I've changed my mind about the rebellion. Every man in the South West should do his utmost now to overcome Russell and his henchmen.'

'What can we do?' I asked.

'My servants tell me Arundell is at Sampford Courtenay recruiting more men to join the surviving rebels. Many from Somerset, commons and even gentry, have answered his call, all determined to resist. Even Russell's own conscripts from Dorset and Somerset have deserted, having no zest for killing their neighbours.'

'Russell will keep the upper hand', I pointed out. 'His mercenaries make arrests all over the South West. Three Exeter merchants in fear have even offered to pay their wages. People are so frightened they try to ingratiate themselves with Russell and the Carews. It's a lost cause, Uncle.'

'Will is right', said my father. 'Keep out of it, Humphrey. He and I are already so deep in this commotion we've nothing to lose. Joanna will need you, and so will Agnes and Thomasine.'

However, Humphrey's family pride had been aroused. 'The Bonville family will not tolerate an upstart like Russell ruling over us.'

'Send provisions, but not men.'

'The state of the South West was never so miserable as it is now. The greed of these Protestant possessioners beggars belief.'

'My poor dear father used to say that if the Church had not grown so rich, landowners would not have coveted its estates', said Joanna. ' Indeed, if the gentry had all been of one mind, the government would have listened to our grievances. Religious reform might have been achieved peacefully.'

'It's too late now to think of what might have been. I shall send men as well as provisions', stated Humphrey.

Joanna set to weeping again, and I felt sorry for her poor husband. He'd always been slow to act, but once his mind was made up nothing would shift him. My aunt would make his life a hell now, and should he be imprisoned she would go into a decline. She had none of Agnes's calculating determination to turn a misfortune to her advantage.

Though we were all facing up to the harsh realities of life, our minds were yet in turmoil. For the first time in his life my father seemed unable to bear up to the evils of humankind. 'I still find it hard to credit that foreign ruffians are being used against our own people coming in peace to present a petition', he kept saying.

'No, John', said Humphrey, 'Not in peace. From the moment Body was slain, and then Hellyons, the government regarded it as armed rebellion.'

'None of our leaders had anything to do with Body or Hellyons. We took on the leadership to keep the peace.'

'Any citizen seizing a pitchfork and marching to change the law is registered a rebel.'

Father Welsh had remained with the besieging force during the battles at Woodbury and Clyst, and I'd assumed he'd now gone to Sampford Courtenay. So we were shocked to hear he was in prison, and that several priests had already been hanged in Exeter as traitors. My blood ran cold when I considered this, and Dick and I determined to go and see for ourselves.

Slipping away early on a beautiful sunny morning as though to take a ride on the moor, we planned to leave our horses at an inn and proceed to Exe Island on foot to make enquiries. Father Welsh was a much loved and respected parish priest, and when we spoke to a trio of women in the street, they told us tearfully he'd been hanged. One of the women mumbled words about Bernard Duffield, the keeper of Russell's mansion just south of the East Gate, being responsible. This man had a most unpleasant reputation, and I feared the worst.

The tall church tower came in sight, standing out against a breezy blue sky across which birds were flying. Suddenly my head swam, and I gripped Dick's arm so hard to stop myself falling that he exclaimed in pain. For on top of the tower was a gallows, and a familiar figure hanging in irons, a short, stocky man clad in a chasuble. When I could bring myself to look again, I could make out a bucket attached to the body. There were other attachments, but I could not see what they were. A group of people in the churchyard weren't gaping at the sight, but standing quietly, their mouths moving in silent prayer. In the street were more people, laughing and chattering. When Dick enquired of a bystander who might be the unfortunate person hanging from the gallows, he answered with fanatical glee, "Tis Father Welsh, the popish servant of the devil, with all Satan's regalia – bell, sprinkler and beads – 'ung about 'im.'

'When was he taken up?' asked Dick.

'Yest'day mornin', hauled up wi' a rope round 'is middle.'

'Who gave the order?'

'Bernard Duffield. 'Ee who set up gallows all over the city for they Catholic traitors. He'll be along come midday to see if this 'un still lives.'

It lacked but a few minutes to twelve, and though I felt sick and shaky at the knees, I stayed to watch Bernard Duffield arrive and mount the stairway within the tower. When he appeared at the top, there followed a sudden expectant silence below, and soon after came the triumphant shout, "Ee do live!' There was a moan of horror from the praying group, and excited exclamations from the crowd.

Behind me I heard a satisfied laugh and the clink of coins as money changed hands between two lads. 'He saved others', one of them blasphemed. 'Himself he cannot save.'

'Master Duffield'll be back tonight', said a woman. 'They do say a man can last three days. Father Welsh be a strong man. 'Ee could chop down a sturdy tree, an' wrestle many a younger fellow.'

'But the thirst, do 'ee think o' the thirst', said another.

We mingled with the group in the churchyard, and with tears running down my face I listened to them murmuring, 'Father, forgive them, for they know not what they do.' And then, 'Requiem aeternam dona eis Domine, et lux perpetua luceat eis.'

But a God who could forgive Russell for this crime was not a God I could worship.

We left hastily and remained silent till we reached Ivybridge. There I told my father in private about how Duffield had been quick to devise the most cruel death for Father Welsh. He spoke not a word, but ashen-faced left me, hobbling, to go to his bedchamber. Looking back I think the call to arms at Sampford Courtenay saved him from madness. He had ever been an optimistic man and full of good spirits till the rebellion. His soul was being crushed by so much cruel disaster.

The citizens of Exeter and those living nearby within reach of Russell's first ruthless wave of punishments, were cowed enough, but men living further afield were made the more courageous by their fury at the wickedness of his actions. Thus new recruits had been hastening towards Sampford Courtenay to join Arundell, who was once again busy setting up ramparts, digging trenches and preparing ordnance. To be slain in battle was a better option for him than to be hanged.

My father had, as I might have guessed, decided to set out for Sampford Courtenay without delay.

'But you're still using a stick', I protested.

'I'll throw it away', he replied. 'Arundell will be depending on my support. It's a matter of honour. We have a slender chance of success, for the government has ordered Russell's army to proceed immediately to the coast to defend the ports against the latest French threat. Anyway, I'm tired of being fussed over by Joanna. And how could I return to Tregarrick? Agnes would press me to join Arundell.'

'Agnes would enjoy making a martyr of you – "My blessed husband who laid down his life for the Faith…"'

'You malign poor Agnes. She tried to be a good mother to you.'

'She overdosed me with religion. As a child I remember her laying a bible on my stomach to make me sleep at night.'

'There was no harm in her *Aves* and *Paternosters* and Masses for the dead.'

'I dare say she'll make just as ardent a Protestant if she has to.'

'Agnes a Protestant! She'd rather die.

'Agnes has her pragmatic side. Behind our backs she'll be treating Thomasine very badly.'

For once my father did not deny it. 'You'd best return to Tregarrick, Will, to take care of Agnes and Thomasine. Who knows what will happen once Russell's executioners reach Cornwall.'

'When will you go?' I asked.

'Tomorrow at dawn, with Humphrey's men.'

Humphrey dreaded more tears from his wife, but she had to be told about the death of Father Welsh.

'Father Welsh – not dear Father Welsh!' she cried out. 'That kind man, always ready to laugh at his own misfortune.'

'I remember him berating John Hammond, that blacksmith from Woodbury, who wanted to set fire to Exeter. Father Welsh would not have his beloved city destroyed. And now the city has destroyed him', said my father.

'Why didn't the citizens rush out to cut him down?' demanded Joanna.

'No one dared', said Humphrey. 'This foul deed has convinced me I must send every man I can raise to fight at Sampford Courtenay.'

'We've done nothing to deserve this fate', wailed Joanna.

'No, my dear. Tyranny takes no note of what people deserve.'

Unbeknown to Humphrey, Joanna had sent a message to Tregarrick describing the dire situation, and to our surprise, Agnes arrived at suppertime that evening, the eleventh day of August. She found us all despondent, but Agnes was not one to sympathise with despair. She was full of enthusiasm for Arundell's plan, and glad to know my father's condition had improved.

'Poor Johnny goes to certain death', announced Joanna.

'As always, a defeatist, are you not, Joanna? And what is Humphrey to do?'

'He is sending men to Sampford Courtenay.'

'*Deo gratias*! At last you've seen sense, Humphrey.'

'Why didn't you bring Thomasine?' I asked.

'She didn't wish to come. She was too busy looking after her menagerie.'

'Did she send a letter?'

'No.'

'I'll not believe it. She would have written.'

'How dare you accuse me of lying! I doubt Thomasine could compose a letter. She's a witch, I'm sure of it. I've seen her dancing in the moonlight with that one-eyed black cat.'

'Dancing?'

'Twirling around on the wet grass in bare feet.'

'How does that make her a witch? She's always liked being outside on a warm night. It is then she sees the otters and badgers.'

'A good Christian doesn't prowl alone at night, consorting with wild…'

'Agnes, you're mistaken over Thomasine', broke in my father angrily. 'She's a strange girl, but that doesn't make her a witch. I'm glad for her to be William's wife.'

'You're all duped by her looks. It's well known her mother was a witch. With Constantine confiscated, William has no home to take her to. And you can be sure I'll not share my manor with a pagan.'

I rose and said in fury, 'You prevented Thomasine from coming to Ivybridge out of malice. I'll not listen to any more of your pious falsehoods.'

'William, I demand that you apologise', said my father. 'Agnes has done her best for you over many years.'

But the time for patching our quarrel was long past. It was open war in future between Agnes and myself.

'No, she suffered me as long as I obeyed her and followed her religion. But I can tell you, Father, I'm heartily sick of religion. It causes more evil than good.'

'Listen to him, John!' Agnes cried indignantly. 'See how he's been bewitched by that girl.'

'I didn't join the rebellion to keep fanatical Catholics in power.'

'No more quarrelling, please!' begged Joanna. 'In these terrible times we should love one another. Come to supper. There's a pig stuffed with eggs and spices, and a salad of cresses and onions, with herring and raisin sauce.'

In this mood of anger we sat down to eat, Joanna doing her best to lift our spirits. We were all conscious it might well be our last family gathering. At the end of the meal we heard a disturbance outside, and who should enter but Thomasine. The Trelawneys' bailiff had been coming to Plymouth and agreed to bring her after Agnes had departed.

'What have you to say now, Agnes?' I exclaimed angrily.

Joanna rose, determined we would have no more dissension in her house. 'Not on our last night together, Will. I forbid it.' And to Thomasine she said, 'We've finished supper, my dear, but you'll be needing sustenance. Sit you down with William, and join us when you've done.'

She chivvied Humphrey, my father and Agnes out of the chamber, and at last I could embrace my darling, who felt more slender than ever, a mere wisp of a girl. A few weeks of separation had seemed like months. In different ways we'd both suffered and changed, perhaps matured for the better. We were more firmly united in our hatred of violence and betrayal, and to our shame, of Agnes, whom we wished dead.

'Why didn't she bring you?' I asked. 'She must have known my father and I would be angered.'

'To punish me for the worst sin I could commit in her eyes.' She paused, and then said, 'I am with child.'

This news filled me with great joy, but also with much disquiet. It was hard to see a way out of our troubles. Thomasine told me Agnes was consumed with a mad jealousy. 'She's trying to make me miscarry, giving me impossible tasks, lifting heavy sacks and carrying full buckets. I feel sick, and then vomit, and can't eat. I must learn more quickly, she says, to be a good housekeeper if I'm to be a wife and mother. At other times she threatens to make sure I never will be. I'm very frightened. If our child is born she'll kill it.'

'No, no, my darling, she wouldn't dare to go that far.'

'I tell you, she will! One night I heard her praying in the chapel room. She was crying and shouting again and again to God, how unfair it was that He had sent me a child and not her. She was the good Christian, and I was the servant of Satan.'

When I told her I was coming back to Tregarrick, Thomasine calmed down and said happily, 'So now we can go to Constantine.'

'No, my darling, for all my father's property has been awarded to Peter Carew, even the estate at Putford. His men raided Wynslade Farm and my poor grandfather died of a heart attack.'

'Oh, how wicked, how very wicked! To do such an evil thing to an ailing old man? I loved him, he was so good to me.'

'We all loved grandfather. His death has reinforced my father's determination to fight on.'

'But we can't live at Tregarrick! Could we not live for a while at Poole House with the Trelawneys? Your grandfather has been kind to me.'

'No, we can't ask him. His property might be confiscated too.'

In a wild flight of fancy, she said, 'We could live in a cottage in Torrington, by the river.'

'With a child, in winter, and no money? It's not possible. If my father dies, Agnes may marry again and leave Tregarrick.'

'Who would want her?'

'Oh, Agnes can be so charming when she likes. And she has money of her own.'

'In the village people are saying King Edward isn't likely to live. The Princess Mary will become Queen and restore the Catholic faith.'

'The Protestant Council will never accept Mary as Queen.'

'What does it matter whether we have a glittering altar or a bare table? Why does religion have to cause so much trouble?'

'Because life is so fleeting and uncertain. Everyone wishes to make sure of salvation in the life to come.'

'Agnes says I'm destined for hell. I wish no harm to anyone, so why should God cast me into hell.'

'You'll not go to hell.'

'To think your poor grandfather Wynslade is dead. Such a dear, kind gentleman. I recall sitting among the flowers in his garden, and him talking to me as though I was a little girl; if I wrote a love poem, he said, and placed it in a bottle and threw it into the river at Putford, it would one day reach Torrington. And there it would be rescued by a handsome young man who would come and claim me as his bride. And now Wynslade Farm is full of wicked strangers, and I shall never again sit by the Torridge and watch the otters.'

'We can still visit Torrington.'

'It won't be the same. It takes time to win their trust. I did so want you to see them. Nothing in heaven could compare to watching an otter swimming by moonlight on a still, warm night.'

'Have patience, Thomasine. We must concentrate on ending the strife in the West, and then on the birth of our child. Be thankful for the few good things in life.'

'We were so happy together at Pelynt. Why did our lives have to be shattered by a few wicked men who want us all to suffer. How can anyone be happy, Will? The world is such a terrible place.'

It seemed shocking to me that a young girl could feel such despair. 'We will be happy again, I promise you.' Hollow words, as I thought of Father Welsh, and knew Thomasine was right. Life would never be sweet and innocent for anyone in the South West for many a long year.

The next day my father, accompanied by a band of Humphrey's tenants, set out for Sampford Courtenay. They had to keep well clear of Exeter for fear of Russell's scouts. Humphrey himself didn't go, for all that Agnes chided him. 'I have my children to think of', he snapped. 'You don't.'

At this, tears welled up in her eyes. But neither Humphrey nor Joanna cared. Further contention erupted when Agnes discovered Dick was to accompany my father instead of escorting her to Tregarrick. 'Dick should be going with us, and William's duty is to go with you and fight for our Faith.'

The following day I travelled by carrier with Agnes and Thomasine to Pelynt. It was a miserable journey, with Thomasine feeling sick and Agnes scolding. 'Sickness or no sickness', she said. 'You'll have to help out at home, now that we have so few servants. Plenty of wood-chopping for you, William. I've been keeping the estate going single-handed.' Then she announced with a gleam in her eye, that she was embroidering another banner of the Five Wounds, and there was a heap of new linen to hem for the lining. 'You'll be fit to sew if nothing else', she told Thomasine. 'The new banner will hang in Pelynt Church as a memorial to John.'

'But my father isn't dead', I said icily.

'If he escapes death at Sampford Courtenay he'll hang.'

'You talk as though you want it to happen!'

'No one escapes Russell's clutches! The ringleaders are sure to die a martyr's death.'

Thomasine burst into tears. 'It's wicked of you to say such things.'

'Do try to behave like a grown woman and not a silly girl.'

'When Father Lambe is replaced by a Protestant you'll certainly not be allowed to hang a banner in the church', I remarked with satisfaction.

'We shall see', replied Agnes grimly.

The only pleasure awaiting us at Tregarrick was the dog, Nonna, who flung herself in ecstasy at Thomasine. That night we secreted her into my bedchamber, caring nothing for what Agnes had said. But in the morning there followed a confrontation, as my room was bare of all the possessions I had left – objects collected and cherished throughout my youth, including the beautiful small-sized bow Dick had fashioned for me when I was eight years old, which had always hung on the wall. Agnes had thrown out everything, hoping I was never going to return. While she was out one day I scoured the manor seeking some of my father's personal possessions, but could find none.

And so the quarrels continued during those bleak days as we waited for news from Sampford Courtenay. It was as well we were given so many tasks, for at bedtime we were too weary to brood. By the twentieth day of August we were desperate, fearing that Dick had been killed, for surely by now he would have reached us. In the event it was Humphrey, not Dick, who arrived first at Tregarrick.

'The news is very bad, as you might expect', he said. 'John and Arundell are in Exeter gaol, awaiting trial in London. Arundell was captured at Launceston, and John at Bodmin. The battle took place on Saturday the seventeenth day of August. A complete rout. The whole brave venture has been a disaster.'

As to the aftermath of the battle, the most terrible rumours were circulating, most of them probably true, judging by the ruthless characters of Russell, Grey, Herbert and Carew. Many rebels had apparently fled up the Exe valley towards Tiverton, led by John Bury and Richard Coffyn. They'd all been captured, and many executed on the spot. The rest were sent to various towns and villages, even as far as Bath, to be hanged, drawn and quartered as a lesson to the people of Somerset, Wiltshire and Dorset. Humphrey had heard that Richard Coffyn was the only one left alive, and he was now in Exeter gaol.

'And how is it you've not been arrested?' demanded Agnes.

'A stroke of luck. Thomas Denys pleaded on my behalf to Russell. I've been spared imprisonment on payment of all my assets bar the manor at Ivybridge. We have had to dispense with servants, and Joanna is sick with worry.'

'I suppose Thomas Denys told Russell you'd not lifted a finger for the cause, that you had been forced to help John against your will, and that you and Joanna will be good Protestants in future?'

'Yes, Agnes', responded Humphrey wearily. 'He probably said all those things to prevent my being imprisoned.'

'How cunning, to have a foot in both camps!'

'I shall use what influence I have to get John acquitted.'

Agnes laughed in derision. 'What influence could you have in London? You and John – two obscure country squires? Who cares for your opinion?'

'I will assure them that John never was a firm Catholic…'

'You traitor! You'd deny Christ to save your skin?'

'God's blood, Agnes, one has to be practical. You know as well as I do John didn't go to fight only to preserve your saints and your relics and your Hail Marys. Now the rebellion has failed what sense is there in his being martyred? I must do all I can to have John and other ringleaders reprieved.

Otherwise we shall remain overrun with landowners who care not a fig for the welfare of our people.'

'And what can you do?'

'I've sent word already to friends of mine who have connections on the Council. Protector Somerset won't remain in control. A contest for power is going on at Westminster. John Dudley is the up-and-coming man. Unfortunately we shall find him as greedy and uncompromising a Protestant as Russell. It will be hard to persuade him to pardon a rebel, but I'll do my best.'

'Who is this John Dudley?'

'The Earl of Warwick, a good soldier, and firm on the question of religious reform. He is all for abolishing bishops. Even you, Agnes, will have to remain silent should he become our ruler.'

'I shall never be silent!'

'If you were to be cast into a filthy rat-ridden dungeon, as John has been, you might well keep your mouth shut.'

'Are you staying the night?' asked Agnes.

'No, no. I must return home to comfort Joanna.'

'Ah, yes, poor Joanna must be comforted. She takes misfortune so hard, having inherited none of her brother's courage – you must excuse me a moment – we are very busy.' Agnes bustled out impatiently.

'How I hate her!' cried Thomasine. 'She said all my pets must be drowned – except Nonna – even my little black cat. She says it was my witch's familiar.'

'Such crazy superstition', said Humphrey.

That evening, as we sat in the parlour after Humphrey had departed, Agnes continued working on her banner, while Thomasine was set to continue hemming the lining.

'Don't expect me to run around after Thomasine at her lying in, or to pay for the upkeep of your bastard, William.'', she said.

'Our child will not be a bastard. We are betrothed.'

'You couldn't wait to satisfy your lust, could you? – Coupling in the woods like brute beasts.' I recalled the dark shape on the steps at Ninny's Grotto.

'You're so jealous of our happiness', exclaimed Thomasine. 'You've been married twice, yet I dare say you've never learnt the joy of lovemaking.'

'And you have everything to learn about marriage. There's more to it than pleasuring yourself in the woods.'

'I know there is. But perhaps if you'd pleasured yourself with John in the woods you might have borne a child. But of course you'd expect a virgin birth, like the Mother of Christ!'

If I'd not been present, Agnes would surely have struck Thomasine, as she hissed, 'How dare you blaspheme! You'll burn in hell, Thomasine Wynslade, like your witch of a mother and your drunk of a father. You come from tainted stock. When John dies, out you go, both of you. I'll not have a brat born of lechery in my house.'

Now my father and Arundell were in gaol and the rebellion over, I felt I must ride to Exeter. I even considered taking Thomasine with me. but it would have been too risky. But I remained at Tregarrick, still hoping Dick would arrive. Eventually, he came – this time without the glimmer of a greeting or a smile, a Dick we scarcely knew for the same man, so shrivelled he looked in his threadbare, filthy clothes, with a matted, rusty-looking beard bristling about his chin. He was almost incoherent, repeating my father's name, constantly blaming himself for his capture. After a meal I put him to bed, where he slept a full twelve hours.

Then he described how he'd stationed himself near the main section of the army, commanded by my father, in a good position on high ground a mile east of Sampford Courtenay. Arundell had kept his troops in the village itself. Grey and Herbert attacked with such force and superior numbers that all the rebels were driven back into the village.

'I were concealed behind an 'edge', he said, 'And then did take refuge in a cottage with two women whose husbands were fightin' with us, as were every able-bodied man from Sampford Courtenay. For a bit it seemed us was givin' more than us got. But then Russell arrived with gurt numbers, an' our men was fleein' in every direction. I seen Sir John leavin' the village by the Okehampton road, an' I were lucky to be showed a short cut from out the back door o' the cottage. Then I rinned with many others till us reached the town. Sir John and Arundell rallied the men an' prepared to make a stand, being certain Russell would send a force after us. An' so 'e did, a force far too big for Arundell to tackle. Every man alive did flee towards Launceston. I left the road and hid in a ditch all night, too weary to rin further.'

Dick stopped speaking for a while, too distraught to continue. But finally he told us he reached Launceston the following morning, only to find Arundell had been arrested and my father had pushed on to Bodmin. By the time Dick had tramped many miles to the town, my father too had been arrested.

'I shouldn't've falled behind', Dick said. 'I should've kept up with Sir John an' helped 'e to escape. I be to blame for his arrest.'

What could I say? His grief was too great for consolation.

Russell was still in Exeter, by all accounts carrying out executions, imprisonments and confiscating the lands and goods of even the humblest of the rebel yeomen. One might have hoped that after so many executions the people of Cornwall would be left to settle down to normal life in spite of their tragic bereavements. It was not to be. Russell had given Anthony Kingston, the provost marshal, a man with a reputation for appalling brutality, orders to crush the spirit and increase the hardship of any family which hadn't given Russell active support. Names were added daily to the endless roll call of hangings – gruesome deaths to which we became so accustomed that our compassion began to freeze. Every man was concerned only for his own skin. But I did almost weep to think of the hanging of Roger Barrett and John Tompson, two priests whom I knew well, who had been governors of our rebel camps outside Exeter.

I was waiting anxiously for Dick to recover his health so we could ride to Exeter to visit my father, for any day now he might be taken to London. At the same time my worries as to Thomasine's welfare increased. Agnes herself was probably living in fear of Anthony Kingston's soldiers, who had permission to raid any property and arrest the owner with no questions asked.

Towards the end of August Dick was fit to travel, though he advised strongly against going to Exeter. However, I felt bound to risk taking food and other comforts to my father. Once he left for London we might never meet again. It preyed on my mind, and even Thomasine understood I must go. So we made preparations to leave. As Dick and I were seeing to our horses in the stables, John Trevanion arrived, the son of Sir Hugh Trevanion, Sheriff of Devon, who'd been on the jury which condemned the Helston rioters. He took little notice of us, for which I was thankful, since he was a staunch supporter of the Protestant religion. He came laden with gifts of poultry and wildfowl, which was surprising, considering Agnes was such a fanatical Catholic.

In her best dress, and giving him her sweetest smiles, Agnes was far too preoccupied at dinner to nag at us. Thus we were able to slip away to spend an hour or so alone together.

'I shall die if you don't return', said Thomasine slowly, with a serious threat in her voice. 'I could not live without you.'

'I'll be back, I promise', I said rashly.

Our plan, on reaching Exeter, was for Dick to take my gifts to the prison, to test the opinion of the gaolers, whether they be sympathetic to the rebel cause or no. Since no one had come to Tregarrick to arrest me, I assumed that my presence at Fenny Bridges and Clyst St Mary had gone unnoticed by Russell. Had I been fighting at Sampford Courtenay, by now I would be hanged or imprisoned. Dick returned to tell me the gaoler was a decent man who would let me in without giving us away.

It was hot and noisome in the tiny cell where my poor father sat chained to a bench. There was little I could say to comfort him. His only hope lay in the testimony of local justices, such as Hugh Pollard, Anthony Harvey and Thomas Denys, who'd known him for years as one of the best landowners in Cornwall. All my desperate feelings for this kind and honest man had to be hidden behind a calm exterior, for fear of causing him to break down. His normally ruddy complexion had turned a yellowish grey, and his eyes were sunken. I could see his wound was still giving him pain. He was glad I hadn't been taken by the provost marshal, but he blamed himself bitterly for not being able to leave me an estate. I told him Dick and I would find a lodging and visit him each day till he left for London. He didn't enquire after Agnes, but instead talked to me after a silence of many years, of my mother, his beloved Jane Trelawney.

'Always be proud, Will', he said, 'Of your Trelawney blood. We Wynslades are an ancient Devon family, but living in Cornwall has taught me much about the toughness, the loyalty, and above all the exceptional courage, of the Cornish people. They've endured the worst life can bring.'

'They are often too fanatical in their superstitions.'

'They are indeed. It is this fanaticism which has kept their spirits high. You have to admire it.'

Dick was waiting for me in the gaoler's lodge, and on leaving we caught sight of a familiar figure coming in. It was Kestell, no doubt arriving to visit Arundell. He glanced at us, but said nothing. A few minutes later, or earlier, and we would have missed him. This random encounter led to my undoing, for the following day as I approached the gaol, two men seized me from behind, and without more ado I was hustled into a cell and left alone in the dark. Later, when Dick was granted entry to me, we agreed it must have been Kestell's betrayal, though as usual we had no hard evidence.

Throughout the rebellion this cunning creature had turned up like an evil spirit to taunt me, a man whose only loyalty was to the devil, whose only aim was to spread as much misery as possible. He didn't even have cause to hate me, other than that he desired to seduce my wife. And what of his master, Arundell, who trusted him completely? What terrible betrayal awaited him who'd raised Kestell up in the world? He'd noted how clever Kestell was as a young boy, but had been utterly deceived as to the man's devious and wicked ways.

So there I was, one of Russell's miserable captives, and not likely to live. For the first time I had to face the reality of cruel judicial death and my own stupidity in coming to Exeter. I had put the noose around my own neck. I'd deserted Thomasine. Then my thoughts went to the hundreds of women now bereft of their husbands and sons, many without a home or a livelihood. Who was I to escape the horrors which had descended on the South West? The only thing to be thankful for was that Dick had not been taken. I wanted him to take a message back to Tregarrick, but there was no time. Dick had determined to travel to London with us. The date had been set for the third day of September. My poor Thomasine would have to fend for herself, possibly for ever.

Nine of us prisoners left at dawn by the South Gate for the journey to London, escorted by guards under the command of Lord Grey. Apart from Arundell, my father and Pomeroy, our party included John Bury, Thomas Holmes, John Wyse, William Fortescue and Richard Coffyn. I hadn't set eyes on the latter since Fenny Bridges. As he was brought out of Exeter gaol it was a sad surprise to see his wretched condition. He could have passed for forty-four instead of twenty-two years of age, so haggard and skeletal did he seem with his right arm in a sling, and two vicious-looking scars on his face. One of these caused his mouth to look so twisted that the smile he tried to give me was more like a grimace of pain.

A single small bell tolled in the cathedral tower. All the bells but one in each church in Devon and Cornwall had been removed, to prevent any future summoning to rebellion. I discovered some time later that the commissioners hadn't dared to provoke the people by bringing down the bells; they'd merely removed the clappers, and sometimes the frames.

We suffered the harrowing pains of having our legs tied together beneath the bellies of our horses, and in this humiliating manner took the road to Honiton, finally leaving Devon just beyond Axminster. Some of us were never to see our homes again. At Fenny Bridges I glanced at the field to our left, thereafter known as Bloody Meadow, and saw the low mound of barely covered grass beneath which were buried so many brave west country men. It seemed to me they were lucky, for it was all over with them. We were still suffering, and would suffer more.

It turned out to be a warm, humid day, but at that early hour one could catch the tantalising scent of autumn. We were barely past the toll house at Honiton when our miserable cavalcade had to halt, because my poor father fainted for the pain in his thigh. One of the guards threw water impatiently at his face, and when he came to, he was permitted to travel with his legs in the stirrups. But still the movement of his horse caused him pain. I even prayed that my father would die on that terrible journey. It was unbearable to think of what he might yet have to endure in London.

As we passed through Axminster we were delayed by a carriage conveying some wealthy personage. A small crowd gathered to jeer, and several lads threw stones at us. Then a pretty, innocent-looking girl of about five years old stepped out close to my father's horse. She held up some kind of cake, saying, 'You must be starved, poor man. You look so thin.' My father was bending down to take the offering, when the guard struck it out of the girl's hand and trampled it under his boot. I expected the child to run away in tears, but she stood her ground, saying loud and clear, 'You be a very wicked man, and you be goin' to hell!' At this, the spectators clapped, and one or two stones were now aimed at the guard, one knocking his helmet off. This incident started as a kindly act, and ended with the guard treating his prisoners with constant petty cruelty for the remainder of the journey, to cover his own public humiliation.

One day, I thought, that intrepid child might grow up to admonish a king or a bishop, and find herself behind bars. Such are the ways of humankind.

It was a relief to reach London on the eighth day of September, in spite of prison awaiting us. Arundell had warned that a hostile mob might pelt us with rubbish. But the streets were empty. Once lodged in the Fleet Prison we were told that this had been the day appointed for the Bishop of London, Edmund Bonner, to preach at St Paul's Cross against the Catholic faith, to test his loyalty to the reformed religion. He failed the test, and was incarcerated in the Marshalsea Prison.

The Fleet lay on a kind of island formed by ditches, on the east bank of the River Fleet. It was a damp, noxious place plagued with mosquitoes in the summer. Men coming from the fresh, clean air of the west country found it particularly unbearable, and yet we had to bear it week after week. Unlike in Exeter gaol, we were all thrust together in one ill-lit chamber, sleeping on straw which was rarely changed. On the first day, the stench from the six buckets placed in the corner for our convenience caused me to vomit. But after a week we became so used to the smell that we scarcely noticed it. Our greatest misery was the food. Had we possessed sufficient funds of money we might have bought tolerable victuals, but we all, even Arundell, had been captured without sufficient coins in our pockets. My father and I had to make do with dry bread soaked in salt beef and a sickening liquid our gaoler called 'pottage'. We could not even allow ourselves to run into debt as the others did, for who would pay? – certainly not Agnes.

In the camps round Exeter we'd all worked well with each other, laughing and joking and sharing whatever food and drink came our way. Each man knew he might be killed in battle the next day, but it was a risk he'd chosen for a cause, and should death catch him out, he'd at least have been in charge of his own mind and body. Now our fate was entirely in the hands of malicious vengeful authority, which would try to wrest every vestige of our pride and dignity before slaughtering us like cattle. If we'd depended on Somerset's leniency, we were to be disappointed, for in a few weeks he was deposed by John Dudley, who, our gaoler remarked with satisfaction, would make mincemeat of us all. If the King should die, however, the Princess Mary might rescue us.

In this atmosphere our comradeship waned. Arundell made it plain he had many friends in high places who would plead for him. Pomeroy expected his friends would do the same. Wyse and Fortescue were certain no one of note would speak for them. Thomas Holmes was only a yeoman from Blisland, not far from Arundell's home at Helland, and was aware he had no chance of pardon. Knowing Arundell of old, he disliked and despised the man for his loud-mouthed arrogance and claim to special privilege as a lord. Holmes resented bitterly that Arundell might be let off. John Bury, a decent man exuding quiet authority, stood back from us all, disdaining to talk of his chances. My father, as always, bore no ill-will, and though he'd no time for Arundell, he was civil enough. That left Richard Coffyn who's already told me his extensive family had disapproved of his joining the rebellion. Perhaps if he'd contacted them they would have rallied to help as best they could, but he was too proud to ask.

'What use would I be to my family now?' he said. 'I've not long to live.' Certainly he looked a very sick man. He was losing weight rapidly, his skin was grey and he coughed incessantly, keeping us all awake at night.

I hated the atmosphere. We should have been supporting each other, but in a matter of life or cruel death, it was too much to ask. We became a morose, even suspicious group. In addition I'd never imagined how swiftly a lice-ridden prisoner deprived of the bare necessities of life can appear, or even become, so much less than a decent human being.

For my part, to keep me from utter depression I depended on the snippets of gossip and news which the gaolers revelled in giving us. Being young and unable as yet to fully believe in my own mortality, I wished to learn something to our advantage, something on which to pin a tiny hope. One of the gaolers whispered to me with gleeful malice that John Dudley had turned out to be a loathsome tyrant. If the King died there would be a revolution. Lord John Russell had acquired Protector Somerset's property in London, and was like to be created Earl of Bedford. He and Dudley were as thick as thieves, and would see us, like the wicked Norfolk rebels, into hell before the year was out.

These Norfolk rebels, I discovered, had been led by one Robert Kett. He'd raised sixteen thousand men to march against statutes which kept the commons in extreme hardship while the nobility and gentry enjoyed much comfort. John Dudley had put down that rebellion in the last week of August with great slaughter. The government had no patience whatever with such protesters, and did nothing to redress their grievances. Kett had been tried and hurried back to Norfolk to be hanged on the seventh day of September. Pomeroy was of the opinion that since our rebellion had been on account of religious reform, the government felt unable to dispense with us so swiftly as Kett's followers. It embarrassed them, as there were plenty amongst the nobility and gentry who considered dying for the old faith to be martyrdom, and they had sympathy for a martyr. Thus unwillingly the government felt constrained to give us time to recant. It wished we had risen instead against poverty, taxation and enclosure. Officially we should have been locked up in the Clink, a prison for religious protesters, but that would have drawn more attention to our plight. I had no care for the difference, except that we were kept waiting so much longer to be hanged.

Having plunged me into gloom, the gaoler would then say that Dudley would have to reckon one day with the Princess Mary, a most obstinate, courageous lady, who should have had the chop two years ago. But rumour had it she was hidden away in a country house with her priests, missals and rosaries, her bells and smells and all the other paraphernalia of the devil – and not even the Archbishop dared stop her. Many declared a daughter of Good King Harry would be better than John Dudley.

During our first weeks in the Fleet, I had devised a letter to Thomasine in my mind, hoping that soon there might be a way of sending it. My father and I had become so used to relying on Dick to deliver messages safely, that it was frustrating not to be able to do so from prison. Even if we'd had the money to bribe one of the gaolers to admit Dick to the Fleet, we couldn't have asked him to go. With money enough we might have found another messenger at least to take a letter to Humphrey Bonville in Devon, who might pass it on to Cornwall. But all was too risky in these unsettled times. Agnes would have been told we were waiting in the Fleet, and no doubt she'd be glad. Remembering John Trevanion's visit, I was sure she had plans for her future. But what of Thomasine's future? There was nothing consoling I could tell her. Even if acquitted, what could I offer her and our child? How much misery the poor girl was already enduring with Agnes. I had to find some kind of work – but where should this be?

Thus we eked out our miserable and shivering existence, for having arrived in the summer, we had no warm garments. During the second week in October, my father, Arundell, John Bury and Thomas Holmes were taken by boat up the river to the Tower. What did this mean? I asked the gaoler. It meant, he said, that they would be tried soon at Westminster. And what of the rest of us? 'As like as not you'll be dispatched at dead of night without trial', he stated with a grin. Was he joking? We could never tell. But Pomeroy thought it held some hope for us. He was still relying on friends to help him, and he hinted he might be able to save me too, by swearing I'd joined the rebellion under duress. My dear father had no such friends, and was never one to beg favours.

Pomeroy was right. On the first day of November the rest of us were pardoned and set free. My first thought was for Thomasine. I had to remain in London for my father's trial, but I wrote to my uncle, and to Thomasine, telling her we would soon be together again. Fortunately the gaoler was in a good mood, and provided pen and paper. Pomeroy promised to put both my letters into Humphrey's hands. How I longed for a letter in return, but I'd no idea where I would be lodging.

Remaining awake all that last night in the Fleet, a treacherous and selfish thought crossed my mind, for which I'm still truly ashamed. Why hadn't I had the courage to refuse to identify myself with the rebellion and kept my head down. If only I'd taken Thomasine to Constantine before it started. We'd plunged ourselves into this insoluble dilemma just for the sake of a prayer book. Yet I knew if I'd had to make the choice again I would have joined the commons in their struggle for basic human rights. People might call it the Prayer Book Rebellion, but it was far more than that.

The gaoler told me Dick had often come to the Fleet in spite of not being permitted to see us. So when I stumbled out of the prison in pouring rain, a filthy starving skeleton, there he was, ready with a borrowed cloak. He took me to his lodging, a flea-ridden, scruffy enough place, but the height of luxury to me. Once a week there was even a bowl of hot water to be had. Dick was lucky. The landlady, Mrs Bates, had taken a liking to him, and let him have the room rent-free. Her husband worked away from home much of the time and she was grateful to Dick for doing much-needed tasks about the ramshackle building. He was also earning a little money for doing repair jobs in the immediate area.

But my relief was short-lived. We had to wait for nearly a month till the trial. My money had long run out, and it was humiliating having to depend on Dick, who even had to buy me clothes at the market, for my old clothes were only fit to be burnt. Becoming Dick's assistant, I felt ashamed for my lack of knowledge and my clumsy fingers. Dick was patient and generous, giving me half of his earnings to restore my dignity. The one talent I possessed could not be put to use, for my harp was at Tregarrick, and such instruments were not cheap.

During his visits to the Fleet, Dick had encountered Rowland Jeynens, who wanted to visit his master, but for some reason was not allowed in. Dick had befriended the young man, who felt lost and alone in London in a miserable lodging house. He refused Dick's advice to return home, being determined to see his master through to the end. Besides, the poor fellow had no home to go to.

On Tuesday the twenty-sixth day of November we went to Westminster for the trial. Dick had been hoping to be called as a witness to speak up on my father's behalf, in particular to insist that his motive had been entirely on the grounds of religion, and that he had intended a peaceful march. It was Russell's actions which turned it into a military venture. But Dick was not required to speak. We might have guessed who would be one of the main witnesses for the prosecution.

It must have been the day Kestell was waiting for: to stand up in the crowded hall to see Lord Humphrey Arundell and Sir John Wynslade condemned. Looking every inch a gentleman in expensive clothes, his manner was both humble and full of false regret that his master should have turned out to be a traitor. His speech was quiet and articulate. He was a most impressive witness, and, for the first time I felt truly sorry for Arundell.

He'd appeared in the dock on the first day looking fairly confident. He, of all us prisoners, had the most influence in high places. And was he not related to the great family of Arundells from Lanherne, the foremost Cornish landowners? Thomas Arundell had been a commissioner for the dissolution of the monasteries. Sir John Arundell was a Privy Councillor. And during the war with France, had not Humphrey Arundell himself given excellent service? He'd also been on the jury which condemned the Helston rioters, which surely proved he was on the side of law and order.

Kestell presented a different story. He repeated, word for word, conversations Arundell had had – threats he had made against Lord Russell. He was an irreligious man and a quarrelsome landowner, only interested in his own glory, a keen military man and nothing else.

'Lord Arundell will tell you', said Kestell, 'That he never desired to lead a rebellion. He was forced into it by an armed mob arriving at his residence in Helland. Also that he was instructed by the Sheriff, Hugh Trevanion, to take on the leadership temporarily, to try and persuade the protesters to lay down their arms. He lies! Calling himself General, he himself mustered, armed and trained men to fight against the government.'

Arundell's confidence flagged and then visibly disappeared, as he realised that Kestell was betraying him. The court knew he was a spy, but since he was but a humble servant with nothing to gain, he was only acting as an honest man should. Imagine, I thought, if Dick had betrayed my father's trust in like manner!

That Kestell gave such a damning picture of Arundell, reflected of course on my father. Without Arundell as a partner he might just have obtained a pardon. No one but Kestell spoke ill of him. And yet how malicious Kestell was. It was all a show on my father's part, he said. He had no interest in religion, as his wife would tell you. He led the rebels, like Arundell, for his own glory. He and Arundell had even abducted two fourteen-year-old twin boys to be used without their parents' knowledge as spies, laying them open to great danger, wherein they were eventually hanged. My father naturally denied this accusation. Then he reminded his accusers that when a ruler turns into a tyrant and neglects to listen to the petitions of his people, it becomes their right in extreme hardship to take up arms against him, provided that they are led by the nobility.

But Kestell had already besmirched the character and motives of our sole member of the nobility who, he said, had deliberately planned to bring his army to besiege Exeter and starve its citizens into submission. Kestell's manner was persuasive, he spoke so earnestly, so full of righteous regret that it mattered little what any other witness said. It was heartbreaking to know that one cunning servant had been able to influence the passage and the outcome of our whole disastrous venture to such an extent. Even Humphrey Bonville was betrayed, for Kestell had been hanging about in the fields after the battle at Clyst, and had seen my uncle helping my father to escape in a cart. Kestell could have been the kind of successful lawyer who for a great enough fee would have acquitted many a villainous murderer. He himself had, I'm sure, been responsible for a number of deaths during the commotion, and now at the end of this trial, he'd virtually condemned Humphrey Arundell and my father to being hanged, drawn and quartered at Tyburn.

From the twenty-sixth day of November till the twenty-seventh day of January Dick and I waited in agony. I could have returned to Tregarrick during that period. But for the first time all thoughts of Thomasine were blotted from my mind. I could think only of my father. Dick and I worked to earn our bread, eating and drinking but little, barely talking and sleeping only to have nightmares.

I was beginning to accept that fate had a grudge against me. But nothing had prepared me for that experience at Tyburn on the twenty-seventh day of January – an experience which cut into my very soul like the sharpest knife. Again and again I relive that freezing day when the icy breath of the spectators rose in a steamy cloud above their heads. Sometimes I wake myself with my own anguished cry, my skin bathed in sweat, with limbs trembling and heart thumping.

Unfortunately, the night before the hangings Mr Bates had returned unexpectedly from one of his working trips away from home to find us all very dismal at supper. On learning from his wife that four rebels were to be executed in the morning, he began to taunt Dick and me with his brand of grizzly humour. 'No place like Tyburn fer a good hangin'', he announced gleefully. 'Don't get too close, mind – wi' four prisoners the stink will be…' and he clasped his hand to his purple nose. '…and you'll get spattered. Wi' a hanging, drawing and quarterin' you get three fer the price o' one. First, the hangin' by the neck till 'alf-dead, and the cuttin' down. Second, the innards cut out o' the body to be burnt. And third, but not least, the cutting off o' the head an' the chopping up o' the body into four parts to be seethed and then displayed at Lunnon Bridge or Westminster as a lesson to us all.' He thrust a piece of meat into his mouth and continued while chewing, 'I know fer a fac' that there was seventy-two thousand villains executed in Good King 'Arry's reign, and still people ain't learnt to be law-abidin'. It's a disgrace!'

'It's a disgrace', I fumed, 'That a Christian country still retains such a barbaric custom, and that men such as you find it amusing.'

'If the archbishop and bishops say a rebel dog should 'ang, who are you to pontificate agin it, young fella?'

I stumbled over a chair to reach Mr Bates, but was stopped in time by Dick, who dragged me from the room.

Rowland Jeynens met us at an appointed spot along the Tyburn Road, and we proceeded to the place of execution. Throughout the whole long-drawn-out agony, Dick stood solid as a rock while the crowd sniggered, gasped, retched and cheered. When my father's turn came, next to last, he put his strong right arm round my waist. As John Wynslade's head was held up aloft for all to see, my legs gave way for a moment, and Dick held me upright. How could Christians allow such a good man as my father to be torn apart? When Humphrey Arundell's head appeared I heard an unearthly shriek, and the croaking words, 'God rest yer soul, dear master!' It must have issued from Rowland, who turned and pushed his way through the mob, sobbing pitifully, poor lad. The souls of those four men would never rest.

Dick, our everlasting fount of compassion, whose face was wet with tears, took my arm. 'Come, us must follow Rowland. He be no better'n a babe-in-arms in London. He'll get 'isself hanged by nightfall if us don't look to 'im.'

I barely remember the rest of that day. We returned to our lodging to collect our meagre possessions. Mrs Bates fed us on bread and dripping and walnuts in salt. Mr Bates told Rowland in a practical, jolly manner to stop snivelling and be grateful it wasn't his limbs being boiled in a pan. Rowland suddenly tugged at Dick's sleeve, saying he had a secret to impart.

'Well, let's have it, my boy', said Dick.

Whereupon Rowland stuttered slowly, with a timid glance in my direction, 'Sir William must go to Tregarrick, where Thomasine Wynslade waits for'n.'

Whoever had spoken to Rowland had given him an all-too-obvious instruction. Of course I would go to Tregarrick, but I had to visit my uncle at Ivybridge first.

'Who gave you this message?' I asked.

''E didn't wish to give 'is name.' And the poor boy looked so agitated that we forbore to press him. He left the Bates' house after supper without another word.

It took us nearly a month journeying to Devon and then Cornwall, mostly on foot, sleeping behind hedges or in barns, fearful of any authority. Mrs Bates had given Dick some extra pay to enable us to eat as we travelled. And once we were lucky enough to stop two days at an inn, where the generous landlord let us sleep for free, with mutton pies thrown in.

The first gibbet we came across was at Yeovil. Thereafter we saw one at Axminster, one on the Honiton road, and six more before reaching Exmouth, all hung with well-seethed human quarters, like to last some while to act as a lesson to the people of East Devon. Even the carrion crows found such remains unappetising. Looking to each side of the road, we could see the burnt-out blackened ruins of farmsteads not yet rebuilt, and tree stumps everywhere. Another innkeeper told us many families were short of food that winter. In the gloomy February dusk the fields looked bleak and deserted, with few sheep to be seen.

We left the Honiton road and dropped down past Aylesbeare Common, and then on to the top of Windmill Hill, from which on a still afternoon we surveyed the land below stretching towards Clyst Heath and the estuary. It was hard to believe this peaceful earth now housed so many dead men – and some women too – that the new grass ready to sprout and the buds preparing to burst into leaf were being succoured with their blood.

Taking the lane to Woodbury, we made our way to the Popham farm in the hope of finding Dick's mother and sister. But when we stopped outside the gate, two unknown dogs barked fiercely and a strange man emerged from a barn and glared at us suspiciously, taking us for vagrant beggars, which in truth we were. On questioning him I discovered that the farm had been awarded to one of Russell's men, since the Pophams had forfeited their right to it by supporting the rebels. There was no chance of food or shelter here, and it was all but dark when we hobbled into Lympstone. By some miraculous stroke of luck we were given a place to sleep by a cottage fire with a widow whose son had perished as one of those nine hundred prisoners on the bank of the Clyst River.

"E only went out to ask why so many church bells was a-ringin', and the nex' I knawed 'e was off with 'is friend to Clyst.' She kept repeating these words, glad for someone new to listen. Those poor lads who went off on an adventure to teach the foreigners a lesson – how were they to know they would be surrounded by highly trained Italian gunners, that they'd be dead by the following evening? How was she to know, poor woman, that the morning after, she and many others would be searching for and burying their relations and friends. The people were so terrified of reprisals that they dared not stay to say prayers over the dead. Neither did they dare bring a body home to be buried in the churchyard.

The mother took all her son's clothes out of a press and begged us to choose anything to tide us over till we reached Ivybridge. I found a pair of boots, some breeches and a shirt. Dick found a shirt and a jerkin.

The rest of our journey passed without event. As I expected, my Aunt Joanna had taken sick with a melancholy likely to be permanent. She'd adored her father and brother too much to recover from their deaths, and she was mourning for her stillborn child, born in December. What had been a happy home was torn apart with misery and recrimination, and what must have seemed like poverty to Joanna. In spite of this, when I went to say goodbye to her, she gave me two diamond rings which no longer fitted her swollen fingers, and a pearl necklace which had belonged to my grandmother Wynslade.

'Take these to sell, dear Will', she said. 'For rest assured, Agnes will give you nothing.'

Dick and I stayed but a single night, not wishing to overburden my uncle with gloomy talk, and he in his turn had little to tell me. He'd heard no news from Tregarrick, and although he'd sent off my letter to Thomasine he feared she might never have received it. And I was anxious to be off to Pelynt.

Once we'd crossed the bridge into Cornwall, I began to talk of where we would go when we'd collected Thomasine from Tregarrick. Even if Agnes permitted us to stay, I told Dick I'd no intention of doing so. To become a servant along with Dick and Thomasine in my father's house would be intolerable. We would go to Trelawne, a mile and a half out of Pelynt, and ask my grandfather to put us up for a day or two, and then travel to a town to find lodgings and work.

But Dick as always took a more practical view. How could we expect Thomasine to walk here and there to find lodging and work? He'd been assuming we'd remain at Tregarrick, at least till Thomasine's child was born. He was well versed in the possible risks of childbirth, whereas I'd grown up with no knowledge of such matters. Besides, my mind had been too overwhelmed with my father's fate to think of Thomasine. I remembered now that my grandfather, being a Catholic, might have suffered during the Commotion. The Trelawneys would be suspect throughout Cornwall, and couldn't be expected to welcome rebels under their roof. It was essential, said Dick, that we shouldn't remove Thomasine from Tregarrick until we'd found suitable accommodation for her lying-in at the end of March. And he reminded me it was already the twenty-fifth day of February! How stupid I'd been not to realise how soon our child was due to arrive in this sorry world. Dick was right. We must remain at Tregarrick for the birth, and for some time after. In the meantime I must visit Looe to sell one of Joanna's rings.

At Tregarrick I'd be able to retrieve various belongings we'd left behind – a chest of clothes and, of course, my precious harp. Thinking of this I suddenly recalled with a flood of relief that I'd also left a small leather bag of jewels inherited from my mother. These would keep us comfortably for a while.

We approached Tregarrick from the north, thus avoiding going down the village street and being recognised. Arriving at dusk, we found the gate locked, and a servant we'd not seen before guarding it. Demanding to be let in, we were given to understand that Lady Agnes Trevanion had gone away, leaving instructions that the gate be barred permanently against me. The man also informed us that Thomasine had left Tregarrick in December. Where had she gone? I asked in desperation. He didn't know. Had she gone with anyone? He gave us the same answer. The only place I could imagine her wanting to go was North Devon. But in December, heavy with child? How could she travel so far? Was she lying dead in a ditch, or in woodland? The only person who could possibly have taken her in was Mary Lee. That must be the answer. We had to return to Devon to find out. We'd been puzzled by the message Rowland Jeynens had given us, that Thomasine was still waiting at Pelynt. But now we guessed that, of course, it was Kestell's doing. My expectation that Kestell would no longer trouble us was dashed. Where was he? And what further mischief was he planning?

Before leaving we created an angry scene, demanding our personal possessions. Dick too had left clothes and some good tools he could well do with. As we argued, a vicious-looking dog appeared behind the gate, barking ferociously. It wasn't one of my father's dogs, and I immediately remembered Nonna. Thomasine had taken Nonna away, said the man, and he threatened to summon more guard dogs if we didn't remove ourselves.

Our final resort was Amy, who fortunately was still employed by Agnes, and was therefore still living with her parents in their cottage on the estate. She told us Agnes had remarried at the beginning of

February, and no longer lived at Tregarrick. Thomasine had been ordered to leave early in December. Thanks to Jake, Amy's father, she'd been taken to Amy's sister, Susanna at Helland Farm. From there she was hoping to reach Torrington. The dog, Nonna, had been kept. Farming on the estate had continued under an efficient new bailiff whom Agnes had employed to make money without any care for the welfare of the servants or tenants. As for our possessions, Agnes had instructed Amy to tie up my clothes in an old sheet. She was to sell them if she wished, together with my harp. Dick's tools were being used by another servant. Everyone at Tregarrick knew, of course, that my father was dead, but Agnes, suspecting I was still alive, had made sure I would not be admitted. Amy had stored the clothes and harp against my return. It was the only good thing to happen to me in many a long month, particularly as I discovered the bag of jewels safe amongst my clothes. So now we would be able to pay the family for feeding us and for being so honest.

Amy told us all that had happened in Cornwall since June. Anthony Kingston, a crude and sadistic man by nature, having been given the liberty to declare strict martial law, had been terrorising the people. Executions without trial had been carried out in as many places in the county as possible to act as a deterrent – and the property of every rebel's family was forfeited. The worst crime, said Amy with tears in her eyes, was the hanging of so many good priests – Simon Morton, Richard Benet, Roger

Barrett, John Tompson, William Alsa, Robert Bochyn, John Barrow, John Woodcock, Robert Boyse… she had the names of all these priests by heart, for each hanging had caused an angry stir in the county.

Then Amy's father related several sickening tales of Kingston's gratuitous cruelty which would never be forgotten. Each instance was based on a similar theme. With smiles and smooth talk, Kingston had led innocent men to believe they were safe, and then suddenly, pouncing on them like a cat playing with a mouse, he'd ordered them to be hanged immediately. The most grotesque had taken place at the mill in Bodmin. The miller, who'd assisted the rebels, had fled on hearing that Kingston was to visit Bodmin. The servant left in charge, who was to pretend to be the miller, was hanged on the spot instead of his master, in spite of protests he'd had nothing to do with the rebellion.

The Cornish people had endured much ill-treatment at the hands of government and landowners in their time, but never had they suffered such a reign of terror as this in every town and village. He reckoned folk everywhere had become suspicious and sullen. The season of Christmas had passed by without joy. Dancing and drinking of ale on church land was prohibited. Cornwall had become a sad and silent place. Father Lambe lived in constant fear of being deprived of his living or worse, and had presided grimly over our bare church at Pelynt, tolling its dismal single bell. But on hearing that the great banner Thomasine had so detested had been cut up to make sacks, I could only think, what a fitting revenge!

We felt in better spirits after eating, but nevertheless, it was unbearably sad to see my beloved home turned into a dismal fortress in the hands of the woman I so hated. Without thinking I walked back to the high wall surrounding the house, and continued round it to the back gate, which gave onto the cobbled yard. Hiding myself behind the wall, I gave a low whistle. It was almost dark, but I recognised the dog, Nonna, bounding out of her shed. At once I regretted my stupidity in calling her, for she stood expectantly, wagging her tail furiously. But the wooden gate was too high and topped with iron spikes. There was no possibility of lifting her over.

Feeling very guilty I turned quickly and, joining Dick, we made our way up the track. Suddenly I heard the padding of feet, and a panting noise behind us, and there was Nonna, trying to leap up at my leg. I knelt down, but as I clasped her to me, I felt a wet stickiness on her fur. We hastily retraced our steps to the cottage, and found that Nonna had three gashes along her back, with several splinters of wood caught in her fur. They were not deep gashes, but they looked ugly. Amy pulled out the splinters and cleaned the wounds, binding a strip of cloth over the dog's back and under her belly. She must have escaped by constantly trying to force her body through the tight space under the rough wood of the gate.

It was seven o'clock by this time, and Amy's parents begged us to stay the night, even though it meant sleeping on the floor. We were most grateful, particularly as Nonna was in no fit state to walk far. Amy informed us the Looe to Launceston carrier was due to pass through Duloe, and we could catch it at the bridge early the following morning.

Sitting in the large dusty cart with half a dozen other travellers, bumping along the stony rutted road with a fine Cornish drizzle dampening our clothes, I was struck at last by the knowledge that there remained no vestige in me of Sir William Wynslade of Constantine. Since the end of the rebellion and my father's death I had lost all the authority I'd ever had. During my time in London, Tregarrick had remained the only beacon of my past life, and it was not until I actually reached my childhood home to find it barred against me that this unsavoury truth penetrated my mind. I had become a wandering vagrant, with no status in the world. Dick, on the other hand, though he'd lost his job and home at Tregarrick, hadn't come down in the world. In whichever town we decided to settle, his skills would be in demand, and his place in the community assured. But Thomasine and I, where did we belong, and what could we do? Thomasine had expected to become Lady of the Manor. Now, what could I give her and our child?

There was little conversation amongst our fellow travellers, though I suspected they all knew each other. No one laughed or even smiled. I had the impression that nearly every life in Cornwall had been destroyed in some way by Russell. Not far from Launceston we crossed the River Inny, and then, to my surprise, the driver turned his horse off the main road, taking a most bumpy track into Launceston.

'Why this way?' I asked the old man sitting next to me on the bench seat.

'Tis on account of Eliza', he answered in a low voice. ''Er that's wearin' a shawl.' I cast a hasty glance at a miserable woman with drooping shoulders and a pinched-looking face. ''Er son were 'anged by the road into town', whispered the old man. 'His corpse be swingin' there yet.'

'By whose order?'

'Anthony Kingston's.'

'What had he done?'

'Escaped with Lord Arundell from Sampford Courtenay, an' made a last stand with he outside Launceston on the Okehampton Road. Eliza's 'usband died at Fenny Bridges. Her got no one left, yet Kingston took 'er cottage as well.'

'Where does she live?'

'With 'er neighbours, but her cannot bide with they for ever. Her threatens to hang herself, and I dare say her'll do it.'

I shuddered, and suddenly remembered Mistress Kylter at Constantine. Had anyone told her of the terrible fate of her twins? Perhaps someone had assured her the boys died in battle. They were dead, that was all she would care about, and I hadn't even spared the time to visit her with some kind words. Some day I'd go, but not until I'd found Thomasine.

As we journeyed closer to Torrington my spirits lifted a little, in the hope of being reunited with Thomasine. It was fortunate she'd never quite become a lady, and wouldn't mind us renting a simple cottage with chickens, a vegetable plot and perhaps a pig – certainly a horse. We could have purchased a couple of horses at Launceston, but decided not to draw attention to ourselves on approaching Torrington.

Besides, we had Nonna to consider. Her wounds showed signs of beginning to heal, and we were able to walk the last two miles into the town. We had a meal at the Black Horse, and asked the innkeeper the way to Mary Lee's house. He regarded us suspiciously, and all he would say was, that Mary Lee was almost a recluse, rarely talking to anyone. Her husband, Henry Lee, the former mayor, hadn't returned, and she knew not how he'd died. We would be lucky if she let us into her home. His words gave me cause for worry, for if Mary Lee was living alone, where was Thomasine?

Standing on the steps of an imposing grey house in South Street, set back on the cliff which rose steeply from the flat green water-meadows far below, we could see the bridge across the wide river, and the thickly wooded hills stretching miles into the distance. As a child I'd been to the Michaelmas fair at Torrington with my grandfather, and had never ceased to wonder at the unique position of the town. Now, looking down at the Torridge I realised why Thomasine loved it so much. Indeed no river in Cornwall could match it.

We had to knock twice before the door opened, and a thin, dark-haired woman with a chalk-white face and huge haunted dark eyes surveyed our travel-worn appearance. Her rigid expression softened a little as Nonna wagged her tail and then licked the trembling hand extended to stroke her. I thanked God for the dog, as Mary Lee asked, 'Do you bring news of Henry?'

'Forgive me, no', I replied. 'But I did meet your husband in one of the camps outside Exeter. You must know already that he fought in the last battle at Sampford Courtenay.'

'Yes, yes, I know that. Some died fighting and some escaped up the Exe Valley, only to be captured and hanged. But how did Henry die?'

'He was a brave man to join the rebellion', was all I could say. I was desperate to enquire about Thomasine, but wary of upsetting Mistress Lee.

'He was a fool, a fool, to throw away his life for a lost cause', she exclaimed bitterly. 'So what do you want with me?'

'My name is William Wynslade, and this is my friend, Dick Popham.'

Mary Lee gasped, and then shrieked, 'It's not possible! You can't be William Wynslade!'

Bewildered, we stood gazing at one another until Mary remembered her manners. 'You had better come in', she said. We moved into a large darkened room, for the curtains were almost drawn to. 'I was told William Wynslade had been hanged in London with his father, John Wynslade.'

People often say life has become a nightmare. We wake from nightmares, but I had a frightening premonition that I would never wake from this one. Standing in the dimly lit room, I listened intently, desperately hoping Thomasine might appear, but in the doom-laden silence that descended on us I became certain she wasn't in the house.

At length Dick ventured, 'Who brought you this news?'

'A former servant of Lord Arundell at Helland – a youth named Rowland Jeynens.'

Dick and I exchanged horrified glances. 'Please sit down, Mistress Lee', I said, 'And tell us, if you will, exactly what he told you.'

Mary put her hand to her forehead and swayed a little. Dick and I took an arm each and helped her into a chair.

'At the end of January an official messenger from Exeter told our deputy mayor that Lord Arundell and three others, John Wynslade, John Bury and Thomas Holmes, had been hanged in London, and that commissioners would be coming to take down our church bells and punish anyone thought to have actively supported the rebellion. Then on the ninth day of February came this Rowland Jeynens.

Immediately we guessed the sickening truth. Not only had Kestell instructed Rowland to tell me to return to Tregarrick; he'd also told him to travel to Torrington with the false news of my death. It was an astonishing revelation. How did he know Thomasine was living with Mary Lee? How did he persuade poor Rowland to travel all the way to Torrington in winter? No wonder Arundell had chosen Kestell to be his spy, so experienced was he in devious ways and persuasive lying.

'What did Rowland Jeynens actually say, Mistress Lee?' I asked.

'He said I was to tell Thomasine Wynslade that he himself had seen William Wynslade hanged, drawn and quartered at Tyburn. He said it twice, quite clearly.'

'Did he leave Torrington the same day?'

'I believe so.'

'Had you given refuge to Thomasine Wynslade?'

'Yes', whispered Mary, 'Yes, I had.'

I began to tremble as my hopes rose. Perhaps Thomasine was in Torrington after all.

'Please continue', urged Dick, very gently. Then Mary told us the whole story, glad, it would appear, to unburden herself at last. I wanted to hear her story, and knew I must curb my impatience.

'She arrived, poor girl, early in December, with child and in such a state. I assured her, may God forgive me, that William Wynslade must surely be alive, and would soon come to find her. With food and rest she revived, and she helped me bear my loss. I hoped William Wynslade would arrive before the birth. But I told her, if he didn't come in time, she could stay here to be delivered.

'Over the Christmas season a friend of hers named John Kestell came three times to see Thomasine. He'd been Lord Arundell's secretary, and was fighting with the rebels until his master's arrest. Thomasine had met him in Cornwall, and when she left Tregarrick, he and his family, who lived on the Helland estate, helped her to reach Torrington. I took to him at once, for he is such a considerate and kind person, with the manners of a real gentleman. I also felt sorry for him, for it was obvious he was smitten with Thomasine. He even bought her a pure white kitten, which pleased her very much.

'At the trial in November of Lord Arundell and his colleagues, Johnny spoke well of his master, to no avail. He didn't remain in London to witness the hangings. He couldn't face such brutality. But I guessed William Wynslade must have stayed, on account of his father. At the end of January, Johnny told us he'd been appointed bailiff somewhere near Hartland, and would be moving in February. We were very glad for him, and Thomasine became a little happier, expecting William Wynslade would reach Torrington by the end of February.

'Then on the ninth day of February that Rowland Jeynens came to shatter all Thomasine's hopes. After he'd gone I was in a terrible state. All the while she'd been upstairs in her attic chamber, the little room she loved because there was a good view of the river. How was I going to tell her the news that William

Wynslade had been hanged? To my great relief, Johnny called in by chance on his way to Hartland and readily offered to break the news to Thomasine for me. I asked him how such a mistake could have been made in the official announcement, and he replied that there had been so many executions in London in the last few years that it wasn't surprising. He knew Rowland Jeynens of course, and assured me that in spite of being somewhat backward, he was completely honest, and what he'd witnessed must be true.

'Johnny went up to Thomasine's chamber, and about half an hour later a door banged. I heard Thomasine shrieking at Johnny on the first floor landing, but couldn't hear what she was saying. I glanced up the stairs and saw her looking very distraught. Then I heard her shout, "Get out of this house, and don't ever set foot in it again!" Johnny ran down the stairs and left hurriedly, saying he would no longer intrude on our grief. Thomasine refused to leave her room that evening, or to have any supper. During the night it was heartrending to listen to her weeping.'

At this point Mary ceased speaking, and regarded me as though I was a ghost, and also with suspicious distaste. Later, when I thought about it, I realised that Dick and I had arrived as muddy, ill-smelling vagrants. I was certainly not the man she'd envisaged as Sir William Wynslade, Thomasine's betrothed. Mary must have been most disappointed. She kept on muttering, 'He's dead. You must be an impostor. I tell you William Wynslade is dead.'

I wished I was dead, for at that moment I sensed there was no one upstairs – Thomasine was dead.

Then Mary had resumed her tale. 'When Thomasine came down in the morning I wanted to give her some little comfort, but she was inconsolable. I have never seen anyone so bitter. I knew from my own grief over Henry how long it might take for her to recover. But she was still so young, so beautiful, with all her life before her. I thought how suitable a husband Johnny would make her, he being such a good person, and clever enough to rise in the world. They'd make such a handsome couple. Soon she'd have a babe to think of, to keep her from fretting too much. I planned to tell Johnny to tread carefully, not to visit too often or to expect anything for some months. But in the end I was sure she would come to realise his worth and marry him. I loved Thomasine, and wanted for her to be happy.'

Mary paused again. Soon she would tell us how Thomasine had died. Didn't her words, *I loved Thomasine,* already prove her death?

'After remaining silent all day', Mary went on, 'That evening Thomasine suddenly accused me of allowing Johnny to go upstairs to tell her the news of William Wynslade's death. "Once he knew Will was dead", she said, "He thought he could just walk into my room and I'd fall into his arms. I am not his whore, nor ever will be, and I never want to see him again. Never! I'd sooner die." I couldn't understand why she'd turned against him, and could only think that so much grief for William, coming on top of all her troubles, had affected her reason. She returned…'

'Tell me how she died', I demanded, interrupting her sharply, for by now I could no longer wait to know.

Mary began to weep silently. 'Jesu, forgive me! Why did I let her go out on such a day in her condition? Why, why? It was all my fault. I should have kept her here.'

On hearing these words a heaviness crept through my limbs as though I'd drunk hemlock.

'She never missed a day going down to the river to look out for otters. There was nothing she didn't know about those creatures – how long they lived, where were their holts, and how they could breed at all times of year. One day it was pouring with rain and very windy, but she still insisted on going. The next morning – it was the twenty-eighth day of February – her body was washed up below Rothern Bridge. She must have slipped and lost her balance in the wind.

'John Kestell attended the funeral, and afterwards came here, beset with guilt for her death, saying, almost in tears, he should never have told her so soon that he loved her. I felt such pity for him, poor man.

'I had a headstone placed on her grave in the churchyard. She was only seventeen, not much more than a child herself. What kind of evil woman is that Agnes Trevanion to have thrown her out in such a wicked way?'

There and then I should have told Mary the truth about Kestell. At the time I was too overwhelmed by Thomasine's death. Lengthy explanations were beyond me. In any case I do believe Mary was so far gone in her infatuation with Kestell's deceptive personality that she would never have thought any evil of him. She still believed I was an impostor. Understandably her mind was in a muddle. Throughout our ensuing relationship she never quite overcame her suspicion and disapproval of me, her only certainty being that Kestell was a good man. What a blessing that Thomasine hadn't been taken in by him.

Frustrated by Mary's views regarding Kestell, I said we would trouble her no longer, but go to see Thomasine's grave and find ourselves a lodging. Nonna got to her feet wagging her tail again, and to our surprise Mary said, 'You may lodge here if you wish. There are rooms aplenty.'

Thanking her kindly, I asked Dick to settle in the house while I went to the churchyard.

Perhaps because it was new, the granite headstone jumped out at me immediately. It was not till I saw the name, *Thomasine Mary Wynslade, daughter of Alice and Edmund Wynslade, 4th June 1532 – 28th February 1550,* that I believed her lost to me for ever, with our fully formed child within her womb. What horrors did they both suffer as the dark rushing waters closed over them? I should have raged then, should have wept, but all feeling had deserted me. It was as though I was contemplating the wife and child of another man.

In the next few days, as Dick and I listened to Mary talking endlessly of her husband and of Thomasine, I was, as they say, numbed by grief. It was Mary who was full of guilty feeling, and it was Dick who struggled to comfort her. I myself had lost the power of speech, other than for strictly practical purposes.

At Mary's request we stayed with her throughout the spring. When it became known that Dick and I were survivors of the rebellion, and that I was William Wynslade, Thomasine's betrothed, we were made welcome in a town recently much given to suspicion of strangers. That I had come too late to Torrington filled them with sympathy. But I couldn't yet respond to their kindly feelings. There was no shortage of jobs Dick could do, especially with my help. We went out of the house early each morning and worked hard all day. At night after a meal with Mary we went thankfully to bed.

I brooded daily over Thomasine. If only, if only... the words raced through my mind together with all the unanswered questions... Should I go to Hartland to confront Kestell and take my revenge? What had motivated him? He knew I would arrive in Torrington sooner or later to confound what he'd forced Rowland to say. In the meantime had he expected that in spite of being heavy with child, Thomasine would succumb to intimacy with him which would end our relationship or sour it for ever? What had taken place in Thomasine's chamber when Kestell went up to tell her of my death? Did she allow him to comfort her? Did he – but no, pray

God it couldn't be – she'd died hating him, but was that owing to guilt? If Kestell came again to Torrington – and I was sure he would – to taunt me by hinting or even swearing Thomasine had given herself to him before Rowland said I was dead, would I believe him? Above all, would I find the courage to kill him, and if I did, would everyone think I'd lost faith in Thomasine? Had I lost faith in her? These questions were driving me into jealous madness.

As the days passed I lost all inclination to be sociable, or to take the slightest pleasure in the lush Devon spring. My grief grew daily, but was stifled within me. Dick, as always, chatted to people in the street, made friends and defended my reclusive character.

For a long time we didn't enter St Michael's, though I visited Thomasine's grave each day. Churches were a cruel reminder of the malicious destruction wrought upon the South West. But one day Dick suggested we look at the changes inside. The rood screen had been ripped out, and the high altar, with its gilded cross and the pyx hanging above it, had been replaced by a communion table which Protestants called the Lord's board, situated in the chancel. A rumour was circulating in Torrington that parliament would soon be passing an act of uniformity, with heavy fines for non-attendance, and imprisonment for non-payment.

As Mary owned suitable stabling, we'd bought horses, enabling us to undertake jobs in the surrounding villages. One Sunday afternoon Dick went alone to Bideford to call on a girl he'd met at the market in Torrington. Meanwhile I rode across the bridge into the forest. I wished to find a secluded plot to build a hut on stilts, hard against the hillside and looking down through a small gap in the trees, to give a sight of the river. We'd reached the decision not to bide with Mary beyond the summer. Dick was hoping to get a permanent, more rewarding job in Torrington with a long-established family business making bows. He planned to rent a cottage in the centre of the town, and was disappointed when I declined to share it. But he understood my reasons. There would be no room for me in any sense of the word if he took a wife. Besides, my increasingly taciturn nature would be a liability.

So he agreed to assist in the construction of a single-roomed hut on the spot I'd chosen. We hired a donkey for two weeks to carry planks of timber along the river and then up a little-used woodland track. All day I worked alone until Dick came to inspect my labour, and to give me instructions for the following day. Only on Sunday did he ride off to Bideford to do his courting. Appropriately her name was Patience, for she had to wait till November to marry Dick.

My hut was exceptionally well built, high up on its strong stilts. The one large room had two small windows and a door giving onto a spacious platform. It was sheltered from the wind and to some extent from the worst of the rain by the thick intertwining spread of branches above it. The most important addition was a rope ladder which I attached firmly to two metal rings on the side of the platform. Rope making was a speciality in Torrington, and mine was necessarily a good stout one.

When the hut was completed, Patience came to see it. She was a good-natured, homely person, slightly overawed by my presence, and puzzled by my lack of easy conversation and inability to enjoy a good laugh. She herself was always full of laughter, which infected Dick but failed to move me. Fortunately Nonna provided a link between us, for Patience was much amused at the way my dog sat herself down obediently in the basket attached to a rope which I then hauled up to the platform. Not surprisingly, the people of Torrington also began to think of me as very strange, living alone in the woods, and looking, with my long unkempt beard, like a wild hermit.

Once a week I'd walk through the town to buy necessities, such as soap, salt or oil for my lamp. Nonna would greet everyone and relieve me of having to say more than a few words. Children in particular loved her, and therefore assumed her master could not be dangerous. Dick said they called me Wild Willy, and talked of my brave exploits in the rebellion. There was a garbled tale of my having evaded the hangman on the gallows and galloped away on a waiting horse provided by a mysterious admirer. Now and again in a window I'd catch sight of a tall, gaunt figure with leathery brown skin and eyes in cavernous sockets, and realise with dismay that this was I.

We paid Mary a small fee for allowing us to keep our horses in her stables. I looked after them, the one task I did for Dick. Sometimes Mary would see me from a window, and we would wave. She too continued to be regarded as something of an oddity, a woman shutting herself up to grieve for the husband who never came home. Yet I sensed there was more to Mary's state of mind than people realised – something to do with Thomasine's death. There was unfinished business between us which should have been aired sooner than it was.

By the end of July my hut was completed and I spent August knocking up rough furniture and utensils to make it into a home. Most of my inherited jewellery had been sold, and it was time to consider how I was to earn a steady living. To rely on odd jobs for ever didn't attract me. I had taken up playing my harp again, and singing some of the old Cornish songs. Ideas for new songs based on Cornish legends came into my mind, which I wrote down. Not surprisingly, they were songs of love and loss, set against the background of the hills, valleys, moors and coast of Devon and Cornwall. Recalling the long winter evenings at Tregarrick, when my father's friends had so enjoyed listening to my performance, I determined to put my talent to use once more. To become a wandering minstrel as in the days of old, visiting manor houses to sing for my supper, might be worth trying from late autumn to early spring.

Sadly, in our new zealous Protestant world, pastimes such as singing and dancing round the bonfires on midsummer's eve, or watching outdoor plays, were frowned upon. All public performances were forbidden as being relics of idle pagan times. Even some of the innocent pastimes of children were regarded with suspicion. Sitting on my platform on warm summer evenings, I began to wonder how I was going to fit into the new system. To live in my hut for half the year I would have to resume my work as a handyman, and possibly make things to sell at Torrington weekly market. I also promised to assist Dick and Patience to dig over their large vegetable plot. Otherwise I could go hunting for my dinner in an ancient part of the forest where black boars lived among small oak trees.

How long would it be before the Protestant minister, recently appointed to replace the old Catholic rector, caught up with my heathen ways? Father Chambre's last public act, I was told, had been to bless the rebels of Torrington and to sprinkle them with holy water as they set out with their Mayor, Henry Lee, in June 1549 to meet up with Arundell at Okehampton. Possibly the upheaval taking place within the church had hastened the old man's death. Had he lived, the best he could hope for was to be deprived of his living, and of course his rectory. No, he was lucky to have quitted this world before being forced to beg his bread.

Fortunately the Protestant minister was a man not too earnest at compelling his flock to give up all their beliefs overnight. There were elderly parishioners and the families of those perished in the rebellion who still refused to partake in the new service. These he left alone during 1550. Dick attended church and came to know the minister, who'd buried my Thomasine and knew a little of my history. Dick exaggerated my misfortunes, telling him my mind had been mightily disturbed and plunged into melancholy by my father's and Thomasine's deaths. Thus the minister, thinking me a madman, didn't venture to admonish me. He was a short, frail-looking man, and I must have seemed a very tall, threatening figure. We only met face to face once during the summer. He bowed his head slightly, murmuring, 'Good day, Master Wynslade', and hurried on.

At the end of September I sold my last piece of jewellery to buy a sheepskin coat, strong boots, leather bottles and saddlebags. I bade a sad farewell to Dick, for in the last fifteen months scarce a day had passed without my seeing him. I told him jokingly to expect me back within a week, but he maintained the venture was worth a try. Parting with Nonna was almost as bad, but she was in good hands with Dick and Patience.

That first day I rode as far as Tavistock and put up at an inn to obtain information regarding the situation in Cornwall. It was not encouraging. The innkeeper grumbled that times were hard. He had two travellers upstairs just arrived to stay overnight, but the local people rarely dropped in for a cup of ale. The spring and summer had been very dreary. Public festivities of all kinds, including wrestling, cockfighting and hurling, together with drinking of ale, were prohibited, and Tavistock was a dead town after dark.

'Us all suffered from that rebellion', he said. 'My two nephews died at Fenny Bridges. I be thankful to 'ave only the two daughters, else I might 'ave lost my livin'.'

At this point the travellers appeared, and taking the table at the opposite end of the room to me, ordered their supper. Immediately the one with his back to me spoke I recognised the voice of Nicholas Udall. The inn parlour, lit by a single smoky oil-lamp, was dark enough to hide my identity, but I doubt he would have known me with a beard.

Udall called for wine, and the two men began to converse in loud, confident voices, as though the innkeeper and I were not present. 'From what I've heard and seen', commented Udall, 'Lord Russell has done a fine job in Cornwall. Thank God he ignored Somerset urging him to deal gently with those rebel savages, otherwise we might still be in the midst of riots.'

'He has indeed made a thorough job of it' returned his companion. 'But in doing so he's wasted many an excellent soldier. Lord Grey said that such was the valour and stoutness of these rebels, that in all the wars he'd been in, he'd never fought in so murderous a fray.'

'Ah, well', said Udall, 'They fight like savages because they are savages. Somerset did not know the Cornish. The only way to keep a Cornishman down is to hang him up!' Udall laughed heartily at his own joke, and continued, 'Russell knows that better than anyone. He'd like to have hanged every man under fifty in the county.'

'But think what a mighty grudge has been left. He had better keep out of Cornwall if he values his life. Personally I don't care for the man. His greed beggars description. You heard, no doubt, he was granted all Somerset's properties?'

'Oh, yes. Still, you have to admire a man who can rise so high from nothing. What was he, after all, in King Harry's time? – just a small landowner in Dorset. Then he proved himself a good soldier in the French wars. And now, look at him! His house in Exeter resembles a castle.'

'A ruthless military man will always get on in this world.'

'The King relied on him to keep order in the West – collecting taxes, press-ganging young lads and so on, and suddenly, there he was – Lord Privy Seal, President of the Council of the West, and Lord High Admiral. And with each promotion came more church lands. Now he's made Earl of Bedford he's a king in the South West. His motto will be *Kill first, explain later.*'

'What a vested interest he had in the destruction of the abbeys – Dunkeswell, Tavistock, Exeter,

Woburn, Thorney, St Albans… D'you realise he even owns this town and thirty manors round about? Russell's writ runs in Cornwall and Devon, no doubt of that. It staggers the imagination.'

'And while it does, for his son Francis is hot on his father's heels, the South West will never again succumb to "papistical superstitions and abuses", as Cranmer so aptly puts it. A splendid achievement!'

My blood boiled as I listened to Udall's opinions. How easy to dub your opponent a savage! Did he ever think of the long, hard, incredibly disciplined training archers have to undergo in order to be marched off at a moment's notice to Scotland, or shipped across to France, often on short rations and ill-clad against the weather, to fight the King's battles? These are the men who won Crecy, Poitiers and Agincourt for such creatures as Udall sitting comfortably at home, pontificating on their savagery. And in a few years they'll be cast aside in favour of gunners, and the authorities won't give a fig for their welfare.

Early the following morning I stopped halfway down the inn staircase leading directly to the parlour, and listened to the conversation below. It seemed Udall and his companion were about to depart, and were discussing the best route to Helland.

I recalled with distaste that Gawen Carew now owned Arundell's manor. Humphrey's family had lost their home, and no doubt Gawen had seized all their goods. The Carews had not been known for generosity or courtesy. It grieved me to think of

Catholic estates transferred so arbitrarily into the hands of such Protestant families as the Tremaynes, Strodes, Fortescues and Yardes. Then I heard Udall ask the innkeeper who I was, and felt great relief when he lied, 'Just a yeoman from North Devon on his way to Plymouth.'

'He looked tall enough to be a Cornish bowman', commented Udall.

I remained on the staircase till they'd gone, wondering what wickedness Udall would be planning with Gawen Carew at Helland. As I was gazing out of the landing window at the vivid pink sky behind a line of dark elms, and thinking there might well be rain on my journey, a sudden guilty thought came to me. During the months at Torrington Dick and I did wonder once or twice what had become of poor Rowland Jeynens. Dick thought Kestell must have paid him well to ensure his silence. I'd agreed, but now began to wonder. It occurred to me the answer might be found at Helland, where Rowland had spent all his life. I'd had no intention of going out of my way to visit Helland, yet now my conscience urged me to go before embarking on my singing career. Thus after a substantial breakfast I rode off towards Bodmin.

I called at Helland Farm, hoping that Susanna might have some news of Rowland. She told me he had indeed returned to Helland in February 1550, after his foolhardy expedition to London. Susanna and Luke agreed that for all his glaring faults, Arundell had looked after Rowland well. Had he not died and lost all his assets, he would probably have left the boy something to live on. As it was, Rowland had been destitute and in a most distressed state on his arrival at Helland. Luke had found him shivering on the wall of Helland Manor and brought him to the farm. That night he developed a fever, and began shouting in delirium that William Wynslade had been hanged. Fortunately Johnny had come home the following day for a short visit, and had assured his parents that I was still alive. On his return to Hartland Johnny had taken Rowland with him, promising to find him work and lodgings. Susanna had been unhappy about letting the boy go, as he was obviously still unwell. But her son had allayed all her fears, and she had helped Rowland up and sent him off in her husband's sheepskin jacket, which he could ill afford.

'So you need have no fear', Luke told me, 'For the boy's safety. Johnny will see to it the lad won't starve.'

Kestell had told his parents of Thomasine's death, and they offered me their condolences for her and for the loss of our child. I was dumbfounded yet again, at Kestell's audacity. So where was Rowland? If any authority was to challenge Kestell, he would have concocted a plausible tale: that the witless boy was prone to running off, no one knew where. But I suspected that somewhere between Helland and Torrington Rowland's corpse must lie buried, another sacrifice added to the thousands of nameless rebels dug into the soil of Cornwall and Devon.

I now resumed my original plan, to visit the Beckets at Cartuther, near Liskeard. Our families had always been good friends, and John Becket would receive me cordially for all that I'd refused to marry his daughter, Honor. The Beckets would know about my father's death, and I dreaded having to talk of it. John's wife and Honor were away in Dorset: instead I was received with courteous gravity by his two younger daughters, Ruth and Katherine, aged twelve and ten. My beard and gaunt appearance, in comparison to how youthful I had looked only three years before, must have astonished them.

To begin with, there was some slight constraint between John Becket and me. He admitted my father had been a good man and a brave one. 'He put me to shame for sure, but I must be honest with you, Will. He was too impulsive, almost too quick to stand up for the weak and the misjudged without thinking of the consequences for himself and his family. Agnes was always striving to keep him from giving away his money and his labour for a lost cause.'

'And yet she pushed him into leading the rebellion, a lost cause if ever there was one', I said bitterly.

Becket, who was aware that Agnes had never cared for me, said, 'Oh, we all knew Agnes was a cunning woman. She could see long ago where all this Protestant commotion was leading. If John hadn't marched off to fight, he would no doubt have stood up for John Moreman and Martin Geoffrey, and been marked down as a troublesome Catholic.'

'She wanted him to die in the rebellion. She as good as said so.'

'For all her religious devotion, as a practical woman she was determined to be on the winning side. She knew John Trevanion had once wanted to wed her, and was still looking for a wife.'

'Well, she lost no time in marrying him.'

'Did you know he intends selling Tregarrick in the spring?'

This news was not surprising. Disaster had struck so often in the last three years, my numbed mind should have been inured to it. And yet a stab of pain did strike me, thinking of the loss of my beloved Tregarrick, soon to be in the hands of strangers.

'It's a bad business', said my host. 'Agnes should have kept it to be given to you after the commotion is well over. But of course Hugh Trevanion had no time for your father, and his son would not care to help you. When it comes to property, Will, how many men can claim a clear conscience?'

'I have accepted my fate, and am glad not to join in the rush for spoil.'

I explained with a certain diffidence my intention of playing my harp and singing wherever I could find a welcome. If John Becket pitied me he didn't show it. Moreover, since he had a cousin and his family arriving the following evening I could entertain them at supper. His daughters, Ruth and Katherine, would certainly be delighted to hear me.

'But don't let Kate monopolise you. She regards the rebellion as an exciting adventure story, and knows little of death. I wish her to remain ignorant of the reality. Anthony Kingston has a lot to answer for in Cornwall. Did you hear of the fate of the deputy mayor of Bodmin, Nicholas Boyer?'

'Not of him, but I did hear of the miller's unfortunate servant.'

'Well, Anthony Kingston invited Boyer to a banquet. Before the meal started, he asked the deputy mayor to have a gallows erected outside. While this was being done, the guests were treated to a long and lavish meal. Then Kingston took Boyer out to the gallows and had him hanged for expressing sympathy with the rebels' cause. A cruel trick to entertain his guests! We live in fear lest Kingston should descend on Cartuther. There have been many unsavoury incidents. Our family intend to remain Catholics, so who knows what will befall us?'

I agreed that to remain Catholic might court suspicion for ever in the future. 'Our Protestant government in London, and most of the gentry in the South West, are not content with having put down the rebellion. They've abolished all our traditional pastimes.'

'Indeed they have', said John, 'The Padstow and Helston May Day festivals and all the village carnivals and sporting competitions.'

'And yet these traditions have nothing to do with religion.'

'The cycle of religious plays has also been forbidden. The reason is, tyrannical governments always regard drama as subversive. Those stories from the Old Testament may seem harmless, but they also give many an opportunity for a dig at authority, usually local authority, but latterly against the government. Even a clown entertaining a crowd in the streets is suspect these days, for a clown's words are always double-edged, and can raise many a laugh at the expense of a pompous mayor.'

'I had best not become a clown, then.'

John laughed, stating I would make a very sad clown.

In the parlour after dinner his daughters wanted to hear of my part in the rebellion. I described the short-lived moments of success at Clyst St Mary, but then passed on hastily to my project of becoming a wandering minstrel.

'Just like the troubadours of old', said Kate.

Towards evening I changed into my new chemise and velvet doublet. When the girls saw me they said I must have a hat to complete the costume. They hurried away, returning with a flat green velvet cap adorned with a bright ostrich feather. Ruth insisted their father would not mind my keeping it, he had a cupboard full of hats, she said. It certainly made me look younger and more jaunty. Then, feeling a little nervous, I tuned my harp and embarked on my musical career. The girls were delighted to hear that several of my lays were about the legends of Cornwall and Brittany. They had lately been reading the romantic tale of Tristram and Iseult, and were particularly moved by my song about Tristram. Ruth would have preferred a happy ending, but Kate thought the story wouldn't have been so beautiful without the tragic death scene. There started an argument as to whether a happy outcome could ever be as beautiful and moving as a tragic one.

'You looked so sad when you were singing about Iseult. Have you had a tragic love affair yourself?' asked Kate.

'Oh, do tell us!' begged Ruth.

'Please, please do!' echoed Kate.

'One day perhaps.'

'I wish you could be happy', said Kate, slipping her tiny hand into mine. 'You mustn't die of your love, like Tristram.'

'Don't worry about me', I replied, smiling. 'There are many other things to be joyful about in this world, and there are different kinds of happiness. Music brings me great contentment.'

'As a minstrel, you could call yourself Sir Tristram. You play on your harp just as well as he did.'

'But Tristram was the most handsome man in Cornwall, and the most clever', declared Ruth, looking at me doubtfully. 'William is rather too tall and bony.'

'I agree', replied Kate. 'And he does have a crooked smile. Nevertheless, I'd as soon have William. Handsome men are far too conceited. I shall always think of him as Sir Tristram.'

And so it was settled that I should announce myself as Sir Tristram.

I remained a week with the Beckets, riding each day to one of the nearby manors to try my luck. I sang at Menheniot, where the Trelawneys used to live, and at Fursdon, St Germans, Treworgey, Trenant and Lanreath, and then again at Cartuther.

At supper once more the Becket daughters monopolised me, and Kate read me extracts from their book about Tristram, which made me smile. – *'Sir Tristram played so melodiously that the whole household arrived for the most part at a run',* read Kate

'It's quite true' agreed Ruth. 'You do play so sweetly that everyone will forgive you for not being so handsome as the real Sir Tristram.' The innocent honesty of these two delightful girls amused and touched me greatly, especially as neither of them had mentioned the ugly scar I bore above my eye.

I left Cartuther on the twelfth day of October, and made my way gradually to Truro and thence to Constantine. To my surprise it wasn't hard to find gentry glad to welcome me into their homes, to provide an evening's entertainment. John Becket had given me a letter of introduction to a manor within a day's journey from Liskeard, and thereafter I had letters of introduction from place to place the length and breadth of Cornwall. There seemed to be a dearth of singing, dancing and juggling groups, once available to bring good cheer to long, dark winter evenings. When the Christmas season approached, more requests came to me than I could accept.

Each night I slept on a pallet in someone's hall, near the fire, never lacking for food or drink. My hosts were curious as to my true identity, for I always announced myself as Sir Tristram. I would smile, saying I remembered having no other name.

Often after a wet and windy ride I felt a desire to eschew humanity for ever, and on entering a manor with all its bustling activity, it was no easy task to conceal my bereavement with a hearty demeanour. Though I met many people, I confided nothing, and all who spoke to me must have felt my strangeness.

On making enquiries at Constantine, I was told Mistress Kylter no longer lived there. She'd been given refuge by a relation at Launceston, for since hearing of the death of her twins she was no longer fit to live alone. Walking down the familiar village street with my hat pulled down almost over my eyes to avoid being recognised, I thought how much grief must reside in so many of the cottages. Every healthy man in Constantine had rallied against the injustice of William Body and every 'furriner' who had ever marched into Cornwall to make life the more harsh for its people. But the death of the Kylter twins was a shocking crime. In the final count it was Kestell's doing, but the fault lay ultimately with Arundell and with me for not packing them off home.

Cornwall in a bad winter is a grim land, its long granite backbone swathed in mists where banks of fathomless dark clouds bear down heavily. The winds feel vicious enough to take not only the clothes but the flesh off one's back. By mid-afternoon dusk shrouds the lead-coloured moor and heath land, and out of this frightening semi-darkness a tall Celtic cross will loom into sight – or maybe a menacing giant boulder, a cairn of jagged rocks or a circle of brooding, ancient standing stones. The land had long since ceased to hold fears for me, but that winter, when my spirits were at their lowest ebb, it seemed to mock me. Even my sure-footed, hardy cob, Verity, had to be urged through black mire and thick fog, since the track was easy to miss. On arrival at my destination it was all I could do to present myself as a normal human being.

Dick told me once that the first time he'd journeyed in winter across Cornwall, he experienced such a mighty relief to be safely back at Woodbury that he resolved never to set foot in Cornwall again. He'd only settled at Tregarrick to work for my father because the fertile hills and woodland between Looe and Pelynt did bear some resemblance to East Devon. Since I'd been visiting so many manors, it became hard to distinguish one from another, but a manor in the area south of Port Isaac, in between Wadebridge and Camelford, stands out owing to an unpleasant experience at the nearby church of St Kew.

I'd been picking up snippets of news each day, and learned to my dismay that in January six commissioners, including Russell's son, Francis, were to be visiting every village church overlooked during previous inspections. The county boasts a great many churches, testimony to the devotion and labour of its people. It was an immense task, particularly in winter, to accomplish such a visitation, for many of the churches had been sited in remote places. But such was the eagerness of the government to seize any remaining church plate, gold or silver crucifixes, jewelled ornaments and embroidered copes and chasubles, that it couldn't await a more clement season for the commissioners to travel.

It was in connection with this visitation that I became involved in an incident at St Kew, which might have turned ugly. As I rode away down a narrow high-banked lane from the nearby manor at Tregellist, the high tower of St Kew church could be seen long before I entered the village. My host suggested I look at the impressive north-east stained glass window, depicting the story of Christ's Passion. He feared that, since the government commissioners were due the following day, the window might be removed, as had all the others in the church.

Crossing the stream by the ford I entered the churchyard, where a large group of men, women and children were gathered. Three horses, together with two packhorses, stood tethered outside the gate. As I dismounted, two men emerged from the church porch, each carrying a heavy sack. They were followed by a young, stern-looking man, whom I recognised as Francis, Russell's son. He stopped and addressed the parishioners, saying, 'We have removed all the objects no longer required for worship – crucifixes, pyxes, censers, chasubles, copes and candlesticks. Sufficient linen has been left to cover the Lord's Table.' He glared round at the semicircle of faces. 'Woe betide you if anything has been hidden away. It will go hard with you, should we discover property belonging to the church.'

Then a weasel-faced man spoke up loudly. 'Ask Eliza Pendoggett where her's hid our second chalice.'

Every eye was turned towards a short, humble-looking woman clad in a threadbare shawl. 'Is it true, Mistress Pendoggett, that you've stolen a chalice belonging to your church?'

'My grandfather, 'e gave that chalice to the church', she uttered in a thin, pathetic voice. 'His initials be engraved on it. He were a poor man, but saved ten years to buy it. 'Tis a small chalice, but I'll not have it stolen by rich men.'

'You had better fetch it, or we shall have to search your cottage.'

''Tis not in my cottage, and I'll not say where 'tis hidden.'

'Then we shall arrest you for theft.'

'Arrest me if you will. I'll not be givin' it up', stated the poor woman defiantly.

Francis Russell glanced nervously round at the villagers, perhaps aware that more had gathered since my arrival, enough indeed to call it a crowd. I found myself stepping forward to confront Russell's obnoxious son. 'I suggest you cease bullying Mistress Pendoggett. This church could do with two chalices. Your sacks are brimming with treasure, and many more will be brimming before you quit Cornwall.'

Frances Russell was surrounded by hostile faces gradually pressing closer. The two men who'd filled the sacks had loaded the two sturdy packhorses, and were ready to proceed. It was clear a riot might have broken out, had I not taken control, for everyone was now looking to me to speak. 'We can only guarantee your life, Sir Francis, if you depart quickly with no further threats.'

He looked sullenly at the people of St Kew as I said, 'Stand back to let Sir Francis pass, my friends.' I watched him go, relieved that another Helston riot had been averted. Then before anyone moved I mounted Verity, waved and rode off towards Port Isaac.

During the last days of February 1551, I reached Launceston and putting up at an inn, the first since Tavistock, I enquired of the innkeeper whether he knew anything of a Mistress Kylter.

'Oh, yes', he replied. 'A sad story. If you go to the castle early, you'll see 'er, the poor soul. Every mornin' from six to nine, never a day missed, since Kylter and Trevian were 'anged.'

And so I did. In icy, driving rain, sitting on a stretch of frozen greyish grass beneath the tower, a white and wizened Mistress Kylter sat cradling a large flat stone, the water running down her wrinkled face and dripping off her sodden white locks of hair. I sat down beside her and spoke some gentle words, but she knew me not. I could still read the faded black inscription on the stone, ending with the words, *God bless you all.* Once I might have shed tears for her, but now I had none left to shed.

Leaving Launceston by the Holsworthy road, I crossed the Tamar into Devon at Nether Bridge, feeling I'd had enough of Cornwall for the present. Its tragedy was too great a weight for my tormented mind. Its ancient exuberance in living despite grinding poverty had been so utterly crushed by Russell and his henchmen that it would be hard to imagine the sons or even the grandsons of our rebels rising again to defend their rights.

On reaching Torrington I didn't cross the bridge at Taddyport, but turned left along the river and into the woods to find my hut. Dick knew I'd planned to return on the first day of March, and with his usual kindness had left bread and meat, a pot of broth and a jar of ale. And best of all, a pair of new boots. He'd also filled my pallet with fresh straw. I soon had a good fire going in my brazier, and I fried rashers of bacon in a skillet balanced on a gridiron.

It was a relief beyond measure to be alone again in my own home, humble though it must have seemed to Dick and his wife. Patience was due to have her first child in August, and Dick was doing very well in the craft of bow making, besides being in demand at Torrington to construct other items of woodwork. He was now so well established in the town he might have lived there all his life. It was hard to believe that only two years before we'd not yet marched away from Pelynt nor had any notion we would never resume our life at Tregarrick.

I was worried lest Nonna should have been so comfortable during the winter in Dick's cottage she would no longer be content with the rigours of my hut. But when Dick and Patience brought her she seemed glad enough to see me, and placed herself obediently in the basket to be hauled up. Through being my only connection to Thomasine, Nonna was particularly dear to me, and I resolved not to leave her behind again. We'd go together on foot. Instead of staying away all the autumn and winter I planned to return to my hut every few weeks for a night or two.

A few days later I ventured into Torrington to place flowers on Thomasine's grave, and after stabling my horse, to see Mary. Dick said she'd sadly neglected her health, not eating enough nor taking exercise. She no longer kept servants, and her house was never cleaned or kept in repair. Dick and Patience had done their best to keep up her spirits, but as time passed she became more miserable. 'She's taken to sitting on the edge of the cliff overlooking Taddyport for hours in dry weather. Something is troubling her over and above her grieving for Henry. You'd best see if you can persuade her to talk,' said Dick.

It being a fine day I found Mary at the top of a cliff path, just above a bank of early primroses. On seeing me approach she greeted me with a wan smile, saying in a somewhat distracted fashion, 'Good day, William Wynslade', as though I'd not been away since October. I sat down beside her, and she said, 'Thomasine used to go down that path and along the river to the little spit of sand and shingle just beyond Rothern Bridge – d'you know it? – to watch the otters. There was one otter came to her call. Oh, such a way she had with wild creatures, that girl. The birds would eat out of her hand.' She paused, and putting her mouth close to my ear, whispered, 'I must tell you more about Thomasine, Will. I must tell you the truth about her.'

I prepared to listen again to the story I thought she'd already told me.

'You remember how a young man named Kestell used to call on me – so well-made he was, with thick curly black hair, such even white teeth, and a smile to melt any woman's heart. John was his name, yes, a good honest name, and he wanted to make a good honest woman of Thomasine. He even bought her a kitten, a lovely pure white kitten. But she would have none of it – left the pretty creature for me to feed.' Mary paused, sighing, and then continued, 'Johnny was rising in the world. He was a bailiff over at Hartland. Thomasine could have married him and been content. But she pined for her William. "He promised to come back to me", she said. "Instead they hanged him and cut him to pieces." "You'll soon have his child", I said, and Johnny would make such a kind stepfather." "I wouldn't marry him if he was the last man on earth" she replied, so bitterly. Why did she turn against him? And he such a good man.

'One dark, dreary afternoon in February, with a gale blowing and rain bucketing down from the blackest of clouds, I found Thomasine in her cloak, standing in the hallway, holding a basket covered with a cloth. "I'm going down to the river to take something for my otter", she explained. I begged her not to venture out. The river was rising, and I feared she would slip and fall in her condition. But she would go.

'By seven o'clock the wind had grown worse, and I raised the alarm. Three men went down this very cliff, but found nothing but the empty basket caught in a bramble.'

Mary's voice had become stifled with sobs, and I put my arm around her shoulders, much concerned for her distress. Then she went on to say, 'On Thomasine's bed I found a letter she'd written to me just before leaving the house.'

'Why didn't you tell me this when I first came to Torrington?'

Mary stared at me, her eyes filled with fear. 'Because she was to have a Christian burial. I didn't want her to be buried like a heathen, and go to hell. When Thomasine was a child, her mother was always ailing. Very frail she was, and I promised that, should she die, I'd see that her daughter was well cared for.'

'What had she written?'

'*I can no longer go on living without William, and I will not bring a child into such an evil world*' Mary quoted in a whisper, and then added, 'She said I'd been a mother to her, and she asked my forgiveness.'

'Did you destroy the letter?' I asked.

'I intended to do so, but that night I slipped it into my missal – Henry's family missal, which has always sat on the stool by my chair. In the morning, when Thomasine's body was found washed up beyond Rothern Bridge, my mind was in such confusion I could do nothing but think of giving her a Christian burial. Everyone in Torrington had liked and pitied Thomasine. They knew she went every day to the river, and no one suggested she might have taken her own life. I was so anxious to have her buried quickly in the churchyard, a proper funeral in the old Catholic rite, like the service old Father Chambre used to conduct when I was young. So proud we were of our Rector, he being physician to King Henry. But the curate insisted on a Protestant burial.

'Johnny's employers gave him compassionate leave to come and help me organise the funeral. He told them Thomasine and I were relatives – and why not? – had it not been for his support I might have collapsed altogether with the worry. He talked of her so sadly, as though they were wed. It seemed the whole of Torrington was present at the burial. But afterwards, when I came home I wondered whether God would strike me down for burying her in sanctified ground. I could not pray, and I felt as though I would go to hell myself.

'And the letter – did you destroy it?' I said, perhaps in too demanding a tone, for Mary shrank back as if she'd been struck.

'When I looked in my missal on the night of the funeral it had disappeared. I turned the whole house upside down, searching for it. Thomasine was safely buried, so I tried to forget the letter. It was then that you came to Torrington.'

'Someone must have stolen that letter, Mary', I said.

'I know, I know, it's always at the back of my mind. It haunts me night and day. But only Johnny and my two servants had entered the house.'

'Have you questioned them?'

'Of course not! How could I accuse Johnny? And I don't want my servants to know there was such a letter. Maybe someone from outside came in – but no, it's quite impossible.'

The poor woman was at her wits' end, and I felt great compassion for her. She'd done so much for my Thomasine, and should not be suffering for it. 'Over a year has passed, Mary', I said gently, 'And nothing has happened. Thomasine's grave is undisturbed, no questions are being asked. You have no need to go on worrying.'

But now my own worries had started, for I knew Kestell had stolen the letter. It would have been cruel to tell Mary at that moment what kind of evil rogue he was. He'd given her comfort, and she'd trusted him. I could only hope he'd leave her alone in future. Was he intending to blackmail Mary? He could no longer harm Thomasine. She was in God's hands. Or was he going to avenge himself on me for Thomasine's faithfulness? What good would it do him? But then, what had he ever gained by his wickedness, except the satisfaction of having deceived and outwitted so many people, playing the devil's game.

In August 1551 Patience was delivered of a healthy boy, baptised with the name of Oliver. I was pleased for Dick, who'd laboured so hard to achieve a home and family of his own, but I was envious too. It seemed to me when I visited their cottage that he and Patience possessed all that could be desired in this world. I thought of my manor at Constantine, where Thomasine and I might have brought up a family in peace and happiness. Dick had many well-deserved friends in and around Torrington, and would always be respected for being an honest man, one who'd survived intact amidst the horrors of this world. I was so thankful that people like Dick and Patience would always be there, small beacons of decency shining in the darkness.

In my hut that summer I experienced a lonely void, yet couldn't bring myself to quit my refuge. Without Nonna I would probably have descended into genuine madness. Thomasine was so right – there's nothing to compare with the unconditional trust and loyalty of an animal – a horse or a dog in particular.

Mary had ceased spending so much time brooding over the past. We'd persuaded her to hire a couple of servants, and she would go with me sometimes to put flowers on Thomasine's grave, underneath the yew trees in a quiet corner of the churchyard. Thus in October I left Torrington, hoping that all would be as well as could be expected for the poor tortured woman.

My travels on foot during the autumn of 1551 took me from Torrington to South Molton, and thence to Wiveliscombe in Somerset. Once on the road I always referred to myself as Sir Tristram. Hiding my identity as a leader in the rebellion enabled me to talk more freely to the many people I encountered on my journeyings. In some places feelings were still running high against Catholics, and in others against Protestants. For my part I attended a few services and found nothing to arouse my indignation in the prayer book. Yet the discussions I sometimes had with educated Protestants left me feeling that these were men full of triumphant enthusiasm for the Protestant faith, but greatly lacking in human understanding or compassion.

Not surprisingly, the small town of South Molton had gladly embraced the new religion, for its minister was a charismatic preacher, his sermons to an eager congregation sometimes lasting two hours. One evening at a nearby manor my host had a guest named John Jewell, a man in his late twenties, born at Berrynarbor, near Ilfracombe. He told me he'd gone up to Merton College, Oxford, at the age of thirteen, and was now a fellow at Corpus. He took it for granted I was a Protestant, for during our conversation he waxed most enthusiastic over the recent demolition of every monastery in Scotland.

Licking his lips with satisfaction, he said, 'Of all that ridiculous theatrical attire, sacrilegious superstition and idolatry, we are seeing to it that not a vestige remains. In just twenty years the whole wicked edifice of Catholicism will finally be brought to the ground, and the arrogance of the papists crushed. Would you not agree?'

'Not entirely.'

'You people in the South West are the most obstinate, the most insolent lovers of idolatry.'

John Jewell went on to speak eagerly of the second prayer book, now in preparation for the coming year, and the proposed act of uniformity, which would insist on every Catholic attending church to hear God's word. 'I was glad to note, Sir Tristram, that at least you attended divine service this last Sunday. Were you not inspired by the words of the minister?'

'He spoke at great length in the most fiery manner', I said.

John Jewell regarded me suspiciously. 'Come, come, man. Do not look so gloomy. After centuries of listening to some sleepy, ignorant parish priest muttering Latin balderdash behind a rood screen, is it not uplifting to comprehend God's truth at last?'

I nodded, but thought only of the huge cost in human life, misery and destruction which had brought us "the true word of God". John Jewell demanded to know my family name, thinking Tristram to be my Christian name, and was not satisfied when I said Sir Tristram was my name as an entertainer. After hearing me playing and singing, he said sharply that such songs were full of fake nostalgia, harping back to childish legend and magic, and I would do better to sing hymns to the glory of God. This John Jewell, I reckoned as I left South Molton, was in line to become a bishop. Let his flock then behave itself, or else!

It was raining heavily as we reached Bish Mill, and Nonna and I could not have looked a more dripping, sorrier sight. The dog who set out from Torrington so eagerly must have been wishing she was spread out in front of Dick's fire. We pressed on, squelching our way through muddy fields beside the River Yeo until we reached Yeo Mill, where we took shelter, and I purchased bread and cheese, and a scrag end of mutton for Nonna. Thereafter we were given two lifts, one with the miller's assistant, and the other with a tinker. The latter lived at Wiveliscombe, to which he was returning after six months on the road. He was hoping, he said, that the remains of two rebels, whose quarters he'd seen hanging from a gallows the last time he entered Wiveliscombe, were removed, for one of the victims had been a cousin of his. Till then I'd not imagined Somerset to be littered with gallows as in Devon and Cornwall, but the tinker said there were sufficient to turn a man's stomach, as far as Bath and Frome, and even in the village of Mells.

I'd been given a letter of introduction to a manor near Wiveliscombe belonging to Sir Edward Whyte, a friend of the Coffyns. My host, who knew my true identity, harboured much sympathy for the rebellion, but his health had prevented him from fighting. He admitted with some shame to having kept his opinions quiet. Once the siege of Exeter had started, tales of the high-handed methods of Russell and the Carews became known, and he told me scores of Somerset men had flocked to join Arundell. Russell had managed to bribe or bully some men into his army, but these had eventually deserted to the rebels. Sir Edward felt it had been necessary not to encourage too many farmers into leaving their land over haymaking and harvesting time, especially after hearing that crops in East Devon had been trampled over, farms burnt and livestock slaughtered. He judged there might well have been some famine over the winter of 1550, and had wished to prevent this in Somerset.

Over a jug of ale, after the household had retired to bed, he described to me many details of the final events of the rebellion. The Sheriff of Somerset, Sir John Thynne, had worked closely with Russell and Carew in carrying out the punishment of rebels captured after the last stand near Tiverton. They were hanged, drawn and quartered in pairs in many towns over Mid and West Somerset, as a lesson to the county. Sir Edward himself had given secret refuge to three rebels who managed to hide and then stagger, starving and exhausted, to his manor.

In spite of the hardship of walking, rather than riding, I found Nonna to be an excellent prop to my singing act, and a marvellous companion at night. The ladies adored her melting, soulful brown eyes, and would even forgive muddy paws on the hems of their trailing gowns.

We worked our way home in time for the Christmas season, which we spent staying with Mary. Dick brought his family on Christmas Eve, and Patience stuffed a festive goose to be roasted in the nearby baker's shop. The delight of watching young Oliver helped us, especially Mary, to feel some joy. On Christmas day we placed flowers against Thomasine's headstone, and for the first time Nonna sat on the grave and whined piteously. What was passing through her mind? I wondered. She couldn't have been aware Thomasine was buried beneath the grass, and yet it seemed as though she did.

Before leaving after Christmas I asked Mary whether Kestell had made an appearance in Torrington. Oh yes, she said, he'd come several times. She'd offered to lend him money to buy himself a plot of land, but he wouldn't take it. Then she told me in confidence she planned leaving him her money and her house, as it was not likely she would live to a great age. My look of astonished disapproval betrayed my opinion, for she rebuked me, saying, 'What have you got against him? He's been like a son to me.'

'Nothing', I lied. 'I hardly know him.'

'I suppose you dislike him because he wanted to marry Thomasine. I can understand that. But do remember the poor man believed you were dead. You must admit it would have been a suitable marriage.'

I shuddered. 'Thomasine killed herself, Mary, because she and I were all and everything to each other.'

By the time I'd returned for the spring and summer of 1552, the Protestant way of religion had superseded the Catholic faith to all outward appearances, and the least bitter memories of the rebellion had begun to fade. In London, John Dudley, now created Duke of Northumberland, continued to rule for King Edward, who became ill in April with the measles, or it might have been smallpox. Such a frail body as his could not sustain disease easily, and by September it was rumoured he had a life-threatening lung complaint, and was no longer appearing in public.

Naturally, people in Torrington were speculating as to who would succeed. There was even talk of Dudley placing Jane Grey, great niece of King Harry, on the throne, overruling the rights of the princesses Mary and Elizabeth. Dick judged that the eldest daughter of King Harry should become queen, in spite of being a Catholic. Russell and Archbishop Cranmer were still busying themselves, seeking to oust any lingering elements of the Catholic religion. What a cruel twist of fate if the Princess Mary were to restore all that the rebels had given their lives for. Far too late, I suspected, except for those Catholics in high places who'd resisted the government and yet survived. Humphrey Arundell's rich relations at Lanherne were still practising Catholics, and were most probably shaking their heads sadly at Humphrey's stupidity in leading a rebellion.

The following autumn of 1552 I left Torrington in the second week of September, earlier than usual, planning to go to Exeter and then work my way round East Devon. It would be a painful journey, revisiting those places which had endured so much. I particularly wanted to know if the people of Clyst St Mary had been able to rebuild their burnt down houses, and whether the land had recovered.

On leaving my hut a sudden whim led me to stuff into my pack the rag doll I'd picked up at Clyst.

I entered Exeter by the east gate, and joined the traffic along Saint Sidwell Street. I had not proceeded very far before two horsemen wearing the Russell livery emerged from a side street to clear a passage for a carriage containing none other than Lord John Russell, the Earl of Bedford. Previously I had only glimpsed Russell on horseback clad in armour. Now, owing to a slight hold-up while an overburdened ox cart shifted itself out of the way, I was able to see him clearly. He wore a black hood surmounted by a wide, flat black velvet double-layered cap, contrasting with his very fine long white beard and heavy white eyebrows, curving down to join the longest, thinnest nose imaginable. His gaze was staring, cruel and arrogant. He was the man, after all, who had saved Exeter, and its citizens must now bow down and obey.

I put up at the White Hart, where in no time I heard all the gossip I needed to know, and one piece of information which filled me with rage, regarding Robert Welsh. Russell had forbidden his body to be taken down from the church tower, and his skeleton still hung there, with the sodden rags of vestments clinging to his bones. The mayor, John Blackaller, had been granted a knighthood, and the sixth day of August was to be commemorated each year as a day of thanksgiving for the delivery of the city. A few weeks before, all the leading officials, clad in their civic robes, had proceeded to the cathedral to hear a special sermon given by Russell's chaplain, Miles Coverdale, now Bishop in place of old Vesey.

On entering Saint Peter's I could see immediately that this fanatical bishop had removed every sign of Catholicism. A Protestant gloom had descended on the place, the extreme opposite of the glitter, vivid colour and scents I remembered. I doubt one stitch of embroidery could have been found on any robe. It was as though a husband suspecting his beautiful, honey-voiced, perfumed and overdressed wife to be a strumpet, had put her away in favour of a plain, scrubbed, unadorned sharp-voiced stick of a wife. Nicholas Udall had complained that it was in the South West where the filth of popery still clung, therefore it was the South West which must be the more strictly cleansed.

As I feared, even after more than two years Clyst St Mary was still a shambles, with nettles and hogweed growing out of cob rubble. Since the menfolk had nearly all been killed, their families had to shift for themselves as best they could, with help from nearby villages. Some cottages and barns had been rebuilt, but much remained to be done. It was impossible to ascertain the spot where the cottage in which I had waited all night had stood. I wandered around the village, but no one stopped to converse with me. People were all too absorbed in the task of preparing for the winter. As I stood on the bridge remembering the poor fellow who'd been shot into the river, I saw a group of little girls returning with baskets of late blackberries. Pulling out the rag doll from my pack, I enquired if anyone recognised it. The girls were nonplussed for a moment, then started to giggle, pushing forward a shy, skinny child they called Mags.

She stared at me, and then snatched away the doll, saying, 'You stole Griselda. You'm a thief!'

'I am indeed, a very wicked thief", I stated gravely, 'But I have treated her with care, and I beg your forgiveness.'.

'Her looks half starved to me.'

'She was pining for you, and wouldn't eat.'

Mags accepted the excuse, and added, 'Did 'ee kill my father?'

'Not I! He and I were fighting against the government forces.'

I felt then as if it would have been right for me to have died instead of her father. 'Show me where you live', I said.

She startled me by bursting into tears. Another girl explained that Mags's mother was still waiting for help to rebuild her cottage. A relation had promised to come soon: in the meantime she had to live with three children in very cramped conditions in a neighbour's outhouse. It struck me forcibly how great was the responsibility of our leaders, who'd decided to commandeer Clyst as their battleground. Though Russell's mercenaries had burnt Mags's cottage, I felt it incumbent on me to help rebuild it.

Thus, instead of playing my harp and singing my songs over East Devon that autumn, I found myself lodging in John Yarde's house. Each day I joined a couple of men from Topsham to build a cottage. Though I'd never built a dwelling of cob before, the skills Dick had taught me were invaluable. It was a lesson in reparation which all soldiers should learn after carelessly destroying a whole village.

By the time Nonna and I left in mid-December I felt I belonged to Clyst almost as much as to Torrington. It was nought but a crude shell of a cottage we'd built for Mags, but her mother was so full of gratitude it humbled me. The child desperately wanted to keep Nonna, who slept each night curled up with Mags for mutual warmth. I explained to her that the dog must decide, and she agreed. I strode away across the bridge well before dawn, and after half an hour Nonna caught me up, and we journeyed on together. Mags would shed a few tears, but in later years might come to realise that even a dog could have prior loyalties.

I returned to my hut in March, and life in Torrington continued as usual. I was too accustomed to the solitary life to contemplate living in the town itself, and, more important, too used to living outside the life of the church. As a man who should have been a fairly wealthy landowner, but now reduced to the status of a partially vagrant peasant, it might have been discomfiting to the people of Torrington to have me in their midst. As I grew more wild-looking and somewhat slow of speech, those that met me in the woods or fishing in the river, probably thought I was mad. But some were kind enough to give Dick gifts of food and clothing for 'poor Sir Tristram, whose wits were addled in that cruel rebellion'.

In June all kinds of rumours were circulating in Devon regarding the King's health and the discontent in London over the machinations of John Dudley, who desired to retain control over Edward's successor. Thus it was that the second half of 1553 turned out to be a momentous time, with yet another great upheaval in religion. In mid-July we received news of the King's death. By this time I couldn't picture him as a king at all, only as a poor lad of fifteen years, coughing up blood and burning with fever, a piteous condition I'd seen in several of my father's tenants.

In May John Dudley had married his son, Guildford, to Lady Jane Grey, determined on her being Queen. Everyone knew what that meant, and most revolted against it. By the nineteenth day of July Queen Jane had lost her crown to the Princess

Mary, who was then welcomed to London on the third day of August with bells and feasting. Even in our remote corner of Devon we felt the joy which spread throughout the country when John Dudley was executed on the twenty-first day of August.

It was a strange experience to have the Catholic Stephen Gardiner as our Archbishop. He had been Bishop of Winchester before being deprived and imprisoned. Strange too was the changeable mood of the citizens of London. They wanted Mary as Queen, yet were loth to return to the Catholic religion for fear of popery. And when Mass was reintroduced in some London churches there were minor riots. As for us in Torrington, after the tyranny of enforced Protestantism it would have been no great task returning to the old faith, but for the new tyranny of our recently appointed Catholic priest, Robin Dyer.

When Dick came to see me one day, shortly before I intended to leave, he wasn't his usual cheerful self. He had much to relate, and none of it good. Father Robin Dyer, it seemed, was very busy in the task of ensuring every parishioner was truly embracing the old faith. To this effect he spent much time going from house to house examining each person's beliefs. He'd noted Thomasine's gravestone in the churchyard, and having heard of

John Wynslade and the other leaders of the rebellion, had asked questions: Who was this Thomasine, and why did she perish so young carrying an unborn child? And where had she been living in Torrington? Father Dyer had a cunning way with words. He knew how to draw out information a person didn't intend to give.

Having discovered Mary Lee had looked after Thomasine till her death by drowning, he spent much time talking to her. Later he questioned Dick, saying he knew Thomasine's history, and wished to know more of William Wynslade. Mary had told Father Dyer that a few days after the execution of John Wynslade, and the false report of his son's death, Thomasine's body had been found in the river. Poor Mary told me she'd continued to suffer much rigorous questioning as to Thomasine's state of mind and her religious beliefs, and finally the poor woman agreed Thomasine might have taken her own life. In that case, Father Dyer said, she had no right to be buried in sanctified ground, and must be reburied on waste land. Dick concluded by warning me that Father Dyer would be coming to examine me as well.

Thus, later that day while sitting in my hut I heard a voice below, shouting, 'William Wynslade, are you there? Greetings in the name of Christ.'

I moved out to my platform and looked down at my visitor, a stout, balding man in a soutane, his protruding forehead glistening with sweat.

'Have you no ladder, William Wynslade?'

In reply I threw down my rope ladder.

'How can I be expected to climb up this?' he asked.

'Speak to me from down there if you wish. Up here I can offer you ale and a stool.'

Let the fellow come up but once and he'll never attempt it again, I thought. Realising I wasn't going to descend, the priest struggled up with my assistance, and heaving himself onto the platform, he lay gasping like a beached fish. Suspecting he'd never been humiliated by a layman, I helped him to his feet – dainty little feet they were – and led him into my hut, where he sank onto a stool.

After half a cup of ale, Father Dyer recovered somewhat. I noted his plump white hands and red-rimmed, watery eyes, and disliked what I saw.

'What do you want with me?' I asked.

'Dick Popham says you've been living as a semi-recluse and vagrant since the rising.'

'It's no concern of yours.'

'It is indeed. I'm your priest.'

'I have no need of a priest. – Where do you come from?'

'Honiton.'

'Did you join the rebellion?'

'I was sent to a seminary before the rebellion, and after it ended I fled to France to finish my training.'

'When did you return?'

'In July, when our blessed Queen Mary came to the throne and restored the true faith.'

'The Catholic faith of our youth will never be restored in the South West. John Russell and his son are seeing to that. You can't pull out religion by the roots, burn them and then hope to replant them. I belong to no sect. I have sworn to eschew religion altogether.'

'Can a man live without God?'

'Better than with God, it would seem, judging by how many priests were hanged from their own steeples for being Catholics and how many will now be threatened with burning for turning Protestant.'

'But you fought in the cause of religion. You risked everything.'

'I fought because my father was a good and just man. I fought because our people were suffering. But even before the Commotion I'd begun to question a faith which seemed to be more about the viciousness and cupidity of men than about the love of one's neighbour.'

'It's understandable you've become bitter, living the life of an outlaw, cut off from the grace of God. But, like the lost sheep, you may return to the fold. I have brought you the Blessed Sacrament.'

'I thank you kindly, but I have no need of it.'

'I can scarce believe you would refuse the Sacrament. Have you taken leave of your senses?'

'In Torrington some do say I'm mad. If grief can drive a man out of his wits then perhaps I am mad. My friends and acquaintances have dubbed me "Sir Tristram", for I'm certainly full of melancholy.'

'Sir Tristram? Was he a Catholic?'

'In the legend we are not told whether he was a faithful Catholic. He became a wanderer, playing his harp, and singing songs of love and death.'

'The love of a woman is a trap to destroy your soul. Return to the love of God. Make the Church your home and you'll recover your spirits. Let me hear your confession, and I'll give you the Sacrament.'

'No, Father Dyer. I've forsaken the Church and have no need of a priest. My church is this woodland, this river. I've found a kinder, gentler god here.'

'You will discover Christ again in the religion of your ancestors. You will pray once more to the saints of our Celtic tradition.'

'Ah, yes, our unfortunate Celtic saints whose shrines have been smashed all over the South West. Let me tell you, I feel the greatest affinity for those saints who lived as hermits. I suspect they chose the solitary life to escape the rigid authority and arrogance of the Church.'

'You malign our blessed saints!'

I gazed at this Catholic priest, thinking that most likely he knew little or nothing of real suffering. He was too newly minted, too shiny. He would need to inhabit a few greasy pockets, to slip through a number of rough, dirty palms, or to be tossed into the air by a couple of cutthroats before he would do as a priest.

I moved my stool closer, and said intensely, hoping to rouse some stirring of concern in his expressionless eyes, 'Tell me, have you ever seen a man hanged? Cut down alive, sliced open – his guts drawn out and burnt before his dying eyes, his quivering heart wrenched from his body as he breathes his last? Have you seen a corpse, still warm with life, chopped in pieces like a side of beef on a butcher's block?'

'I haven't, and pray God I never shall', he replied fastidiously, yet without a shudder.

'But no doubt you've watched a heretic burn?'

'Certainly, in France. To save the soul the body must burn!'

'You lack God's greatest gift – imagination.'

'What do you mean?'

'Compassion born of love for God's creation can only act through the imagination.'

'Betrayal of God is the ultimate sin. The body must be chastened to cleanse the soul.'

I moved away from him, saying softly, 'And have you ever stood by a river on a still, warm night and watched an otter swimming by moonlight?'

'No, what use would that be?'

'Witnessing my father, John Wynslade, being hanged, convinced me there can be little hope for humanity. I even have my doubts as to whether there is a God of love. But one thing is certain: I require no church or priest to help me to a conclusion or to guide my life.'

'Have you lost faith in Christ?'

'I revere Christ. Who could do otherwise?'

'He died for our sins.'

'No, he was put to a bloody death because he was a good man – and humanity cannot stand a good man. The sins of this world are too great for any one person to atone for them. '

'You utter terrible blasphemy! It was God Himself who died for our sins.'

'Your Church would burn me now for heresy. But when Queen Mary dies, the Protestants would hang me for a Papist's son.'

'Your sufferings have affected your mind. The devil has your soul!'

'No, Father Dyer, my soul is no longer the concern of the Church or the devil. As a young lad, in the summer I used to roam on Bursdon Moor and run up and down the barrows. Two thousand years before Christ our ancestors lived on that wild moorland and buried their dead in those mounds. They hunted and killed for survival, and life was hard. Then one day someone conceived the idea of a vengeful god who demanded obedience and sacrifice in return for sunshine and rain and fertility. Religion was born, and life became even more harsh as man gained another reason for killing, as a means of controlling and crushing his enemies and for seizing property and goods.'

'You're talking of pagan gods, before Christ came to tell us of the nature of the One True God.'

'Christ came and told us to love our neighbour, to forgive our enemies, to succour the poor and suffering – but who listens? – Do you?'

'You talk so strangely. Solitude has done you no good. If you determine to remain cut off from the grace of God you'll be eternally damned.'

'The grace of God can reach me without the help of the Church. Must God be dependent on prelates and priests? Did no one receive grace in the centuries before Christ?'

'God only reveals himself fully through our Lord and Saviour.'

'I no longer believe that. How can we tell how God reveals himself to others? – I shock you. You could have saved yourself the trouble of seeking me out. – Let's talk of something else.'

'Where do you go in winter?'

'I travel from manor to manor, playing my harp, like Sir Tristram, and singing my songs.'

'What do you do here all the summer?'

'I snare rabbits, hunt wild boar and catch fish. The Torridge is full of salmon, and the streams abound with trout..'

'It's very silent in these woods.'

'Not when you live here. A busy, noisy life goes on beneath the undergrowth.'

'Nevertheless a lonely life.'

'There's sufficient wild life – brocks, fitches, vairs and suchlike to keep me company.'

'I know little about wild creatures.'

'When you live a solitary life in a place like this you discover a whole new world. A harsh world for the most part, but not dishonest and scheming and greedy like the world of men. On summer evenings I watch the kestrel winnowing across the valley. I recognise all the birds which inhabit this area – kingfisher, cormorant, jackdaw, heron, redwing, fieldfare, corncrake, greenfinch...'

'Truly, can there really be so many kinds? One bird looks much the same as another to me.'

'And you a priest! How can you face your Maker when you know so little of his creation?'

'I've never had time to study nature.'

'You don't need to study nature to notice the trees and the flowers and the wild creatures. Did you never go fishing as a child?'

'Never. '

'Watching a brown carp or a perch or a red-finned roach or a pike darting beneath clear water is to watch a miracle. – How did you occupy yourself as a child?'

'I went to Mass and studied the Bible.'

'Nothing more?'

'I do remember a pond my brother and I used to visit, where we caught tadpoles.'

'Pollywiggles, Thomasine used to call them. And now you catch souls!'

'Why did you choose this place as your refuge?'

'This is the place Thomasine loved. She used to sit on the river's edge at night and watch the otter cubs at play. She's buried in the churchyard.'

'Yes, I've seen Thomasine Wynslade's grave. She was your wife, I take it.'

'I regarded her as such. We were betrothed. But she's dead, and my unborn child with her.'

'How did she come to die so young?'

'After the Rebellion was crushed, my father and I were arrested and thrown into Exeter gaol. Nine of us, including our commander, Humphrey Arundell, were then sent up to London for trial. A month later, my father, together with Arundell, Holmes and Bury, were moved to the Tower.'

'A sad business. How did you come to be released?'

'A friend secured my pardon.'

'So you returned to the West Country?'

'I remained in London with Dick Popham until my father's trial at Westminster. He stood before the bar with Arundell. Their lives might have been spared, but for Arundell's secretary, Kestell, who gave false witness against them.'

'Then you came to Torrington to be reunited with Thomasine?'

'Yes. But by the time I came to Mary Lee's house, she'd died.'

'Did she fall into the river?'

'She went out in stormy weather, and must have slipped. The bank is steep.'

'There are those at Torrington – I might mention a Catholic gentleman named John Kestell – who whisper it was no accident, that she shouldn't be buried in their churchyard. I've spoken to Mary Lee, and she admits Thomasine threatened to take her own life when she heard you'd been hanged.'

So Kestell was already at work again.

'No one saw her die', I said. 'Maybe she did take her own life – and who could blame her?'

'If she did, her burial should be on your conscience. Let her body be exhumed and buried in unsanctified ground. It's a sin to take one's own life. It's murder to kill an unborn child.'

'Would Christ have dug up my Thomasine's body and reburied it on waste ground?'

'He would have to. The Church commands it.'

'The Church commands it! Who is this great authority, the Church, that even Christ would have to obey it? In each century the Church has been governed by a group of cunning, bigoted, selfish, cruel men who revel in the power of life and death, who rejoice in terrorising people's lives on earth. – Where, in the Bible, is suicide condemned?'

My voice was raised in anger, but Father Dyer continued doggedly, showing no emotion.

'Life is God's precious gift to us, and only He can take it from us. If Thomasine had only trusted in God and waited, you would have come back to her.'

'What could I have offered her? A tainted outlaw with no money and no home?'

'God would have provided.'

'God is not so quick to help the poor – Thomasine could not stomach cruelty of any kind, to humans or to animals. She'd seen some of Russell's gibbets. My death in London was preying on her mind.'

'She succumbed to despair, the greatest of sins. Despair comes because we don't trust God. Her body must be reburied.'

'I'll not do it. The day the world truly obeys Christ's commands will be the day the power of the Church collapses. As long as a class of men, calling themselves the arbiters of truth, is permitted to hold power over us, so long will evil thrive in this world. – And you I suspect, Robin Dyer, are one of those men!'

'I have been sadly misled as to your character, William Wynslade.' Father Dyer rose and regarded me with fanatical pity. 'Solitude has filled you with despair and evil heresies. Your soul is in dire peril. '

'What do you intend to do?'

'I have no choice but to report you to Bishop Turbeville.'

'How you would enjoy watching me burn as a heretic!'

'It would be my duty, should you be condemned.'

'And you will dig up Thomasine's body?'

'It must be done. – I'll go now. Pray assist me down your ladder.'

I rose, and having helped the man to get his feet firmly on the top rung I watched him proceed down at a snail's pace. He missed the bottom rung and fell heavily to the ground, his tiny feet waving in the air. I couldn't help but laugh at the undignified sight as he staggered up.

'You'll pay for this, William Wynslade', he muttered as he scurried away.

That evening I thought over Father Dyer's threats, and decided he would probably not act on them. There was no proof Thomasine had taken her own life. His brand of Catholic zeal had won him little support in Torrington, which might have been surprising, considering the support the town had given to the rebellion. Mary once told me that certain farmers round about had risked hiding some of the church treasures when it became known that Protestant commissioners were coming to strip the church. None of these had yet been returned, though it was now safe to do so. Anyone possessing the new Protestant prayer book was advised to conceal it, and to accept the Catholic rituals. There was a definite reluctance for people to commit themselves wholeheartedly to the Catholic or the Protestant faith. They preferred to wait and see. Mary Tudor might marry, bear children and enable the Catholic faith to be revived for future generations. But the rumour persisted that the Queen was set on marrying King Philip of Spain, an idea abhorrent to all Protestants, and even to those Catholics with no wish to be under the dominance of Spain or the Pope.

We knew little, of course, of what was taking place in London, but I guessed it must have been an uncertain time. Devoted Catholic gentry returning from exile, and those who had risked remaining in the country throughout Edward's reign, were now free to practise their religion and to influence the government. Committed Protestants, on the other hand, were presumably fleeing to the continent – certainly John Russell and his son, Francis had gone to Geneva. A large number of Protestants who'd acquired Catholic property and goods remained in England, paying lip service to Catholic practices. The Queen might well be suspicious of these, but could hardly confiscate their gains. For the time being, in spite of all the uncertainties, it appeared that the citizens of London had taken Queen Mary to their hearts.

The following morning I began to feel uneasy about Thomasine's grave. Instead of making preparations to depart, I went to Dick's cottage and informed Patience I wouldn't be going until the end of October, mentioning that Father Dyer was the reason for my delay. Dick was glad I'd stayed. He'd long been making furniture in his spare time, and was planning to start up a furniture business. He wanted me to go into partnership with him, and asked me to accompany him some days later to a small manor house near Titchberry, within walking distance of Hartland Point. He'd hired an ox-cart to deliver some pieces of furniture to the new owner. On the way we discussed the partnership, and I promised to give him an answer by March. I suspected he considered it was time I ceased my travelling minstrel life and settled down to an honest day's work! If I were to do so, working with Dick would be the only occupation I could consider.

'Who's the new owner at Titchberry?' I asked. But all Dick knew was that he was a bachelor from Cornwall. He'd never seen him, having only dealt with his bailiff.

I had taken the excellent longbow Dick had made me, to try my hand at boar hunting in the forest behind Hartland. Dick dropped me in the village, and we arranged to meet later in the day. By that time he'd discovered that John Kestell was the owner of the manor. It was a severe blow to find he was still in the vicinity, and would turn up any day now in Torrington to cause trouble in his new guise of landowner. How, I wondered, had he procured the money to buy the manor near Titchberry? Not honestly, I'm sure, and I wondered what were to be his future ambitions. That he still possessed

Thomasine's farewell note to Mary had often troubled me. but as I'd heard nothing of him for some while I hoped he'd moved well away. And to think that now Dick was actually making his furniture!

'That man should have been sent out of this world long ago,' was Dick's only comment, as we entered Torrington. Was he hinting I should have been the one to do it? Dick, of all men, who along with my father had taught me so much of fairness and decency and Christian compassion, yet was now advocating murder! Kestell was the only person I had ever desired to kill. It may be Dick and I were the only people who knew the full extent of his wickedness, and yet I'd held back for so long. Was it for lack of opportunity or fear of being hanged? There had been opportunity enough during those weeks we camped outside Exeter, once it was clear to me he'd betrayed the Kylter twins. If I had killed him then, Thomasine might still have been alive, and our child born. This thought was an everlasting torment to me. Dick must think me an arrant coward. He himself, the kindest of men, would surely have despatched Kestell had he been in my place. And so that night in bed, unable to sleep, the argument in my mind continued. A decision must be reached. And yet once more I put it off. Maybe in the spring I would act. In my absence Dick would keep his ears open for any news of Kestell.

Dick and I were still stabling our horses at Mary's, and one or other of us would go to the house each day. Often I would call in to see how she was. Since her interviews with Father Dyer it seemed she was reverting to her old unhappy mood. Confession and absolution brought her no peace of mind. Religion had roused her conscience, but then kept her in agony.

The weather soon became too inclement for me to stay in my hut, and finally I left, thinking that perhaps new surroundings and concentration on my music would be good for me.

Towards the end of November, on my way home to sleep for two nights at Dick's cottage before proceeding to Barnstaple, I decided to sample a Latin Mass for the first time since Father Lambe's final Mass at Pelynt the day before one of Agnes's banners was torn down by Protestant commissioners. It had been my intention to attend a service at St Andrew's in Alwington in memory of old times. It was a church I had worshipped in with Jacquet and Richard Coffyn, their home, Portledge Manor, being nearby. However, I had no wish to encounter Jacquet or her family in the church. There was no knowing what gossip they might have heard about my life in Torrington. I had hoped Jacquet might call at Mary's house, so I could have described her brother's unhappy sojourn in the Fleet and his possible demise in London after being set free. I couldn't understand why she kept her distance. I doubted it was because I'd come down in the world. Dick suggested she might still be cherishing a romantic notion of me which my relationship with Thomasine had dashed, and then perhaps revived.

Whatever her motive, I avoided Alwington, and went instead to St Swithun's at Littleham, a few miles further on towards Torrington, just above the River Yeo. The greyish-black stones in which the small church had been built were in keeping with that most gloomy saturated Sunday morning, so typical of a winter day in North Devon. Even when it ceases to rain the air is so heavily laden with moisture that every object inside and out feels cold and clammy to the touch. The flagstones in St Swithun's were heaving with damp, as though the foundations were swimming about beneath them. In the tiny sanctuary next to the equally tiny Lady chapel, bereft of their beautiful rood screen since the desecration in 1549, the Catholic priest looked forlorn and grey, and smelt of mould. Even the rich colour and texture of his vestments had lost their vibrancy, probably owing to having been hidden away during the Rebellion in some chest recently fetched up from the dank earth.

How very different was this dismal scene from those early summer mornings when the Coffyn children and I had sat at the back of St Andrew's at Alwington, watching the sun filtering brilliant streaks of colour across the warm flagstones, and lighting up Jacquet's fine brown hair. How full of hope and joy had life been then!

Now unable to pray, I felt at my lowest ebb since I first saw Thomasine's grave and knew for certain she was gone for ever. A shivering, wet Nonna awaited me in the porch. She'd been restless all night, whining so piteously at intervals that I feared she might be ill. I made a sudden decision to return to Torrington for good. I'd become weary of my life as Sir Tristram. Mary would take me as a lodger and I would settle down to work in partnership with Dick. But reordering my future didn't make it the less bleak.

Nonna and I walked the few miles to Torrington under dripping overhanging trees, with the river alongside or within reach all the way. However, its being the main thoroughfare from Bideford to Torrington, we were soon overtaken by carts, one of which gave us a lift. We arrived well before midday, and made for Mary's house. I met her coming out, without cloak or hood, in a very agitated state. She grabbed my arm before I could speak and pulled me along the road, her feet in their flimsy shoes splashing through the puddles. 'Come', she cried, 'Come and see what they're doing to Thomasine's grave! We must hurry and stop Father Dyer. He is accusing me of hiding her crime! He has her letter, Will! How could he have come by it?'

She was urging me to hurry, but in fact I was having to almost carry her along the High Street and into the cobbled passageway running along beside the church wall. We could hear voices in the churchyard, and over the hedge saw a large crowd of people pressed together in dark cloaks, hoods and shawls, standing within and without the wall. In the corner of the churchyard where Thomasine's grave lay under the yew trees, something was happening.

'Look!' said Mary. 'They've dug up the earth from her grave.'

I'd twice dreamt of Robin Dyer disinterring Thomasine's body. And now there he stood in reality, at the head of her grave, beside a great pile of dark soil glistening in the rain. Four men were struggling with ropes to heave the coffin up onto the grass.

When it was done the rain ceased, and a sudden expectant hush descended on the crowd. Father Dyer drew a small scroll of paper from a little bag tied to his belt. 'We are here today, my people', he intoned weightily, 'To witness the exhumation of Thomasine Wynslade's body. She was not entitled to a Christian burial, since she committed a felony and a murder in taking her own life.' He waved the paper in the air and continued, 'I have foolproof evidence here to read to you, a letter written from Thomasine Wynslade to Mistress Mary Lee, who wickedly concealed it…'

But Father Dyer never did read it aloud, for a great cry was heard from Mary, who shouted, 'You thief! You damned thieving priest! That's my property!'

A boiling fury had been building up in me from the moment I saw the desecrated grave, and as Mary was speaking I leapt over the hedge with that energy only burning hatred can provide, and snatched the paper from Father Dyer's hand. Then tearing it up, I scattered the shreds into the grave.

Coming together with Mary's agonised shout, my action was so sudden and shocking that no one spoke or stirred. Now was my chance to sway the crowd, which like all crowds could so easily have wrenched open the coffin, seized Thomasine's remains and carried them off to the Commons to be buried like a dog's carcase. At that moment Nonna, who was sitting beside the coffin, let out a single wolf-like howl of anguish, an unearthly sound I had never heard from her before.

'Thomasine's body', I said firmly, 'Has lain quietly at peace in her grave for over two years. Her soul is with God, her bones remain in the coffin. Your priest, Father Dyer, who has come to meddle with our lives like a Spanish inquisitor, wishes to rebury a good and innocent girl on waste ground. To what purpose, and to what good? You people of Torrington, whose sons Henry Lee led off to give their lives for the Catholic faith, is this the kind of religion you'd have had them die for? Is God a god of revenge, or is he a god of compassion? Would Christ have dug up the body of Thomasine?'

'No!' came a woman's voice from the crowd.

Encouraged, I went on. 'Robin Dyer says he would, because the church demands it. What, or who, is this church? Archbishops, bishops and priests, who make the rules. I say to you, look to Christ before you allow a wicked and useless act to take place.'

'Amen to that!' muttered several voices.

'Let the coffin be re-interred!' I commanded. This was accomplished in silence, until the last sod of turf was laid. 'Requiescat in Pace', I said.

Then Father Dyer turned and walked out of the churchyard, those nearest him drawing back to let him pass. There was a stir, and some murmuring to be heard, and had the priest quickened his pace along Calf Street he might have been chased, and who knows what could have happened. The tragic incident at Sampford Courtenay came to mind. Fortunately, Father Dyer didn't run, and the people let him go, moving away themselves in different directions. I put my arm around Mary and walked her back along the High Street and into South Street. It had begun to rain again, and she was wet through and shivering.

Outside the Black Horse, who should we see but Kestell. I might have guessed he'd have been at hand to gloat over the result of his stealing Thomasine's letter from between the pages of Mary's missal, and giving, or perhaps even selling it to Father Dyer. The plan had failed. Judging by the sour expression on his face he must have been feeling most aggrieved. No doubt he'd been assured that I was always away from October to March. Nevertheless, he managed to offer Mary a civil greeting, and an assurance that he'd be calling on her soon. She smiled weakly, but didn't stop.

I feared Mary had caught a chill, and when we reached her house the servant girl, Eliza, took her straight up to bed. She sipped a little hot broth while I built up the fire in her room to a cheerful blaze.

The long drawn out anxiety she'd suffered had taken its toll, and the next day she was running a fever, and we had to call a physician. I rarely left the house during her illness, but on one occasion when I was away for an hour, Eliza told me Kestell had called, and after he left Mary had sent for her attorney.

That evening, as I sat with her, she said, somewhat resentfully, 'Johnny came to see me this morning, and told me he'd bought a manor house near Hartland. As he won't be needing my house I've decided to leave it to you, Will. It's time you moved out of that hut in the woods.'

I thanked her, and then asked, 'Does Kestell know you're leaving money to him?'

'Oh yes.'

'And that you've changed your mind about the house?'

'No, I didn't tell him that. But it shouldn't disappoint him. I've left him money enough.'

Mary died soon after, She would have no priest at her bedside, and it grieved me beyond measure to think that Father Dyer's pestering her over Thomasine's burial had probably hastened her demise, making her last years so miserable. I wondered if Mary had begun to mistrust Kestell, and if not, should I have let her die thinking so well of him? It was a hard question to answer.

Two days after the exhumation it was discovered that Father Dyer had quit the town for good. Another priest arrived to take his place, and it was he who buried poor Mary. She was placed on a bier before the altar in the church with candles lit at her head and foot all night. Then her funeral was conducted according to the old Catholic rite, with a bell tolling and the mourners carrying candles in procession. It not being known how Henry Lee had died, or where his remains were buried, the people of Torrington flocked instead to his wife's traditional Catholic funeral Nothing more was ever said about Thomasine's grave.

Dick and Patience were delighted to hear I owned a house, though Kestell's undeserved inheritance was a blow indeed. They themselves had done much for Mary, as had other friends in Torrington. Having a house with stables and working and storage space enabled me to go into an equal partnership with Dick. I would now have a better status in the town, declared Patience, and could abandon my wild ways and learn to be a gentleman again. She was right, of course, but how long would I be able to sustain my new role as a respectable citizen and property owner?

The Christmas season came and went. Mary's house was in need of repair, but it would have to wait for the spring. Inside I set the two servants I had retained, to cleaning the unused rooms. Dick moved all his tools from the barn he'd been renting, to my house, and during the short days of January and February I began to learn the craft of fine carpentry. But when darkness fell in the late afternoon, and the wind blew across the Torridge valley, rattling furiously at my windows, I would often sit in a gloomy trance all evening, despising and hating myself.

Early one evening Patience arrived with her son to bring me some jars of blackberry preserve she'd made. Oliver was now running around and beginning to talk sense, and he wanted me to play with him. But I continued to sit gloomily in my chair, only half listening to the child prattling on.

Patience rarely spoke more than a few words to me, and I was expecting her to leave when she approached me, saying briskly, 'William Wynslade, you should be ashamed of yoursel'! Thank the Lord I be married to Dick. I could not be doin' with a man like you. If Thomasine could see you now, her'd be off to find 'erself a new man. Compared to many, you'm a lucky person. You do have a sound body, a good 'ouse, work and friends. You could get a wife and beget children if your face wasn't always as long as a poker.

'Yes, us all know poor William Wynslade did suffer so much in the Commotion, losing his father and his betrothed and many friends and acquaintances. 'E did witness terrible deeds. But what of the ones who died, or was maimed for life? What about Dick? 'E experienced as many 'orrors as you. 'E didn't lose his betrothed, 'tis true, but 'ad 'e done so 'e'd never 'ave gone into a decline. He's a one to say, life's hard, but if you 'ave your health and your wits there do come a time to stop whinin' and moanin'. So you'd best get on wi' life and make yourself useful. Most of all, you should set an example to the chillern. They 'ave to grow up in this world, and it's up to folk like you to give 'em some 'ope. What sort of example be you to Oliver?' She paused, and then went on, 'Did you ever think of Dick's feelin's all through the Commotion? I'll warrant 'e were the steady, cheerful 'elper, never grumblin' or expectin' sympathy for his own miseries. Dick were just a servant, weren't he?'

'Never!', I answered heatedly, rising from my chair. 'He was my best friend.'

'Not till you ceased bein' Sir William Wynslade o' Constantine did 'e really become your equal. If you want to keep 'is respect you should stop thinkin' about the past and do somethin' for the future in Torrington.'

She lifted Oliver up to give me a kiss, and moved to the door. Then she turned and looked me in the eye, saying, 'You'd best settle your debt with Kestell, or Dick will have to do it for you. – I'll bring 'ee an apple pie next time I come.'

All she'd said was true, and it had taken courage for her to say it. How selfish had been my attitude to someone who was the most saintly person I'd ever met, a man so modest he'd have laughed with disbelief had he heard me say so. I doubt Dick had a single enemy, and yet all our family had taken him for granted, and each one, even Agnes, had depended on him, not only in the daily monotonies of life on the estate, but also in every crisis.

My thoughts turned to all the Celtic saints we revered for miracles or martyrdom, some so legendary I doubt they ever happened. For the first time I saw that the true saints of this world were the unsung ordinary men and women, particularly the women, who lived lives of hard work and sacrifice laced with compassion, cheerfulness and common sense seeking no reward. Thinking of these led me on to remember all the lowly priests who, prior to the rebellion, had been living lives of devoted service to their parishioners. Those who'd dared to speak out against injustice now lay in unmarked graves, while saints such as Neot, Cadoc, Petroc and Geroe would be commemorated in the statues and stained glass which had been preserved. But who would remember Martin Geoffrey, John Moreman or dear Father Welsh? Would legends grow around them? These were decent clergy, who knew what a hanging under Russell meant, and yet spoke out. The relics of St Petroc are sacred for all time, but what of Robert Welsh's tortured bones?

I spent some hours pondering these things, and came to the conclusion that I must follow Patience's advice and cease nurturing my own miseries. I had a mission to fulfil, a mission avoided far too long – to rid the world of Kestell. I could go to his manor and challenge him to a fair fight. But would it be fair? His physique was infinitely inferior to mine. He would demand to know how I'd offended him. He would call me a madman. How could one kill a man as devious and cunning as Kestell?

The partnership Dick and I were to share was soon to become official, with a sign outside our workshop at Mary's house. He was already trusted and well liked, and I had no wish to damage his reputation in any way. However, it was Dick himself who brought up the subject, 'Us must kill Kestell as soon as possible', he said one day to my great surprise, 'Afore the viper plans 'is next attack on you, and on me too. 'Is whole enjoyment in life do lie in subtle provocation. He wants the furniture we make, so he'll bide 'is time, keeping us both anxious.'

'What do you suggest?' I asked, amazed and grateful that Dick intended our partnership to include disposing of Kestell.

'On market day he always rides home by way of Pillmouth, then down along the River Yeo. As you know, it be a dark track overhung with trees. Us could easily hide in the woods and put an arrow through 'is heart.'

'He might try another route home', I said.

'No, it seems he be hoping to marry one of they daughters at Orleigh Court, and always calls there. He be much put out that Mary left her house to you. He needs a rich wife. The latest news, I'm afeared, is that he hopes to purchase the Wynslade Manor at Buckland Brewer from Peter Carew.'

This was a blow to my self-esteem. I wasn't destined to join the local gentry, yet I didn't relish the idea of the Wynslade name being wiped out. And Kestell would certainly wipe it out.

We laid our plans for killing him with the utmost care. It was essential that we shouldn't be caught in the act, or even come under suspicion. Dick had no enemies, but my enemies would now become his. They may have already. The people who disliked me, other than Kestell, were only those who disapproved of my appearance and my way of life. Outsiders like me were not entirely to be trusted. My ownership of Mary's house, however, and my forthcoming partnership with Dick, were giving me an air of respectability.

Kestell, according to Dick, had already become quite the gentleman. His apparel looked every bit as sumptuous at that of the best Torrington society. His well-fitting doublets were made of the finest velvet, his jerkins in the softest leather, and his cloak was trimmed with beaver fur. He'd established connections with merchants and landowners, and had long term ambitions, I'm sure, to become one of Torrington's leaders – perhaps even Mayor. His ability to insinuate himself into society in general, or with someone of importance in particular, would soon give him the power to ruin Dick's business once he'd acquired all the furniture he needed. Dick admitted that at Pelynt he'd been taken in by Kestell, whereas now he distrusted his every word. Even if I myself hadn't been living in Torrington, Dick wouldn't have wished to continue living in the town with a man like Kestell.

'Us have been innocent too long', sighed Dick. 'And now us must become assassins if us be to preserve not only ourselves but others.'

Once we'd made up our minds to assassinate Kestell, we investigated his habit of coming to

Torrington each market day. He had interests in several businesses, he arrived early, lunched late and drank a fair amount – but usually left Torrington well before dusk.

Having chosen a particular market day, we'd also planned an alibi. Dick made it known that he and I would be gone from Torrington all day, delivering timber in the Hartland direction. We set out early, and by midday had dumped our load. Looking back on that day, I can barely recall where we went with the empty cart, who we met, who we spoke to, nor in which inn we took our dinner. My mind was entirely riveted on the murder we were to commit before nightfall.

Dick, to my surprise, retained his usual calm cheerfulness. As far as I knew he'd never premeditated killing anyone in his life. Yet on our journey back to Torrington he spoke as though shooting an arrow through a man's heart was much the same as killing a rabbit. We reached Littleham, two miles from our destination, and separated at the church of St Swithun. I was to make my way by footpath to the woods. Dick had planned where to leave the cart, and at which oak tree to join me. All went accordingly, and we sat for a good hour on a felled trunk awaiting our victim. My heart was knocking so loudly at my ribs, it was a wonder Dick didn't remark on it. He did tell me he'd rehearsed this waiting the previous week, and jokingly admitted he'd almost done the deed alone to save me the trouble. I felt ashamed for wishing he had, just as years ago he used to cover up for me to save my honour.

It began to rain, but then turned to snow. Flakes fell softly through the trees, and I lost all sense of time in the strange half-light. I fixed my eye on the clear white ribbon of road as a horse's hooves could be heard, slightly muffled by the powdering of snow. I prepared to aim, but the rider was not Kestell, and neither was the next and last traveller we saw before dark, a man leading two donkeys. Sweat was pouring off me – was it from great disappointment, or perhaps from great relief?

We waited for some while after night fell, wondering if another horseman might pass, for though it was now too dark to risk an arrow, we were curious to know if Kestell was to pass by that night. But all was silent, and we went to retrieve the cart from a copse just beyond Edge Mill.

'Us can try again next week', said Dick in a dismal tone when we reached Mary's house. For having made up our minds to kill Kestell, the waiting was going to be intolerable, even for Dick's patient temperament. But it was even more of a blow when we discovered Kestell was to be away for a month, which would take us into the spring, with its longer days. We had to fulfil orders for furniture, and Patience's second child was due, bringing new problems. I felt very guilty, as it was owing to my feud that Dick had become involved with Kestell. I'd brought ill fortune to everyone I cared for. Someone told us Kestell had two irons in the fire – that is, the possibility of an even wealthier wife in the Midlands. The chance of my catching him lessened.

On the morrow, Eliza came to me with a small linen bag she'd found under a blanket at the bottom of the chest in Thomasine's attic room. I wept like a child as I laid out a number of tiny garments on my bed – woolly bonnets and jackets, bibs and nightwear – for Thomasine had spent her time knitting and sewing while waiting for me to return. At the bottom of the bag were two sheets of a letter, which I laid out on the table and stared at in amazement and joy, for they were part of a letter written to me on the ninth day of February, 1551.

My own dearest love,

I have written many letters to you, some in my mind and some on paper, since that day you left Tregarrick to travel to Exeter Gaol to visit your father with such tragic consequences.

I am living in Torrington now, with Mary Lee, who was, as you know, my mother's greatest friend, and who has been like a mother to me.

At last there is a good chance of this letter reaching you. Amy is expecting you to arrive at Pelynt towards the end of February. Mary has a friend, Martin Bray, who is travelling tomorrow to Liskeard and has offered to ride to Pelynt and deliver this letter to Amy. Now I must relate all that has happened since we were together.

From the moment we heard at Pelynt that the leaders of the rebellion were to be sent to London for trial, Agnes behaved as though your father was already dead. You know how she is, so I will not describe it in detail. Suffice to say she made my life more of a hell than ever. She swore that if you and Dick arrived at Tregarrick she would bar your entry. She erected a high fence around the house, bought two fierce guard dogs and sacked all your father's servants. John Trevanion called to see her often, and I heard her telling him I was useless, weak-witted and little better than a whore.

By the end of November we still had no news of a trial. Agnes became more impatient each day, for she wanted the death of your father confirmed, so as to make plans to marry John Trevanion. She taunted me with the hope that you too would be condemned. We had terrible quarrels, and on the third day of December she threw me out, threatening to have me locked up if I accused her of cruelty. All the servants were frightened of her and feared she had the power to bring the law down on them if they spoke on my behalf. Amy was my only friend, and promised to tell you I had gone to Torrington.

Amy's father, Jake, risked taking me in his ox-cart to Bodmin, and from there I was to make my way to Helland Farm, where, as you know, Luke and Susanna are tenants on the estate which belonged to Humphrey Arundell before it was stolen by Gawen Carew. Amy said her sister's husband would help me to reach Torrington.

You will be vexed to hear what happened to me at the farm, though it was none of my fault. I insisted Jake drop me at Helland Bridge, just north of Bodmin, for he was in a hurry to return home. The farm was only a short way down a signposted track. Having not eaten anything since breakfast at five, a few minutes after getting down from the cart I felt so sick that I fainted, and the next thing I knew someone was lifting and then carrying me in his arms. All was blackness after that, till I awoke lying on a bed in a warm room lit by an oil lamp. A woman I recognised as Susanna had just brought in some hot broth which she placed on the table beside me. At the foot of the bed a man I assumed to be Luke was massaging my frozen feet, which were gradually gaining some feeling. But when he raised his head I saw it was Kestell.

Susanna kissed me, saying how lucky her son had found me down at the bridge, or I might still be there lying in the cold and wet. I don't care for John Kestell, and his manners are much too forward, but I had reason to be grateful to him that day.

I stayed two nights with Susanna and Luke. Kestell had attended the trial in November, and said he had spoken up for Arundell and your father. But sadly both had been sentenced to hang on the twenty-seventh day of January. He also told me he had served the Arundell family since the age of ten, and had been treated in many respects like a son. Susanna was so proud of him, and boasted how everyone at Helland had loved Johnny. If Arundell hadn't lost his property, she said, Johnny was to have been bailiff at Helland. I began to think, oh, so mistakenly, Will, that perhaps there must be some good in him for the family to love and trust him so much.

At length I came to Torrington and was greeted like a long lost daughter. Mary was grieving for her husband.

but since no one had been to tell her of his death she had not quite lost hope.

On the thirtieth day of January official news arrived that your father had been hanged. What a terrible ordeal for you, yet I cannot help but feel such joy that you have been spared.

To my surprise, Kestell visited me several times at Torrington. Mary was captivated by his charm, and much taken with the way he grieved for Arundell. She wished he had been her son. He certainly listened to her troubles very patiently, and sometimes even made her smile. Mary said she had never met such a kind, considerate person.

I have tried to like Johnny, but when we are alone he continues to make suggestive remarks and has even said you are not worthy to be my husband. But he says these things in such a jocular fashion that I never know whether to take him seriously.

However, one comment he made has disturbed me beyond measure. He said that I have a large mole on my right hip, which he had kissed. When I said he was lying, he reminded me of the occasion when I fainted and he had carried me to Helland Farm. So now I dread seeing him, and I wish to leave this house as soon as possible. Come to me quickly, Will, we have been too long apart, and I cannot bear it any longer.

Someone has arrived. I fear I can hear Johnny's voice in the parlour. I shall refuse to go down...

I felt such agony, looking at Thomasine's unfinished letter. I could not bear it either. She must have left off writing when Kestell came up to her room to tell her the false news of my death. How cruel to think that when he'd gone she couldn't continue the letter. For according to that devil, Kestell, she would have been writing to a dead man. And now this letter from my dearest Thomasine had become a letter to me from a dead woman.

At that moment I made a vow not to rest till I myself, alone and by my own hand, had killed John Kestell.

If I was to succeed in killing Kestell, I wasn't going to hang for it. What satisfaction that would have given him! Yet, if I had been hanged, it would have been worth it to rid the world of such an evil rogue. Since our failed attempt to assassinate him during the summer of '53, and a further attempt foiled owing to his being away for a month, Dick hadn't mentioned the subject. When I informed him in January '54 that I intended carrying out the deed myself, he agreed it was the only way for me to find peace of mind. If I didn't do it, I might as well count myself morally and physically defeated by Kestell. His ingenuity would find new ways of humiliating me.

After Russell's successful crushing of the Rebellion, the Protestant leaders in London had struggled to dominate politics and to reorder religion by force throughout the country. The burgesses of Torrington, coming from well-respected Catholic families such as the Wheelers, the Vaux, the Worsleys and the Wayes, had to practise a fine balancing act with the Protestant authorities. Successive leaders of the town had long been hoping to gain greater autonomy in local government, and the crowning of Mary Tudor as a Catholic queen brought a sigh of relief to the town. Torrington was beginning to prosper again as a centre of the cloth trade, light industry and agriculture in North Devon. There was a strong move towards acquiring a government charter of incorporation, especially as James Bassett, a Privy Councillor and a friend of Stephen Gardiner, the Archbishop, had recently been granted the Manor of Torrington by Queen Mary. In addition, the knowledge that Mary Lee's husband, Henry, had sacrificed his life for the Catholic cause, would influence the government. It was expected that a charter might be granted towards the end of the year.

In January 1554 it became known that Sir John Kestell, as he now termed himself, had purchased the Wynslade Manor at Buckland Brewer, together with the farm at East Putford. He'd ceased living permanently at Titchberry Manor, and now only used it as an occasional summer residence to entertain the local gentry. Residing at Buckland Brewer brought him into daily contact with the long-established Coffyn family, who owned several manors in the area. He proposed to join the famous Portledge Hunt the following autumn, and in the meantime was negotiating a marriage between himself and Jacquet Coffyn.

I'd not laid eyes on Jacquet since we were children. Since returning to North Devon after the Rebellion I made no attempt to contact the Coffyn family, feeling ashamed of my lowly situation. I would have liked to offer my condolences to Jacquet for the loss of her brother, particularly since, as in Mary's case, the family never discovered how he'd died or where he was buried. If my mind hadn't been so disturbed by the possibility of my father being hanged, I should have taken the trouble to find out what happened to Richard after we left the Fleet. The poor man had probably died in some back street lodging, a tragic ending for a man who had endured so much. It was hard to know what I should have told Jacquet. The family might never have been informed that Richard was in prison in the Fleet. They might prefer to think Richard had died in battle. Those who have never fought always seem to think there is more nobility in saying 'My brother died in battle' rather than 'My brother was strung up', or 'My brother coughed himself to death.'

When not at his manor at Buckland Brewer, Kestell was much in evidence in Torrington, busying himself with local affairs. Having been secretary to Humphrey Arundell for some while, he was now able to make himself useful in the drawing up of documents, and soon began to take on some local administration. I would see him on many occasions, impeccably attired, strutting the streets with a genial smile, giving a Good Day here and a Good Day there. He went out of his way to acknowledge me with a nod and a smirk, lording his superior position over me.

His bailiff would arrive at our workshop to order yet more furniture for Kestell's second manor. He treated us as inferiors, though we had the reputation of making the best furniture in North Devon. Once Jacquet came with the bailiff, but not surprisingly she didn't acknowledge our childhood friendship. I pitied her, thinking I could relieve her of Kestell if I could only catch him alone. But he never seemed to be alone, and he knew he was safe in company. It galled me to think he probably judged me too cowardly to do it.

During a warm dry spell in July I visited my hut, which I'd neglected for nearly a year. I'd been thinking young Oliver was now old enough to take great pleasure in climbing up the ladder and generally using it as a playhouse. But first it was necessary for me to examine the structure for safety. It was astonishing how swiftly the woodland had taken over my old home, as though nature had angrily determined to wipe out all vestige of human touch. Even the path to it was almost indiscernible. It was lucky chance that no one had dismantled it for timber. Creepers, cleavers and brambles had twined themselves over, under and between the boards; clematis and honeysuckle had gained a hold –

blossomed and fruited and blossomed again. My rope ladder, left folded neatly on its hooks, had almost become a plant in itself, so intertwined was it with bindweed.

Behind a curtain of dusty cobwebs the skeleton of a dormouse lay on the floor amidst piles of dead flies. Propped in one corner stood my old bow, the first I'd made under Dick's guidance. And in my roughly made cupboard, a quiver. I felt nostalgic for those days when I'd lived in my hut. It was the kind of life which seemed to suit me best, secluded from the wicked, devious ways of society. Since emerging from my solitary existence, moving into Mary's house (I could never think of it as mine) and taking up a full-time craft, I'd never really integrated with humanity. What use was I to anyone? Dick humoured me, Patience despised me, and the people of Torrington tolerated me. I'd become expert at making furniture, but as regards marketing our wares, answering buyers' questions and generally making myself pleasant, I possessed no skill nor desire to communicate.

Once I'd reclaimed my hut from nature, I began to wonder whether I might resume my old life. On a sunny day, sitting by the river, looking across at the green Commons dotted with sheep, watching men steeping the hedges at Taddyport, it certainly became a tempting proposition to live alone in the forest. Dick and I had sited the hut in such a perfect position, with so clear a vantage point down to the Torridge. Yet when I stood at the river's edge I could scarcely make out the hut above, so shrouded was it in greenery. Only when smoke arose from my brazier would anyone know of my existence. I almost wished I'd not promised to bring Oliver to my lair, for once the child saw its potential for play, there would be no possibility of my moving back into it.

Early one fine evening I was sitting on my platform holding the bow, and thinking of using it again to shoot game in the forest. Suddenly, looking down through the gap between the trees to the river, I had the shock of seeing Kestell, standing on the path in the dazzling sunlight. He was looking straight up towards the hut, but can't have seen it. I was caught unawares, and for a moment I was mesmerised by his unexpected presence. Had he been told exactly where the hut was positioned? He must have been, for he began to pick his way up towards me through the thorny bushy undergrowth. I had to act quickly, for he was the perfect target.

Halfway up the incline lay a particularly steep few feet of ground, where Kestell had to bend in order to grab hold of an exposed tree root to help himself upwards. When he stood upright once more, he seemed to be looking at me with a taunting smile. Could he see me within the darkness of the trees? Perhaps he could, and yet... But it was now or never, for he was moving nearer, and I couldn't have brought myself to shoot at close range. Then, though my whole body was shaking, I surprised myself by my rapid response in fitting an arrow to my bow.

My shaft struck home, straight through the heart – that heart Kestell never possessed other than as a pumping machine for his malice. The body doubled up and tumbled down the hill, collapsing face down by the riverside. Descending the ladder, I leapt down through the trees, and turned Kestell's body over. It seemed to me he had a surprised, almost aggrieved look in his eyes, as though he couldn't believe that anyone should want to take his life. Even though he was no longer a young man, it was astonishing how smooth and unlined was his skin. Experience had not marked his face as it had mine. He had not wept or laughed enough. With my boot I nudged his body into the slow-moving water, where it was borne away into the evening sunshine. A river doesn't discriminate. It had carried away an innocent, sweet girl, and now it carried away this evil creature, Kestell. It couldn't have been a more secret act had it been carefully planned. I stood in a trance, hardly believing my luck after all these years. How easy it had been!

Then I took the long way back to Torrington, west to Rothern Bridge and across the commons to Dick's cottage, where he and I puzzled over what mischief Kestell might have been up to in the woods. For the present we must say nothing. Maybe the inquest would reveal his motive.

But nothing of note was ever discovered, for there had been no witnesses to my deed. . One of Kestell's servants did mention that the day before his death he'd been asking about William Wynslade's hut, where it was and why he'd lived as a recluse.

This caused me great disquiet, for I presumed people would connect me with Kestell's death. No one knew, of course, the exact spot where he'd fallen into the water, but they reckoned it might have been within sight of the hut. I awaited being questioned, but no interrogation came. No one mentioned his death to me. It was mystifying. As for Kestell himself, if he'd been curious about my hut, what mischief had he been planning? I'd killed him just in time.

Most of Torrington turned out to the funeral. Dick and I stood discreetly in the street outside St Michael's, watching people enter the church. Jacquet was there with her father and the rest of the local Coffyn family.

It would seem that every now and again a warped personality such as Kestell's is born, already holding a grudge against humanity, while at the same time possessing a dangerous gift for charming and manipulating people to his or her own advantage. Not till his death did I find out how feared Kestell had been in Torrington. It was strange how everyone had wanted to please him, to be his friend, while at the same time hating him. Stories of blackmail, fraud, threats of violence and violence itself circulated. Dick did his best to ascertain the truth of these rumours, but even now some people were afraid to talk. A conspiratorial silence descended on the town.

Having achieved my aim of ridding the world of Kestell, I expected to feel liberated and at peace with myself. Had I not proved that I could kill a man when necessary, that I was not a coward? I should have rejoiced, but a great unease persisted. I continued to work without zest in obligation to Dick, and I lost all desire to bring Oliver to my hut. At the back of my mind was the conviction that sooner or later I'd be accused of murdering Kestell, and I imagined how everyone would attend my hanging, while keeping quiet about Kestell's real nature. This would be his final victory.

At the end of August an archery contest was held on the common, in addition to the usual wrestling and outhurling, ending with a feast and noisy revels. Initially I'd no intention of competing, particularly as I certainly had no wish to draw attention to myself as being a skilled bowman. For the same reason neither did Dick, since he was in a working partnership with me. But when he was drinking ale at the Black Horse, his friends began to pester him to compete, and to persuade me to do the same. A tall Cornishman like myself would surely defeat everyone, they said. Why, they said, there wasn't another Cornish bowman in the whole of Torrington. Surely I wouldn't let Cornwall down. And so the banter went on in the run-up to the contest. So I did some practising, and reluctantly appeared on the common at the appointed time, protesting I was only half Cornish. But they insisted my Trelawney blood would suffice.

It was a bright blustery day, and I could see clearly across the river to where my hut lay concealed. I was using my best bow with steel-headed arrows. People had been betting on me, the only archer from the famous band of Cornish archers, though at this point in my life I felt more of a Devon man. But I recalled the pride I'd experienced after the battle of Fenny Bridges in East Devon, at the way we stood up to Russell and his henchmen.

When it came to my turn in the contest I was surprised at how easily I managed to hit the mark, with five shots a minute at a distance of two hundred yards. Even Dick did not achieve this, and soon the onlookers were clapping and cheering me as I received the trophy from Sir James Basset, of Torrington Manor.

He shook my hand, and then winked at me with a grin, saying in a low voice, 'Your marksmanship, for which we are heartily grateful, may not have saved the day at Clyst, but it certainly saved it here in Torrington. You could not have sited a hut more conveniently. We are indebted to you and Dick Popham…, and should you ever need an alibi…'

And so the burden of discovery lifted, and I strode home across the common, Nonna at my heels, with a lighter heart than I'd had for years. Then behind me came running Jacquet, who said she was sorry for ignoring me for so long. Her husband had told her unpleasant tales about me.

'And do you still believe them?' I asked.

'No, I never did, but it was easier to pretend. Let us be friends again.'

She was still the same sweet, rather timid girl, and I was glad to be on good terms with her again. If

Thomasine had never lived, I might have married a girl like Jacquet. But then Thomasine had lived…

Patience caught up with me now, saying Dick and I had done well. Then she smiled at me for the first time, adding, 'If you want to come to our place for a bite o' supper, us'll be glad. There's a steak an' onion pie, and some o' Dick's beans.'

Then Nonna started to race ahead, and I ran too, easily keeping pace with her. I was still young and fit. As Patience had said, I had best stop moping, and get on with life. For when all was said and done, I'd been one of the lucky ones in all our Great Commotion in the West.